D1020771

INTERN

BONNIE HEARN HILL

INTERN

MIRA®

ISBN 1-55166-691-X

INTERN

Visit us at www.mirabooks.com

Printed in U.S.A.

First Printing: February 2003
10 9 8 7 6 5 4 3 2 1

To Hazel Dixon-Cooper,
sister of the soul

ACKNOWLEDGMENTS

Intern and I lucked out with a winning team.
Here's to all of you.

Amy Moore-Benson, my gifted, mind-reading editor;

Laura Dail, my agent, sounding board, cheerleader, friend;

Tania Charzewski, the promotions queen,
whose enthusiasm is contagious;

Meg Bertini, Hazel Dixon-Cooper and Larry Hill,
talented writers who put their own work on hold
to brainstorm with me;

Sandi King, Lieutenant Mel King and Dr. M. M.,
my sources;

Larry Paquette;

Genevieve Choate;

M.J. Rose;

Mary Jane Clark;

The Tuesday Night Writers: Long may we wave;

And to Dianne Moggy and MIRA Books,
who believed in my story and extended above-and-beyond efforts
to make this novel a reality.

The Girl

Eric was late, but April didn't mind. This must be how marriage would feel—waiting for your man to come home, knowing you'd sleep beside him all night, share coffee in the morning. How had she ever gotten so lucky?

His condo still held the heat of another record-breaking Valley scorcher. She showered with the bergamot gel he loved, then took the bottle of gin from the freezer and splashed some into the martini shaker they'd bought the week before. Nude at the window of his condo, she admired the silvery reflection of her body against the backdrop of early evening. Her hair was still damp, but she piled it on her head anyway. When he walked through the door, she'd be waiting on the other side, just like this. Her hair wouldn't matter once they hit the bed.

She dug through the private drawer, found the thigh-high stockings and eased them up over her legs. Then the hootchie mama high heels, and the necklace he said matched her hair, a large topaz chunk on a gold chain.

She glanced down at the coppery bush between her legs, considered the scissors on the bar. Did she dare?

The telephone rang. April fought the impulse to grab it.

She let the machine answer, her fingers dancing like air above the receiver, ready to pounce the instant she heard his voice.

But it wasn't his voice. It was hers.

2 days

The Senator

Eric and Suzanne attended *Phantom of the Opera* that Sunday night, a fund-raiser for a major hospital. It was one of the governor's pet projects, which meant they had to not just show up, but stay, even though Suzanne would be driving back home alone later. He'd already seen *Phantom* too many times in San Francisco, and this version didn't come close. Had it not been for Suzanne's continual nudging, he would have dozed off for sure.

At intermission, they made small talk with others who'd attended for the same reason they had. Suzanne clung to his arm, and he wondered if she might be having one of her dizzy spells. If so, you'd never know it. She wore her chestnut hair twisted into a knot at the back of her head, tendrils so natural looking they could have been sketched along the side of her face.

He didn't want to think how much the long paisley skirt and top had set him back, but Suzanne was good at recycling her clothes. She kept a list and tried to avoid wearing the same outfits too close together.

The governor, on the other hand, had only two words in her color vocabulary: black and navy. Tonight it was navy, with pearls. With her church-lady suits and grandma-gray hair, she might come across as harmless at first glance, but the birdlike blue eyes told a different story. She kept a running ledger sheet in her head, and Eric always sensed she'd placed him on the debit side.

"When are we going to see that new car of yours?" the governor asked. "I understand you went all out."

"I call it my midlife Chrysler." Eric sipped his club soda. He didn't like to drink on Sundays. Besides, it looked better this way.

"A Jag, is it?"

"Ford owns the company now. It was an indulgent purchase, but I'm on the road so much, I thought I might as well step up."

"Have you seen how fast it can go?"

"Oh, yes." And meeting the governor's probing gaze. "Within the speed limit, of course."

"Of course. I'm sure you're an excellent driver."

"I like to think I am."

"Is there anything your husband doesn't do well?" she asked Suzanne.

"Yes." His wife turned to him, her smile enigmatic. "Relaxing is not Eric's strong suit. I'm afraid he's a bit of a workaholic."

Perfect answer. A point for Suzanne. He started to reward her with a smile, but was interrupted by the arrival of the theater manager.

"I'm sorry to interrupt, Governor, Senator," he said in a breathless voice. He handed a portable telephone to Eric. "It's your aide."

"April Wayne?" he asked.

"Tom Spencer. He says it's important."

"Then I'm sure it is." The lights dimmed. Time for the next act. Mercifully he was saved. "Don't wait for me," he told the others. "I'll be right in."

"Told you," Suzanne said to the governor.

"What's going on?" Eric said into the phone, once the group had moved out of earshot.

"It's April," Tom said. "Her mom's been calling the office. She was supposed to be home last night, but she never got there. She's not answering her phone, either."

Shit. Eric felt sweat break out along his upper lip. "Are you sure? Did you try her cell?"

"Just got voice mail." Tom paused. "Her mom's pretty shook up. She wants you to call her. I explained that you're tied up tonight, and she got pretty rude. She left a number."

"I'll call her in the morning," Eric said. "Her mother expects the poor kid to scurry home every weekend. Maybe she decided to do something else for a change."

"She didn't say anything to you?"

"I didn't ask. Tell you what. Call Gloria Wayne back and explain my situation. Say I'm sure April will be back at work tomorrow, and that I'll have her give her mother a call then."

"What if she's not?"

"She will be. Just get that woman off my back, okay?"

"Sure thing."

He hung up, then dialed the phone. April's recorded message answered, followed by a series of beeps, signaling there were other messages—probably Gloria Wayne trying to control her daughter's life, as usual. "Hi, April," he said. "This is Eric. It's Sunday night, and your mother's trying to get in touch with you. If you haven't already, you'd better give her a call. See you tomorrow. Bye."

Eric made his way through the darkened theater, navigating over legs and feet until he reached his chair. Sweat washed over his palms, and he fought the urge to loosen his collar. Suddenly he wished he'd opted for wine over club soda. It would all work out, though. He just needed to concentrate on one task at a time.

He settled in the seat next to Suzanne, breathing in her fragrance, like the smell of soft rain.

"Anything important?" she whispered.

He shook his head and reached for her hand. No reason to worry her. "Just business," he said.

5 days

The Wife

I am getting my hair colored when I hear about it. Berta, my hairdresser, and I fell into the every-other Wednesday routine years ago when political functions and charity events began to take over my weekends. With another campaign trail looming ahead, Berta's decided it's time to update my look. Perhaps I need to go a shade richer, she suggests, in her pseudo-indifferent manner.

"I don't think so," I say, surveying my shrinking face above the plastic purple smock. "This election won't depend on my hair color, and I don't want to face the cameras looking like a tarted-up old woman."

"Oh, you ain't old, Suzanne, and you are a real brunette." Berta frowns at me in the mirror. "You got the coloring for it."

"*Was* a real brunette," I say. "I can deal with age. The main thing, Berta, I just don't want to embarrass myself."

"I can dig that."

A small knot of a woman, Berta's retained her old speech patterns. It's a matter of pride to her, a nod to the past she never intends to forget. She's been putting herself through college styling hair, mine included, and moonlighting as a psychic. Out of respect for Eric's more conventional beliefs, I've never asked about that part of her life.

"You want more chestnut in it, don't you?" she says. "Think I've been putting in too much gold?"

I meet her eyes in the gilt-edge mirror. "Just not too dark—it seems a little less brassy, don't you think?"

"Okay. Can't argue with the Pisces lady today."

I decide not to ask what that means as she starts to paint the paste on my roots.

"Wonder what color it really is," I say, "underneath all this denial."

"Better'n mine. Look at this stuff." She tosses her head. In the mirror, I check out her masses of silver and slate.

"Look like an old voodoo lady, don't I? I'd go blond again, but I stand out too much at school with it. "

"Just don't ever stop cutting my hair when you get that degree."

"You know I won't."

As we talk, the tiny television on the table in front of the mirror broadcasts some talk show in a low monotone. Berta always turns it down when I come; she turns it up for people with whom she doesn't want to talk.

She hears the newscaster before I do. Swivels her head toward the television. Says, "Dear God."

"What?" I ask. Then I see him. My husband. "That's weird. He hadn't planned a press conference."

He's laughing. It can't be that bad. Can't be. Then they cut to something else. Another photo explodes in my face, a black-and-white photograph of a young woman trying to look serious, smooth neck, deep V-neck drape, a bundle of curls.

16

"She got red hair?" Berta whispers.

"Who? I don't know. Who is that?"

The announcer's voice breaks in. "April Wayne, an intern in State Senator Eric Barry's office in Sacramento, was reported missing today by her mother in Pleasant View." A damning pause, then, "Senator Barry, who lives in Sacramento, while his wife, Suzanne, maintains the family residence in Pleasant View, was last seen with Miss Wayne Friday night in a Sacramento bar."

A photograph of our home sweeps over the screen.

"Eric," I whisper. We talked this morning. Why didn't he tell me his aide is missing?

I think back. We were together Saturday. What was he doing out with her Friday? That was the night I tried to call him, the night I've tried to erase from my memory.

Berta places her hand on my shoulder, hard, as if pressing something into me.

"You okay?"

I nod, my mouth numb, frozen. The tiny television crackles.

"Senator Barry's two aides, Tom Spencer and Nancy Vasquez, say he knows nothing about the disappearance of Miss Wayne, whom he describes as a family friend and an asset to his staff."

As suddenly as it started, the newscast finishes. I realize I'm trembling.

"Take the dye off," I tell Berta. "Now."

She nods. "Go take care of your business, and I'll finish the job later on, come to your house if I have to."

"Thank you," I say. I don't know what else to add as she washes the color from my hair and pats me dry with a towel.

"You want a wig?" she asks.

"Why?"

"So no one will recognize you. I got one you can borrow. It's an Afro."

At that, we both laugh, a nervous burst that releases some of the tension building in me.

"Give me the damned Afro," I say, "but this is ridiculous." At least it will cover my wet head in case someone recognizes me.

"Who knows? You might even like it. Everybody be saying you're the swami woman instead of me."

She helps me secure it, and we check out the new woman in the mirror. She's younger than I, with wide, deep-blue eyes, fine lines, and a straight, shocked mouth that looks ready to scream.

"It works," Berta says. "I wouldn't know you in a crowd."

"I wouldn't know me, either," I say.

For a moment I feel as if I'm going to cry. She puts her arms around me, gives me a hug. She smells of black opium, a musk-like oil she's been wearing since the day I met her, one that stands out, even in this cubicle of fragrance.

"What would I do without you?" I say.

"You don't worry about that. You just worry about taking care of your own self for a change. Better leave out the back."

I go through the shop's back door and get into my car. When I turn onto our street, I see two large vans outside the house. Television crews. Damn. I consider making a run for the garage and decide against it. Several blocks later, I pull to the side of the road, my heart hammering, a full-fledge panic attack coming on, strangling me. I can't breathe. Okay, okay, I either have to do something or curl up here for the rest of my life in a ball in my car wearing this ludicrous wig. That is not going to happen, not this time.

I take out my cell phone and dial his number in Sacramento. The machine picks up on the third ring, just as it did Friday night.

"This is Eric. Leave a message and I'll call you back." Short, sweet, and very unlisted.

"Damn it, Eric," I say.

"Suzanne, wait." I hear him click off the machine. "I've been trying to call you. Where have you been?"

"Where have *you* been?" I shout into the phone.

"It's okay, Suze. A girl who worked for me disappeared, and the media blew it out of proportion. It's going to be all right. Where are you? We'll go away somewhere until this blows over, just the two of us. We'll go away and talk."

"Talk about what?" I demand. "There are reporters all over the place. Eric, what have you done?"

6 days

The Mother

One officer stood at the door of April's apartment. The other, younger but with less hair than the first, ushered them inside.

"Don't touch anything," he cautioned them.

"Now, wait a minute." Jack stopped just inside the door and gestured toward the large room—the Erte prints in black lacquer frames, the wrought-iron staircase semicircling to the sleeping loft. "This is our daughter's apartment. We aren't exactly intruders."

"And there's been no sign of intruders, sir. This is just a precautionary measure."

The boredom in his voice, the by-rote quality of his speech reassured Gloria. April wasn't really missing, he seemed to say. This charade was merely precautionary. Face it, neither officer would be here if it were anybody else's daughter. No, that wasn't true. The official attention was due to only one fact: April had last been seen with her boss, that bastard Eric Barry, Friday night.

Barry was the reason for whatever stunt April had pulled, of that Gloria was sure. He'd done something, said something to set off April's hair-trigger temper. Now she'd pulled a disappearing act, punishing them all for his ill treatment of her.

The testosterone-charged air between Jack and the officer would only hinder their cause. Gloria moved ahead of them into the room she knew so well. She caught a reflection of herself in the mirrored wall across from April's glass dining table. With her dark auburn hair and calf-grazing charcoal pants, she matched this place. For a ridiculous second, guilt threatened to overcome her as she took in the decor she'd painstakingly planned—the Art Deco prints from old Harper's Bazaar covers, the one good piece of art, a bold-gestured Larry Hill original with calligraphic slashes of burnt umber and Payne's gray.

God, had she decorated her daughter's first apartment, not for April, but for a younger version of herself? Had she created the arty sanctuary *she* would have chosen had the times and her own circumstances given her an opportunity to remain single after college? Guilt, a voice reminded her. This was just guilt. Listen to it, and she'd be lost before she started.

Jack remained uncharacteristically silent. He glared at the officer as if they were two dogs in a stare-down contest over a bone. She'd have to be the one to speak up. That was a first.

"So, what would you like us to do?"

The officer acknowledged her with surprise and a certain amount of relief in his brown eyes. "Just look around. Let me know if anything's disturbed or missing."

"Looks like always," Jack said. "Doesn't it look like always, honey?"

"From what I can tell."

There was something she wanted to check, though. She took the lead on the stairs, careful not to touch the railing. Just a precautionary measure, that's all. April's daybed was made, the flowered Ralph Lauren spread Gloria had found too frivolous for the tone of the place tucked defiantly into it.

"Is she always this neat?" the officer asked.

Jack croaked out an undecipherable answer. What the hell was wrong with him?

"Always," Gloria said.

"Everything on this table the same?"

Gloria glanced at it. Yes, that's what she'd been looking for, the photo of April, Jack, her and the bastard, taken just six months before. "It looks that way," she said.

"You want to check out her clothes?"

Bile rose to the back of Gloria's throat. "Sure," she said. "I'm not as up-to-date on her wardrobe as I am on her furnishings."

The closet stood open. They moved closer. The summer closet. April, always well organized, rotated her clothes from one to the other. This was all jeans, tops, a light jacket, and, yes, a man's windbreaker. What should she say? Was it too soon to speak? No, she must. This was her daughter.

"That's not hers," she said, pointing at it.

"We didn't think so."

If this were some damned test of her veracity, they could bring it on. Her fear began to solidify into anger.

"Anything else?"

She walked into the closet, all the way in the back where her daughter's folded sweaters spent the winter. The barren back shelf sported only a taupe faux sixties' macramé handbag and April's luggage—three bags they'd bought together. Suddenly she felt ill. Wherever April had gone, she hadn't packed for the trip. Unless she were going with someone, unless that person had done the packing.

She started to walk out of the closet, then saw it, dangling from a hanger like a formless black ghost. She stole a look at the door where the officer stood. He'd clearly seen it, too. It was what she'd call a cat suit, black stretch lace from neck to wrist to toes. The type of suit one would have to sit down and inch into from the top, it had only one other opening, and that was at the crotch, an opening that was trimmed in bright red maribou.

"You recognize that?" the officer asked.

"What?" Jack asked in a voice that didn't sound anything like his own.

"No." She walked out of the closet. April was an adult, a sexually active one. She might not always make the right choices. Who did at her age? But she had a right to her fantasies, and she could wear anything she wanted in or out of bed. Just let her come home, damn it, before they had to go through any more of this.

The officer mumbled into his telephone. "Press outside," he said, and looking at Jack, "Sorry, folks."

"Can't we get out the back or something?" Jack demanded.

"They're out there, too. Best way is just walk through them. We'll get you in your car as fast as we can, and we'll be in touch."

Jack took Gloria's elbow, and in that moist cupping of his palm, she could feel his fear. Her body stiffened, resisting the impulse to absorb his jagged emotions by osmosis. No, she wouldn't. Jack wasn't going to be here for her today. April wasn't. She had to find someone, something, or she'd run out of here screaming.

The officer opened the door and they ducked the lights, heading for their cars. "Mrs. Wayne. Mr. Wayne. Wait." In the lights of the cameras, the eager faces behind the notepads and the microphones, she found her strength. She wouldn't have to tell them everything, of course. April would be home soon. She needed to give them only enough to put the pressure on the bastard, to keep the story before the public.

"Hurry." Jack nudged her forward.

She stopped, staring into the lights. She could do this. It was no different than making a speech to a room of designers, presenting a plan to a new client. The media could be their allies, not their enemies. Jack couldn't see that from the cave of silence into which he'd withdrawn. She could, though. The media, even more than the police, more than her own husband, would be her strength.

A crass young man, barely April's age, stood out in front of her, his blond hair gelled to the max. "Are you the mother?" he asked. A woman in a plum-colored suit came in from the other side. As if aware of the young man's rudeness, she asked, "Mrs. Wayne, would you be willing to talk to us for a moment?"

Gloria looked from one to the other. "Yes," she said. And, "Yes."

6 days

The Wife

After the business of checking in and unpacking, we have only the dying sun outside, nothing to say to each other. After I called him, he told me to just come up to Sacramento. I did, and without even discussing plans or possibilities, rode all the way here to Mendocino with him. Why? Because it's my job, and I actually want to get away for a couple of days. By the time we return, this whole missing-intern thing will have blown over.

Melinda knocks and pokes her head in the door.

"Need anything?" she asks. "I'm leaving for a while."

Melinda's parents own this motel. We've watched her grow up over the course of our summers here. She's a poli-sci major, and for the last two summers, she's begged Eric for a job. He has no turnover, though. His staff loves him. Everyone loves him. I love him, and I really do think this will all blow over.

Reporters in the Valley are looking for us, and it's possible they'll track us here. Melinda lets us park our car in the motel garage and asks if she can give us a lift anywhere.

"We'll probably walk," I say.

She plucks at the grape-colored sweatshirt over her jeans, pushes back her wind-whipped hair. I feel she wants to say more to me, to offer something of herself. All she manages is, "Okay. Well, call me if it gets dark and you need a ride back."

After she leaves, he goes out on the balcony, his back to me, as if trying to stare down the black water of Noyo Harbor. I should say something, but I'm drained, too tired.

"Melinda's right about the weather."

He doesn't turn. I detect the gritty gray stubble beneath the blond of his hair, the longer top layer tousled like an afterthought. Its real purpose is to make him look taller, like the lifts in his shoes, his slim Italian jackets, his noble posture.

"How's the ocean?"

"Still there."

"Want me to join you?"

"If you like."

He stands with his elbows on the weathered redwood railing, looking out past the seal's bark toward the back of a white boat, heading out to sea. I come up behind him, trying to get a glimpse of what he sees.

"We need to eat," I say.

"I suppose so." He moves closer to the edge, more comfortable than I would be next to such a sheer drop, more trusting of the wood that supports his weight.

If he's as innocent as he says, why isn't he telling me what's going on? I am close to snapping. For one moment, I think of how it would feel to take a quick step closer, make one sudden move, and push. I know I couldn't do it, though. I'd get dizzy, go over myself, screaming all the way down.

"You're damned quiet," he says.

"Just waiting."

"For what?"

"Your choice."

"For what, dinner?"

"What else?"

He sighs. "There's that same place down on the harbor. It's still light. Shall we walk?"

"It will be dark when we come back. Last time the path wasn't lit."

"They fixed it."

"When?"

"I don't remember. There are lights now."

The son of a bitch. We spent our honeymoon here, almost every anniversary after that.

Not so long ago, I couldn't have done this. My knees would be shaking so badly I'd be unable to continue on the path. I would have hidden within the safety of the room. I would have been paralyzed, choked with what I thought was fear but which was really anxiety. Dr. Kellogg, when I could hear him, taught me a great deal. Fear is real. Anxiety is not, although it makes effective use of the same characteristic symptoms.

I'm better now, in spite of everything. What I'm feeling tonight as I smell the ocean and try to walk faster—this is fear, and I know the difference.

As we walk, he puffs ahead of me, as if to clear a trail, but probably out of habit from the days when I used to suffer panic attacks in high places and grab on to him, talonlike. He forgets I haven't grabbed on to him for a long time. Out of curiosity more than anything else, I watch his trim ass clench beneath the light-colored pants he wears like skin. There is much familiar about that ass, but it feels like I am studying the body of a stranger, too.

Finally the path curves downhill. We're practically walk-running now, around clumps of white poppies folding inside themselves for the night. I'd love to stop, pull one up and take it home. Wouldn't help, though. These fragile creatures are the weaklings of the plant world, flowers too frail for our valley.

Soon, we're sitting over fresh salmon that I lack the appetite to appreciate. Beyond the window, the harbor opening reminds me of all the nights we spent here, all the meals and the conversations we've shared. It's a Northern California ocean, churning and blue-gray, not the tamer aqua waters along Santa Barbara and San Diego.

"We'll need a statement," he says, as if asking me to pass the sugar.

I jump at the sound of his voice. "A statement? For what?"

"For me. From you. Your belief in me. Your faith in our marriage."

"Whatever you want." His eyes widen slightly. They are the color of amber. I pick up my fork. "Want me to write something down?"

"No, no need for that. Tom and Nancy already wrote one. All you have to do is sign it, and we'll fax it back." He shrugs like a ten-year-old boy. "Sorry, I should have mentioned it sooner."

"No problem." I say it like the checker making change at the grocery store. But of course there is a problem, a big problem, his problem, which is our problem now.

"So tell me who wrote this statement—certainly not Tom and Nancy in unison?"

"Tom, I think. I have it right here."

He does, too. It's slapped before me like a hand of stud poker. I lift the first page. The language is all support, all political. It even mentions the proposed farm bill Eric's thinking of supporting.

He gives me one of his dazzlers across the table. I want to believe in the face, the eyes, the voice, but I can't.

"I appreciate this, Suzanne. It will help."

"Tell me," I ask, my voice steadier than I feel. "When did they put the lights on the path?"

He looks down at his coffee before he answers. Finally he says, "You haven't asked if I did it."

"Did what?"

"Whatever it is they think I did."

Now I am the one who has to look away.

Fort Bragg and Mendocino were our places, but they were mine first. I was surprised when he suggested we come here this weekend, but now I know why. He needs the isolation and the ocean. Through the years, I've watched him try to get attention here and fail, seen him try to light up our corner table with his charisma. Tonight he's visibly grateful for the wood and water detracting from his golden-boy looks. He seems to fade into his chair. I suggest we call Melinda to pick us up, and he agrees. The dining room has grown noisy with good-natured locals having what looks like their weekly free-for-all.

More noise awaits us as we step onto the porch.

"Eric? Senator Barry?" We turn in the direction of the female voice, look into searchlight-bright intensity.

"Suzanne. Mrs. Barry, please."

I turn away from the deceiving light, march down the stairs as if I know where I am going, but more of them block my path.

"Any comments on April Wayne's disappearance, Mrs. Barry?"

Some kid is directly before me, shoving a microphone like a spoonful of food toward my mouth. I feel it come back, the dizzy, spinning, jelly-legged feeling I've fought since adolescence. I'm going to faint or die in front of all these people.

"I'm sorry," I say, meaning the panic attack, the missing girl, my missing life. Why am I apologizing?

"Please." I feel Eric's hand at my elbow. "My wife is ill."

"With what?"

I try to see beyond the woman's brittle blond hair.

Other customers turn to look.

29

"You know who that is, don't you?" asks a man in a flannel shirt.

I look through the lights, the bleached hair, and spot Melinda. She has pulled the station wagon up in front of the restaurant. The doors are open. We run for it. I scramble into the front. I hear Eric hit the back seat, slamming the door behind him. The media has overlooked this battered wagon that now is our salvation.

"No seat belts in the back," Melinda says as she takes off.

"Don't apologize," I say, and realize I don't have much of a voice, either. "Oh, God. Thank you."

She reaches over, takes my hand in her cool one, and I begin to tremble. I turn to the window to hide my face, and I hear her say, "You'll be all right."

"Should we risk the night here or make a run for it right now?" Eric asks after Melinda drops us off.

His blond hair sticks from his head in a fine fuzz. A Kennedy wannabe, I think, looking at his faded boyish features I would have once called earnest. But then, I chastise myself for delivering even more cruelty upon him.

We leave the sliding door to the balcony open, and the scent of the ocean sweeps into the room. We will sneak out tomorrow before the press finds out where we're staying. Tom and Nancy will issue my message of support, and they can swarm over them for a while. Eric's got to get back to Sacramento. I'll return to the house in the Valley alone, refusing to answer the door, having my meals brought in. I can't think about that now.

Someone, probably Melinda, has left a bottle of lotion on the bedside table. Lavender and chamomile. I sit in bed, naked from the waist up. Eric watches as I massage the lotion into my arms, my shoulders, my breasts. My skin turns to meat, to tissue, as I touch it. I can see my age in the grain of it, and so can he. He takes the bottle from me. Neither of us says a word.

He makes sex easy, without conversation, with very little

sound whatsoever. He smells of soap and salt and a sour long-ing I no longer recognize.

When it is over, the sea air washes over me. Silently I beg it to cleanse my body and soul of his scent.

10 days

The Senator

Eric got up when Denny came into the restaurant, and they hugged. He didn't like touching other men, but people around Denny did things his way.

All day he'd been dealing with pressures from both sides of the upcoming farm vote. As he went through the motions, he couldn't get this mess off his mind. His workday played out before the watchful press, all clamoring for an opportunity to shove a microphone in his face. They waited outside his condo, his office, even the men's room in the Capitol building, cameras and lights and questions over a girl who'd been gone barely a week.

This was his last stop of the day, a necessary one. He'd taken only enough time to change into a pair of comfortable jeans before ducking out in a car he'd borrowed from Tom Spencer, his aide.

Denny still wore his suit, but he'd removed his jacket and tie and rolled up his sleeves. His round baby face and short hair made him look soft, almost callow. But Denny was astute enough to understand not just legal consequences, but political ones, as well. And, in spite of his chubby nice-guy appearance, he was street-dog mean when he had to be.

"So talk to me," Denny said. "How are the twins? How's Suzanne?"

"The girls are at school. We've talked, and I've told them it'll be over soon. Suzanne's in my corner."

"Good. You'll need her."

"She's coming here this weekend. We'll face this thing together." Denny's face looked shiny, and Eric, too, felt flushed with wine and the heat of the kitchen. "But what am I going to do, man?"

Denny put down his wine. "Depends."

"On what?"

"On whether you've committed a crime."

"And if I have?"

"I'll advise you not to talk to the police. Keep quiet."

"And if I haven't?"

"You don't want another Clinton situation. I'd speak up right away. Tell them everything they want to know."

"Even if it destroys my career?"

Denny didn't answer. Eric knew what that meant. He had no career left to save. For a minute, it didn't matter. He'd stepped into a court much larger than he'd ever imagined. He couldn't let himself think about that, didn't dare start dwelling on how he got here or what it would ultimately mean.

"You don't owe the media anything," Denny said. "Your private life isn't anyone's business, but you've seen the polls. You've dominated in your district until now. But people are losing faith in you. And fast."

"The media can kiss my ass."

Denny offered the carafe, and Eric put his glass out for more.

33

Rot-gut wine never tasted so good. Maybe at least he'd be able to sleep tonight. He took a slug of it. "I'm not a killer, Denny."

"And the rest of it?"

"None of your fucking business."

"Do you know where she is?"

"No."

"When was the last time you saw her?"

"Sometime last week."

"What day?"

"I don't recall."

"Come on, that's my line. She disappeared on a Saturday. She was seen having a drink with you on Friday, late. That the last time you saw her?"

"Yeah."

"What was her state of mind?"

"Fine. Not suicidal, if that's what you mean."

"That's what I mean. Was she pregnant?"

"Jesus, man."

"That's what they'll ask you. Get used to it."

His head started to throb. The man beside him wanted to help, but his job had conditioned him to treat everyone, even him, as the guilty party. He sat across from him at the narrow bar, his pudgy hands toying with his car keys.

"Denny, I need your help," he said. "I'm not rich, but I'll figure out something."

"First of all, talk to the cops," he said. "Tell them the truth and cooperate in every way. You don't want to end up in front of a grand jury."

"And then?"

"Pray she turns up." His lawyer glanced up quickly, shot out another question as an afterthought. "You don't think she's hiding out, trying to embarrass you publicly, do you?"

"No," he said. "Absolutely not."

"Then, let's hope she's okay and that whatever happened had nothing to do with you. It's possible, you know."

Possible. It sounded like such an odd, fuzzy word. He wanted to grab for it, to hold on for dear life, but he knew better. "When should I talk to the cops?"

"As soon as you can. They're going to want to talk to Suzanne, too."

"I know."

"What you need," Denny said, "is somebody to field questions for you, prepare statements."

"There's Tom and Nancy."

"Aides in blue jeans?"

Eric looked down at his own.

"Nothing personal. They're fine kicking shit with the farmers in your district, but for this, you need a pro."

"You know anyone?" he asked.

"Anne Ashley. She's handled some high-profile situations, defused them pretty well."

"Tell me."

Before Denny could answer, a waiter dashed past them toward the kitchen.

"Cameras outside," he shouted at them as he passed. "Carlo, get out here."

Carlo Luigi, the owner, blew out of the kitchen and into the restaurant like a dark, tight storm. They could hear the commotion from their hiding place.

"Get your ass out of my restaurant," Eric heard Carlo demand. "If I wanted press back here, I'd invite them."

"We heard Mr. Petroni was in here tonight," a male voice replied. "We understand he's representing Eric Barry."

Denny motioned to Eric, and they slipped out the back door as Carlo launched into a tirade in Italian. A van waited outside, at least only one this time. How had they found him so fast?

"Call you," he said to Denny, and he jumped into his borrowed car.

Eric drove as if someone were pursuing him, then slowed down. No one needed to follow him. They knew where he lived, where he worked, where his wife lived. They could always find him, and since he couldn't get away from them, he needed to prepare for the inevitable.

He pulled into the underground garage and took the stairs up to the first floor. Think of it as a to-do list. That was the way to get the chores done. Don't write it down, of course. Never write down anything again.

He'd already gotten rid of the notes and the cards, tossed them on the spot, although he'd told April he kept them in his safe-deposit box. Thank God he'd been smart about something.

Now, he had to look at the condo the way the cops would. The heart-shaped wind chime over the patio was the first to go. He tossed it into a grocery bag, then lifted the soft fabric from the back of a bar stool—a black kimono, one sleeve almost entirely ripped off. He walked down the hall and paused in front of a photo of John F. Kennedy, taken back when there'd been hope in the world.

The gin bottle on the bar hadn't moved since he'd returned home last Friday. Maybe that's what he needed, that and a little Etta James, a little sweet Etta and her "Tell Mama."

He slid onto the white leather sofa across from the bar. The gin burned just enough to remind him it wasn't his last job of the night. He'd do what he could and face the jackals tomorrow. Etta segued into "Pushover." Shit, he was drinking too much, remembering.

His telephone bleeped. Wait for the message; that's what he'd always told April. He didn't want the wrong person hearing her voice. The few people who had this number were friends, weren't they?

Maybe it was Suzanne. Her voice might even soothe him now.

He picked it up and settled back on the sofa. "This is Eric," he said.

"Hi, baby." The voice tinkled in his ear. "It's me, Holly."

11 days

The Mother

Gloria was on the treadmill, trying to think of only her breathing, her body. The running at least made her feel she was in control of something. It was Tuesday, her first day out of the house since she'd spoken to April almost two weeks before. She wasn't handling it any better than she handled life inside the house. She'd promised Karen they'd come to the gym just as they always did, keep up the routine. Oh, God, just the routine. Just pay attention to the routine, and do whatever it takes. Pray, beg, borrow, steal. Get her baby back.

"Hey," she yelled over at Karen.

"What? You think I can talk, do this and chew gum at the same time?"

Karen's gray sweats clung to her, dark where her perspiration had acted as glue. Her blue-black hair capped her head like a bowl. They could be twins, their clients always said, except that she was a redhead and Karen a brunette. And, their clients no doubt added behind their backs, she was straight and Karen gay.

Today, though, without makeup, Karen looked young enough to be her daughter. God, no, that wasn't what she meant. At once, she visualized April's face, her sly, feline smile, the coppery cascade of hair that flowed like a gown.

"Stop for a minute." Gloria jumped on the side rail of her treadmill and waited until Karen had done the same.

"You ever been to that Cut and Caboodle place down on Herndon?" she asked, barely able to breathe through the pain.

"The hair salon? Only once, to get a pedicure. It costs more than I make an hour."

"I'll give you a raise."

"I didn't mean that, honey."

"I know."

"I don't have to tell you how much I love my job. I'm a lifer."

Karen's pale blue eyes clouded, and she looked away. This is what tragedy did to you, made you edit your own sentences, turn over every word in your mind before you spoke. Gloria felt her throat tighten, heard the treadmill whirring below her, with no runner, no destination.

"You ever go to that woman at the salon?"

"Berta?" The color drained from Karen's face. "Don't even think about it, Glo."

"Why not?"

"Because there's something not right about it. They'll find April, once—"

"Once?" She left the question hanging.

"Once Barry tells the truth, or somebody tells the truth. I mean, they're sure to find her, and you don't have to go to a psychic to make that happen."

"I have to find her now, Karen. I have to know."

"You really think that woman can help?"

"She's helped the cops before."

"I just hate to see you go through any more pain. Jack wouldn't want you doing something this crazy, would he?"

"Before this happened, Jack and I hadn't spoken more than a civil sentence to each other in ten years."

"Oh."

She'd expected surprise to register in Karen's face, or at least sorrow. What she saw was closer to embarrassment. For which one of them, she wondered.

"Was it that obvious?"

"Well, you know, Gloria, you work with someone, you pick up things."

Gloria removed the treadmill key and stepped onto the floor. "My point exactly. That Berta woman has helped them find people before. At this point, I'll try anything."

"I'm going with you then." Karen followed her down the row of machines to the front door.

It was a tempting offer. She'd been to only one psychic in her life, and that was in college when all she wanted to know about the future was how soon she'd meet the right man. As much as she trusted Karen, she hadn't told her everything she knew, and she couldn't risk having her hear whatever she and the woman discussed.

"I think I'd better do this by myself," she said.

"You sure?" Karen watched her eyes as if she could find the truth there. "Aren't you scared?"

"Yes," she said. "I am."

The Girl

April trembled as she listened to the deceptively cheerful voice. "Hi, Eric. I hoped I'd catch you. Give me a call on my cell phone when you get this. Bye."

Psycho Suzanne. The realization hit her like a blow. No. Not tonight. The very mention of his wife's name could send Eric on a one-stop trip to depression. April couldn't let it happen again.

"Shit," she said aloud. She didn't feel right erasing the message. It might be important, maybe something about the twins.

She returned to the white-tiled bar, picked up the martini shaker and poured the icy liquid into the glass.

Her kimono hung over the back of the bar stool, arms at its sides, like the wings of a black satin bird. She spread it on the white leather seat, slid her bare butt onto it and took a sip of the wicked gin. Naked, she thought. Naked as sin.

A rumble erupted outside. April rose from the stool and pulled open the French doors behind the bar to the patio. Warm rain fell soft as mist on her face, moving down her cheeks to her bare shoulders. It reminded her of a song Eric sometimes had her sing to him before they fell asleep, a song that was popular when her mom was in college in 1972—"It Never Rains in Southern California."

The mist on her face grew cold. The air seemed charged with the threat of an earthquake or worse. The ringing phone inside reminded her that she was preening nude on a patio that wasn't even hers yet.

Of course she should let the machine take the call, but this one had to be her Eric. She couldn't wait.

She burst through the French doors on the third ring, just in time to hear Suzanne's voice again.

"Eric?" Her tone sharper now, questioning. "Still not there, I guess, but I'm still trying. Call me back, sweetie."

Sweetie?

Two messages already. The rain beat harder against the patio. April closed the French doors and returned to the bar, pouring herself another martini.

She looked at the clock above the bar. Almost seven. He should be here. She needed to find that silly party mood she'd lost in the course of the phone calls. Her identity, her world seemed set on a timer waiting to click into action when he walked through the door.

Okay, admit it. She was a little scared. She left her drink and returned to the phone in the alcove beside the doors.

She was starting to feel kind of blurry around the edges. She punched in the number slowly, by heart. When she heard the voice on the other end, she let out the breath she didn't know she'd been holding. "Mama?" she said. "It's me."

12 days

The Mother

The first thing Berta asked after draping Gloria in violet plastic was, "You got trouble with your car?"

The question, totally incorrect, relieved and disappointed her. "No," she said.

"Guess it ain't happened yet. Don't worry. You'll be prepared when it do."

"I'm not here about my car."

Damn, if only she were. If only it could be that easy.

"I know who you are," the woman said, sizing her up in the mirror. "I seen the papers. You want a haircut or you want me to do the cards?"

Her directness embarrassed Gloria. "I don't know how it works," she said, meeting her eyes in the mirror. "How much it costs."

"Prices for services are posted there." She nodded in the direction of a water-spattered piece of paper taped beside the mirror. "You want to do the cards, that's twenty dollars for twenty minutes. You don't need no cut right now, but I could do a better job than the guy who's been doing you."

"How do you know it's a man?"

"Don't have to be a psychic for that. I can tell you who he is and how much he charges and what kind of color he tells you is best because he makes a bigger commission on it." She said it wearily as if reading off a grocery list.

"The color's from Italy."

"And it fades faster than what I use, like it's starting to do on you right now," she said. "I don't have no fancy shop or shampoo girls. I just rent this booth, and I don't charge no seventy bucks a visit, but my work's as good as anyone's."

"I'm sure it is. Of course you know I'm not here about my hair. I need your help, someone's help."

"I know." Still standing behind her, she placed a hand on each of Gloria's shoulders, then leaned her head back, eyes closed, as if she were singing. "Who's GG? Is that you?"

"GG? I used to call my grandmother that."

"No, that's not it." Berta opened her eyes.

The disappointment hurt more than she'd expected. Gloria realized how much hope she'd put into this visit. "I don't know any GG," she said, feeling almost apologetic.

"She don't call you that, your girl? Two G-words? Your name's Gloria, right? Don't she call you Glamorous Gloria or something with two G's in it?"

"No, I'm sorry."

"Whatever you say. Maybe she never told you." She turned the large chair around until they were facing each other, then studied her with pecan-colored eyes. "I don't need no cards for you."

"Why not?"

"Because you already have the answer in your heart. You got to tell them people what you know."

"And my daughter?" Gloria had to tear the question out of herself.

Berta shook her head, eyes closed again. "You got to tell them people right away. Tell them people everything. He think nobody else knows about it. When you tell the truth, others will come forward. You have to be first. Don't be afraid. That's the message you're supposed to hear from me."

Gloria was still shaking when she reached her car. No reason for it, no great revelation, as she'd been hoping. She really hadn't learned anything from this so-called psychic. Anyone would have given the same advice. Even Jack had said that very morning, "If you're trying to protect April or me or anyone, tell whatever you know." She had wished then that she could sob out her story to him, but she knew whatever comfort he offered would be momentary. Ultimately he'd blame her, as he blamed her for every unhappiness he'd ever suffered.

Why couldn't she do it? What kept her from telling Jack the truth, issuing a statement to the press? Because of April, of course. She wanted her daughter to breeze in the front door, apologizing profusely, explaining that she'd been out of town for a week and hadn't even read a newspaper. She was capable of that.

Gloria got in the car and turned the key. Nothing. She felt an odd tingle as the battery clicked its impotent response. It could be a coincidence. For a moment, she wondered if Berta had an accomplice who swept through the parking lot disconnecting the batteries of her clients, but she knew better. Berta hadn't shown any special interest in Gloria's tragedy, treating it like another case of dandruff or split ends. Just her luck to get an indifferent psychic.

She wasn't surprised when Jack didn't answer the phone. He was supposed to talk to an attorney today, a thought that terrified her. If they had an attorney, this wouldn't be a mistake,

45

a matter of crossed signals, a misunderstanding. It would be legal or illegal, the kind of story the media already thought it was.

When she reached her and explained her situation, Karen almost convinced her that she'd been waiting all afternoon for a chance to spend even more of her free time dealing with her boss's problems.

"I'll make it up to you," Gloria said, "if I ever get out of this nightmare."

"Don't worry about it." They were walking from the garage that had installed the new battery to Gloria's car, Karen still wearing her sweats after another workout. "So how was the psychic?"

"Not so hot. She did say I'd have car trouble, though."

"No way." Karen stopped, turned to her. "She predicted the dead battery?"

"So it was a lucky guess. She didn't say anything else I could use, nothing about April."

"Nothing at all?"

She sighed and continued across the hot asphalt toward the Camry. "Not much, except something about GG. She suggested that April calls me something with two Gs in it, Glamorous Gloria or something."

"Glorious Gloria?" Karen gripped her arm and spoke in a rush of words. "Is that what she meant? April calls you that behind your back all the time, Glo. It's a pet name, only not always complimentary. Glorious Gloria." She repeated it like a prayer.

The words hit her like blows. She couldn't collapse. She was standing in the middle of a parking lot on one of the hottest days in June. Karen looked frightened, worried that she'd blurted out too much.

"She called me Glorious Gloria?" she managed to ask. "For sure?"

Karen nodded. "For sure, honey. I'm sorry. I didn't think it was important, or I would have told you."

"It isn't important," she said. "It doesn't matter. All that matters is that now I know what I have to do next."

The Parlor Game
Mother Says April Had Affair With Senator

They were still talking about the article at the bar that night. Harold joined in, but he knew the conversation would keep the crew drinking longer than their usual beer or two after work. He could use the business.

"Another round?" he asked.

"Why not? I'll take a Foster's," said Kent Dishman, and to the others who sat around the horseshoe of a bar, "She'll be back when the excitement blows over."

He was a blond, husky but not-too-bright guy, who'd gone to school with April and spent his summers working in his father's grocery store. April was a good kid, he said, and smart. She wouldn't be taking any chances, not even in Sacramento, wouldn't go anywhere with somebody she didn't know.

"Her mom decorated our house several years ago," said Janie Stuart, another student who spent her summers working at a shopping center boutique and chasing Kent. "If it was Barry, he'd better say his prayers."

"You think Gloria Wayne is that mean?" asked Heather Garabedian, who also worked at the boutique.

"A first-class bitch. I thought interior designers were supposed to put the customers first, but she made it clear that if we worked with her, she called the shots."

"Like how?" Heather asked.

"She thought her taste was better than my mom's. She as much as called her crass." She waved the question away as she signaled him. "Could I have another margarita, please, Harold Bear?"

She was the type of young lady who liked to swear and make shocking statements, call a grown man by a stupid name. Still, she never had the facts to back up anything she said. She got away with it because of her looks and her folks' money.

Harold had seen dozens just like her pass through the bar, using their drinks, and in the old days, their cigarettes as props. Down the road, the props would take over. Unless Janie got very lucky, nailed a good man who'd put up with her theatrics, she could end up like the magpies at the other end of the bar, who visited nightly to socialize with the bottle more than with each other.

"Mrs. Wayne seems okay." Whitey Reynolds, a few years older than the rest, worked at the grocery store full-time since he'd got into town. He'd probably been brunette once, but his hair had already gone silver. With the youthful face and that almost shocking hair, he'd be a good-looking guy if he'd ever smile. He had something wrong with his mouth that made him self-conscious, covering it every time he spoke so that everything came out a mumble. Harold had seen it before, but usually older guys with false teeth. Hell, that was it. The poor bastard had false teeth.

"You know Barry's wife?" the Garabedian girl asked Kent.

"She used to come into the store a lot, not now, though," Kent said. "We deliver her groceries. My dad's been friends with her for years."

"You've been in her house?" Janie asked. "Is it weird?"

"It's just a house."

"You think Suzanne knew what he was up to? Maybe she killed April. She was supposed to be there last weekend, wasn't she?" Janie lifted her margarita, the same color as the tank top she was wearing. "Let's all put, say, ten dollars in a kitty, and make our guesses as to what we think happened. Harold Bear can hang on to the money, and when the truth comes out, the winner takes all."

"Nobody killed April," Kent said. "She'll be back."

"What if the truth doesn't come out?" Heather Garabedian asked. "Or what if we're all wrong?"

"Then Harold gets a big tip. Here's my guess. Suzanne Barry came in, found her husband with April and killed her. The two of them hid the body. What do you say, Kent?"

"I'm not sure I like this game." He drained his glass. "A nice girl, a girl I know, is missing, and it's not funny."

"No, it's not funny. It's terrible. What do you think happened to her?" Janie's voice grated with liquor. "You must have an idea."

Harold caught Kent's eye, and the kid nodded an order for another Foster's. "I bet they had a fight. Maybe she was mad that the wife was there. She took off and is hiding somewhere, maybe working as a cocktail waitress in the Caribbean or somewhere. When she finds out all the fuss she caused, she'll come back."

"No," Heather said. "She'd never do that to her parents."

"You always think the best of everyone," Janie said. "What do you think happened, then?"

"I think she was pregnant." She enunciated carefully as if trying to undermine the liquor's effect on her speech, a girl who was not and would probably never be accustomed to drinking. "And she got an abortion, but something went wrong, and she died."

"Oh please. Where did you get that idea, Marjorie Morningstar?" Janie's sharp laugh startled him. "Women today get abortions on their lunch hours."

"It's what I think happened, okay?"

Janie sighed and lifted her glass, as if to toast Heather's innocence. "Okay, okay. Whitey, you've been awfully quiet. What do you think?"

"Suicide."

"Suicide? You can't believe that."

He put his hand to his lips, mumbled through his fingers. "He broke her heart," he said. "He led her on and then dumped her, and she killed herself because she couldn't live with the humiliation. That's the kind of dog he is."

"What do you think, Harold Bear?" Janie asked. He hated the name, hated her snide reference to the way he looked.

"I hope they find her soon," he said, "and I'll drink to that. You buying, my dear?"

Harold walked behind the bar but kept listening. A profitable Wednesday began to take shape.

13 days

The Senator

Holly Yost was one of the few women he'd ever met who looked sexier in a long skirt than a short one. This one had some kind of a gauzy black fabric printed with ferns and exotic apricot-colored flowers, almost the same color as her short fluff of hair.

He sat in the lobby on an uncomfortable, padded bench. Even in sunglasses and pretending to read a newspaper, he felt conspicuous, although in hotels of this caliber, people were more interested in their own business than in those around them. What a grim irony, after all the money he'd spent over the years on name recognition, that it had taken this to make him a household word.

Holly had wanted to meet on the old steamboat where they'd stayed the last time she was in town, but he was concerned that it was too small, too visible. It would take only one person to recognize him, and he couldn't chance that right now.

She moved across the lobby looking like a model in one of the hotel's glossy brochures. They'd met a year ago at a place very much like this when Holly, an event planner, had been in charge of a convention where he was the keynote speaker. During the walking tour of Sacramento's Old Town, the two of them had slipped back to her room. He couldn't remember what he'd spoken on at the conference that night, but he could still recall every moment of what they'd done that afternoon. He'd known then she was not just a convention lay. They had a good thing, and she could stick around.

He hadn't expected her until next week, but she'd arranged this site inspection as soon as she'd heard about his problem. She'd gotten someone else at the agency to handle the convention in Dallas, she'd said on the phone. Dallas, Denver, La-Jolla. He never turned down an opportunity to see her, and he never missed her when she was gone. There was something pleasantly unsubstantial about Holly. She appeared and disappeared like lovely flashes of light.

Without looking in his direction, she stepped before the elevator and pressed the up button. He quickly crossed the room, still holding his newspaper. The minute they were inside and the doors slapped shut, she wrapped herself around him.

"No," he said, pushing her away. "Can't risk it."

As he spoke, the elevator bumped to a stop, and an older couple got in. There was a time he would have felt a rush from being so close to being caught in what his mother would have called a compromising position. Today, he felt terror. The couple chattered all the way to nine, Holly's floor. She got off, and he stayed on for one more floor, his usual pattern. He took the stairs back to the ninth floor, realizing that his heart was beating rapidly, and not with excitement.

She'd left the door open. He closed it behind him, clicked on the Do Not Disturb sign, and let out a sigh, trying to quell the flutter within his chest.

"Baby," she said. "You're scared to death."

He leaned against the solid door. "I don't know what I am."

"You need a drink," she said. "I have some Domaine Chandon on ice over there. Want it in the spa?"

"I'm not exactly in a Domaine Chandon kind of mood."

"I understand." Disappointment clouded her hazel eyes. "You in a spa kind of mood by any chance?"

Her lower lip pouted slightly, as if she had bitten it. Her eyes held him. He stirred. This wasn't part of his plan, but perhaps if they were closer, it would be easier to talk.

"Maybe I'll try some of that champagne, after all," he said.

Her eyes brightened, and she crossed the room to where he stood. "Anything you say, baby. Mind unbuttoning me?"

He did, enjoying a lingering kiss. It would be okay now. She'd do what he said.

The hotel bathroom was spread out in a long rectangle divided by two sliding doors. The spa took up almost the entire last section. Glass bricks along the side caught the diffused afternoon light. He settled in the corner so that the jets pummeled his shoulders.

She poured in a turquoise-tinted liquid that burst into foam when it hit the water. Then she slid in beside him.

"You need to relax." Her legs sliced through the bubbles. Where the jet had sprayed her cheeks, faint freckles dotted her pale skin. She was the youngest-looking thirty-five-year-old he'd ever seen.

"You look about twelve," he said.

"You want a twelve-year-old tonight, I can be twelve." Sparkly foam capped her nipples. She slid her hand along his leg, leaned her face closer to the water.

"Want to play submarine?"

"I'm sorry," he said. "It's wonderful to see you, to be with you."

"But you're not in the mood?"

"I don't know. This thing has really gotten out of hand."

"But you didn't really sleep with that intern, did you?" Her eyes widened. Her bangs clung to her forehead, pasted down by the steam. No one worth a damn could lie to that face.

"Of course not," he said. "I told you on the phone."

"Her mother made it up so that the police would put the pressure on you."

"You can't blame her. She wants her daughter. If it were one of my kids, I'd probably do the same thing."

"No, you wouldn't lie. You're too decent." She reached for the bottle, poured more of the sparkling wine into his glass. "There must be something we can do," she said. "I have an old friend who's a wonderful lawyer."

"I already have an attorney."

"What does he say to do?"

"Just keep my mouth shut and my nose clean."

She lifted a toe from the water. "Not too clean, I hope."

"Holly." His voice sounded stern. Soften it, he cautioned himself. Don't be so pious. "Honey, we're going to have to cool it for a while."

Her glass was poised at her lips. Something in her eyes flickered. "For how long a while?"

"Until this plays itself out."

"Until they find her or she shows up on her own?"

"Right."

She seemed to process the information, the glass still at her lips. Finally she nodded, took a sip and placed it beside her on the edge of the tiled spa. "So you're ending it."

"I just— My lawyer thinks we need to cool it for a while. I still love you, Holly. I want you in my life always."

"What about your wife?"

"I told you about that. Suzanne is taking this very hard."

"So you can't divorce her now?" she asked in a voice that said she already knew the answer.

"I'm sorry." At that moment, he was, too, truly sorry he couldn't be free, couldn't be the man of Holly's dreams.

"You said early next year."

"I didn't expect this to happen."

She slid next to him on the bench, took his face in both of her hands. "Baby, I want to face it with you. I want to help."

"There's only one thing you can do for me, and it's more important than anything anyone else can do." There, he'd said it.

"What's that?"

"Keep this to yourself, all of it. Don't say anything to anyone, not even your best friend."

"You're my best friend, Eric. When can I see you?"

"I don't know. I don't even know when I can call or e-mail. My future depends on this. You can't say a word."

Her eyes narrowed. "How long do you expect me to wait for you?"

"You're a young, beautiful woman," he said. "I have no right to expect anything, but I can hope."

"Eric, baby." She breathed his name into his ear, ran her warm, wet lips over his throat. "You know I'd never do anything to hurt you. I'll just be so lonely."

"Maybe it won't be that long, but if it is, you have to promise me."

"I promise. I won't say anything."

"Not about any of it?"

"No, especially not that. I wouldn't do anything to hurt you. I love you too much."

Her mouth tasted of the wine, sweet and effervescent. He drank her greedily, pulled her to him. She slipped from his arms and rose from the spa, bubbles still clinging to her flesh.

"Come on."

That was all it took. He followed her, letting the water run where it may, not taking time to dry off.

She paused before the bed, and he kissed her again, felt her against him, taller than he as they stood flesh to flesh like that, her long fingers stroking him, her nipples pressed against his chest. Tall and fragile, warm and ripe, a field of fruit.

She stretched out on the bed, beckoned to him.

"Oh, start with my toes," she begged, a little girl again. God, how could he give this up?

Her toenails gleamed with peach-colored nail polish. He slipped a toe into his mouth, heard her moan as he raked his tongue across the soft flesh. He wanted to tantalize her, give her enough to make her remember her promise to stay silent.

He moved his lips along her smooth legs, a garden of fragrances filling his nostrils until his frenzy was all that mattered.

"Sweet little girl," he said. "Sweet little baby."

She reached down, guiding his head to the soft, smooth mound.

"Did you notice I shaved it?"

"God, yes. I could hardly think of anything else."

"Nice and clean," she whispered, "just the way you like it."

14 days

The Wife

A photograph of our home is in the newspaper today. It was like catching my own reflection in a store window, when I least expect it, and finding myself lacking in a major, almost spiritual way that transcends my physical shortcomings. This home doesn't appear the way it feels, either, at least not the way it feels to me. A flat, taupe, one-dimensional series of rectangles, it looks too big for the gardenia bushes clumped to one side of it. Now it is closed, heavy drapes pulled over the front windows so the reporters and the generally curious cannot look in my windows. God, they're looking in my windows. What do they think they're going to see?

I wonder where I was when that photograph was taken, sequestered in the bedroom as reporters boldly rang the bell? Soaking in the tub, hiding in my bubbles? Barry's Wife Refuses

To Talk reads the headline. I'm not sure I have the stamina for the story that follows, but I try it, anyway.

Senator Eric Barry's wife, Suzanne, still has not returned reporters' calls regarding the disappearance of twenty-three-year-old intern April Wayne. The missing intern's mother, Gloria Wayne, has issued a statement saying that her daughter confided to her that she was involved in a romantic relationship with Barry. Through his aides, Barry says he is willing to cooperate with the Sacramento police in any way. He does not return reporters' telephone calls. The Sacramento police are still treating the disappearance as a missing persons case.

Why are they calling me? What do they want?

Within the shadowed, draped rooms, I run the vacuum over the carpets, scour the tile with white vinegar. I want to come home to a clean house, not that newspaper house, that flat, hopeless block of plaster and wood.

The back doorbell rings—two short blasts, one long, the code.

I forgot to cancel the grocery delivery. The bell sounds friendly, though, and I wonder if I forgot on purpose just so I could see another human. This is the way I eat now, the way I socialize. My friends don't call. They're politicians' wives, too, and they fear that having a husband in trouble can be contagious. They're right, still I hope this is not the way I would have treated them.

I go through the den, its photographs of the twins, my parents, Eric's mother, us, the decent art I've been able to accumulate over time—grassy greens and deep violets—the jungle colors that absorb the noise inside me. My home, damn it, until two weeks ago.

"I'm sorry," I tell the delivery boy. "I'm leaving town this afternoon. I should have called."

"No problem," he says, the mantra of the young. Nothing is a problem anymore.

"I'll be back Monday."

"See you then," he says, then he is on the way back to the driveway.

It's his attempt at courtesy, maybe more. He offers what he can, as they all have, Melinda in Mendocino, Eric's aides, Tom and Nancy, even Berta. I can only thank them, only act as if it matters.

After the grocery boy, the gardener arrives, quietly, as if entering a graveyard. When he turns the blower on, he tries not to look at the house, as if the honesty of his noise will break it apart. I know that he knows. Everybody knows.

Over the noise in the backyard, I place the call I've been putting off. I make the appointment.

Panic sets in during the drive. If I can't get across town, how can I drive the three hours to Sacramento? Because, I tell myself in the rational self-speak I've learned over the years, Highway 99 is much easier to drive than any street in Pleasant View.

The drivers in our city seem to get more aggressive by the day, and that's not just something I've made up to rationalize my aversion to driving. The number of flagrant red-light runners has grown so rapidly that the police department installed video cameras at strategic intersections to catch violators in the act.

Pleasant View itself is a joke. This is the San Joaquin, Valley of the mad, a three-hundred-mile strip of violence and bigotry between Sacramento and Bakersfield. We produce eighty percent of California's wine and probably drink ninety percent. Farm labor supports us and the rest of the world, yet too many farm workers died in traffic accidents before the government, my husband included, decided to step in and enforce safety laws for labor vans. Driving across town to the medical center makes me feel I'm taking my life, my sanity, in my hands.

"Because I need them," I say.

The doctor is not one I've seen before. He's small and nervous with thick, yeasty skin and a heavy five-o'clock shadow.

I wonder if I should have a family doctor, someone I can call by his first name, someone who would understand or pretend to. I chose anonymity, thinking an impersonal approach would be easier on me. Now I question the wisdom of that decision. Was it just another easy way out?

"What was the date of your last Xanax prescription?"

I reach in my purse, hand him the amber plastic container. "I don't abuse them."

"I wasn't suggesting that. You seem to have plenty left."

"It's an old prescription. I get a little anxious that they might lose their potency."

"They should be fine." He's toying with me. He has to know about my very public problem.

"I need to be sure they are," I say. "I've had a rocky time lately."

A knowing nod. "Are you in therapy?"

"Not at the present."

"Perhaps you need to schedule a session."

"Yes," I say. "I think that would be a good idea."

"When would you like to come in?"

"I usually see Dr. Kellogg," I say. "I'll make an appointment with him."

"Very well." His face sets in a professional mask. He takes me in, and I stiffen in the chair, straightening the ivory silk shirt, smoothing the legs of my slacks. "Is there anything you'd like to talk about today?"

"No."

"Have the attacks increased recently?"

"I said I want to see Dr. Kellogg."

"I'm just asking a question. Have they increased?"

"Yes, they have."

"For how long?"

"A little over a week now."

"You're sure of that?"

"Of course, I'm sure. Maybe that's the only thing in my life right now of which I'm absolutely sure. You want to debate that, too, Doctor?"

"I'm not here to debate with you. I'm here to try to help." He presses his lips together like a comedian who has just delivered a magnificent punch line.

Through the window behind him, I can see traffic below us, racing along in the world of the sane, people who can walk up escalators and drive across bridges without feeling their very foundation has decomposed.

"What do I have to do?"

"Not a thing. I do believe you should schedule an appointment with Dr. Kellogg, though."

"I agree, and I'll take care of that."

His long fingers inch toward his prescription pad, then pause. He picks up a file, mine, I assume. Why this heat in my cheeks, this sudden flush of shame? I haven't done anything wrong.

Finally, his sharp hand darts out, scribbles the prescription before my eyes.

"Thank you," I say, as I take the paper from his hand. At last, I can get away from this place, from him.

I reach the door in a couple of steps, hear his chair scrape across the carpet as he rises from his desk.

"You might want to think about couples counseling," he says.

I stop as if someone has knocked me against that door I'm ready to open. Perhaps I've misunderstood. I must have.

"Think about what?"

"Couples counseling, you and the senator, considering." He gives me the tight, compressed smile again.

"Doctor," I begin.

"Yes?"

"Fuck you."

I watch the shock register on his face, then I close the door of his office behind me and hurry down the hall to the elevator.

I'm stunned as I reach the downstairs pharmacy and its long, pathetic line to the drug counter.

"I want my Prozac," a large woman in a floral dress chants from at least four people ahead of me.

I've never said those two words—*fuck you*—to anyone, except, perhaps, when I was very young, learning to swear, never, ever as an adult. Now, here I am, a respectable woman, a woman you'd probably pass in a restaurant or the grocery store, or in this very pharmacy, without question or comment. And I just said, "Fuck you," to a psychiatrist I met for the first time today.

Something about the way the self-important smirk on his face froze the instant I spoke makes me laugh out loud as I walk with my small white paper bag toward the parking lot where my dark green car hides among even darker green shadows.

I'm going off the deep end. So why am I laughing aloud? Why am I able to smile for the first time since the day when I heard that girl's voice?

I sit in my car, almost giddy. Enough of that. I have a drive to make, a husband to face. I twist and pull open the cap on the Xanax container, dig out the cotton and shake a pill into my hand. I swallow it without water, anticipating the bitterness. The taste reminds me of what my mother used to say when I complained the iodine she'd put on my cuts burned. "That means it's working."

Work fast, bitter little pill. Work fast.

17 days

The Mother

Gloria had been inside the *Valley Voice* office only once before, as part of a tour for local interior designers, right after the building had been remodeled. It looked like something out of Home Depot, albeit, high-end Home Depot. Cherry wood lined the front office where several clerks sat at recessed computers. Clean, uncluttered, yet warm. It was a good look for this place, the interior designer in her said. The mother side waited in silent terror.

Jack had offered to come with her, but she didn't want to have to worry about both of them falling apart, which seemed to happen more frequently when they were together. She could do this. She had to do this. Mind over matter. One foot in front of the other, walk up to the security guard before the revolving doors, tell him she had an appointment with Rich Ryder.

There. It was done. She waited while the guard made the call announcing her arrival.

"Rich will meet you in the cafeteria," he said. "It's down the hall, to your right."

She followed the shiny hall, its walls lined with framed front pages of significant events. Wars, assassinations. She prayed her daughter's face would never be on this wall next to Roosevelt, Kennedy, the Twin Towers, the children kidnapped on the Chowchilla school bus.

They had spoken only by phone. She wondered if the reporter would recognize her, dressed in the long batik-print dress she'd made this spring from drapery fabric and in which she now seemed to have taken up residence. Grief had affected her grooming, too. She couldn't manage to wash her hair, and today was the first time since April's disappearance that she'd put on lipstick. Dressing, undressing, showers, makeup—it was all too much work. But today, she'd forced herself to do it all, for the sake of this appointment, for the sake of her daughter.

As she entered the cafeteria, she heard a voice behind her, "Mrs. Wayne."

A husky man strode down the hall, catching up with her at the entrance to the cafeteria. "Rich Ryder," he said, and she introduced herself. He wore a purple shirt that did nothing for his ruddy complexion, and his pale eyes looked weary. Still his manner was professional and polite. He offered her coffee, which she declined, and a seat on the patio, which she accepted.

"We'll have more privacy out here," he said, as they pulled up white plastic chairs at a table beneath an umbrella.

"Privacy is a luxury I no longer enjoy, Mr. Ryder."

"I'm sorry. It's all you could do. Your coming forward has at least put Barry on the defensive." He pulled out a long, thin notebook and placed it to his right side on the table. "I'm not trying to patronize you. I know it must be painful to discuss all of this."

His voice was gruff, as if it had done battle with too many cigarettes, too much whiskey over the years.

"My husband and I discussed it, and we know it's the only way," she said. "I'm not going to lie. We're using you. The more stories you print, the more pressure will be put on the police to find my daughter."

"Are you willing to talk about April's relationship with the senator?"

"I'll tell you anything as long as you keep writing the stories. I also want you to print that we want Eric Barry to take a lie detector test. He lied about his relationship with our daughter. I just know he's withholding other information that's crucial to finding her."

Ryder's right hand scribbled while his eyes remained focused on her face. "You gave me very few details on the phone, only that they had a relationship."

"I was still stunned. I hadn't even told my husband." That's right. She'd confided in this reporter that day on the phone before she'd even told Jack. What had she been thinking?

"When did you find out about it?"

"The Friday night she disappeared. She called me from his apartment in Sacramento."

His eyebrows shot up, and she could tell by the tightening of his lips that he wanted to swear. "You're sure of that?"

"It's where she said she was. There was no reason to lie. She said she was in love with him. I told her that was insane, reminded her that he was married."

"What did you say?"

"We argued." She started to choke up, tried again. Just sit straight up in the chair, she told herself. Look at his red, flushed face, his light blue eyes. Don't think. Just talk. "She told me to butt out of her life, that she was grown and I couldn't tell her who to fall in love with. I reminded her that we were still sup-

65

porting her, paying for her place in Sacramento." She could hear April's voice, the strident insolence, her own judgmental admonitions. The last words she had with her baby were spoken in anger. "Oh, God, I can't go into this."

"Would you like some water?" His voice was kind, hushed.

"I'll be all right. I just need to say it."

"Go on when you're ready, then."

"She said I'd better not try to make her choose between him and us, because—because he was her best friend." Her voice trailed off. She couldn't say more. She shook her head, unable to speak. "You don't understand," she said. "No one can understand unless they've been there."

"I know." For the first time, she looked into his eyes, not just at them, and what she saw there smoldered with something real. She had to look away. "I know it doesn't matter to you," he said, his voice husky, "but this isn't just another story for me. I've been where you are, and I understand how it makes you feel, how helpless, how full of hate."

"Tell me," she said. Why had she done that? Was there a private club for people who had been through what she had, something you didn't even know you'd joined until you met a fellow member?

"I can't," he said. "I shouldn't have said what I did. This is about your life, your daughter. I just want you to know that I'm not some journalist out there trying to win an award. I want to bring this guy down for a lot of reasons, and I'm going to do anything I can to make it happen."

"Then write about this," she said. "Write about it every day, and I'll try to think of something new to tell you. Keep that bastard's name in print, and keep April in the public's mind."

He nodded solemnly, his eyes no longer visible, just shadows now. "You can count on it," he said.

21 days

The Wife

I arrive in Sacramento on Friday night. Eric greets me at the door like the guest that I am, leads me into the Etta James music I turned him on to years before. At last, my love had come along, just like in the song. That's what I believed then, what I've wanted to believe through all the years that followed. Now, the music makes me want to stop pretending and demand answers to my unasked questions.

Gloria Wayne's haunted, televised face confronts me daily, her silent husband at her side. The police are demanding to talk to Eric again, saying he has not been forthcoming. The girls want to come home. But I don't dare allow anyone else into this nightmare until I know more than I do now.

What about Gloria Wayne, I want to ask? What about the things she's telling the newspaper about you and her daughter? What really happened between you and April?

* * *

The condominium has an unfinished look, as if he's in the middle of moving in or out. I settle at the white-tiled bar and try to decide what's changed since the last time I was here.

"What happened to the wind chimes?" I ask.

"What wind chimes?" He's on the other side, blue sleeves rolled up, cutting limes for some drink he's making with gin. He's forgotten I haven't touched hard liquor for years.

"The heart-shaped ones that used to hang above the French doors."

"Didn't know that's what they were called. I tossed them out. You always thought they were tacky."

"But you said they came with the place."

"I got tired of them, okay?" He drops the knife with a clatter.

"You painted, too." I'm grasping now, trying to make conversation.

"Just a few touch-ups. It was starting to look dreary." He pushes the chunky tumbler across the bar at me. It's cute, contemporary, and as far as I can tell, new. "Taste this."

I do. The drink is strong with gin and lime, and I know I'll never be able to finish it. "Great," I say, deciding to keep my opinions to myself. No matter. I need to be sober tonight.

"Sorry we can't go anywhere. We'll have to eat in."

"I don't want to go anywhere."

"Denny will be over later. We can all talk, get our stories straight."

"What kind of stories?"

"We need to decide what we're going to tell the police."

"You don't have to answer to the police," I say. "You're not a suspect."

"No, but I'm going to have to talk to them. You, too, maybe. My back's against the wall."

"You're worried about getting the governor's endorsement?"

"Kiss that one goodbye. I'm worried about my job, my pension, my life. The Waynes are putting so much pressure on me that I have to say something, and not just through my aides this time."

I peer over the bar at him, my handsome husband, looking domestic with his rolled-up sleeves and his cocktails. I used to kid myself into thinking I could tell when he lied. Now I haven't a clue. "Do you know anything about that girl's disappearance?" I ask.

"No. Absolutely not."

"And you never had an affair with her?"

"Damn it, Suzanne. Would you quit badgering me?"

"I have to know. I'll stand by you, if you'll tell me the truth about what happened."

"You don't trust me?"

"I called here that Friday," I say. "She answered the phone."

"Shit."

"My sentiments exactly." They aren't my sentiments, though. I've been hoping against hope that he'll explain it all away. It's not going to happen, and at this moment, I hate him for that.

Our conversation has made him aggressive. He's never been much of a drinker—neither of us is—but he gulps the gin as if it contains some magic elixir that can save him. There's a wildness to his eyes I've never seen in person, only on the news, caught in the reflection of the TV cameras.

"Let's sit on the balcony," I say.

"All right. I'll bring the drinks."

We go outside, settle on a stiff rattan love seat I haven't seen before. I don't want to ask any more questions, don't want to know.

It would be a lovely night if we weren't here in this unthinkable situation. The sky is still rinsed clean by the sudden showers that blew in from Mexico last week. We'll have more, too, an oddity for this time of year, an omen, Berta might say. Still, it's a relief from the relentless sun. The air smells so fresh and sweet with rain that you could almost wash your face in it.

"I want you to tell them you were here that Friday night," he says without preamble.

"Why?"

"Because I need an alibi, and so do you, for that matter. You were home alone. I was home alone. Neither one of us can prove where we were that night."

My face burns, but I refuse to turn away. "What was she doing here?" I ask.

"She was my aide. She had a key, as most of my staff members do. Not a very good idea, perhaps, but it's not a crime."

"She called me a bitch. Hung up on me."

He sighs. "She's a strange one. I knew I was going to have to fire her. But the issue, Suzanne, is that I didn't do anything to harm her, and I need my wife's support."

I sit silently, holding my drink, wondering how we could possibly be having this conversation. I love my husband.

"I don't know," I say.

The doorbell chimes. "It's Denny," he says, his voice soft, conspiratorial. "Just tell him what we agreed on."

"That I was here that Friday?"

"Yes. You were supposed to be. It will be easy to verify. No one knows you postponed your trip, do they?"

"I don't think you should lie to Denny," I say.

"Try living this nightmare, and you'll see why I'm ready to do anything."

"I am living it," I reply, but he's not listening.

With a sigh, he heads for the door. "I'm just glad my mother's not alive to see this," he says.

"Yes," I say. "So am I."

I force myself to take a sip of the gin. I'm not sure how much more I can handle. I can hear the buzz of their conversation as Eric makes Denny a drink and their voices come closer.

"Have you told her yet?" Denny asks, as I sit silently waiting for them.

"No, I thought perhaps you could do it." Then their voices blend and soften to whispers.

I take a long swallow of the bitter drink, and from the balcony where I sit, the sky is mad with stars.

Although Denny Petroni is about ten years younger than we are, he settled into middle age early, losing all but the thin horseshoe of dark hair on the top of his head, packing on the comfortable stomach that presses against his monogrammed shirt. Clothes and food have always been his vices, and he goes through more of both as he ages. I don't know him well, and listening to him speak tonight doesn't bring me comfort.

I tell Denny what Eric's steady gaze insists I must, that I spent Friday night here. I am a good wife, a good partner, but the fear I've been feeling since this started is turning to anger.

"You both have alibis," Denny says. "That's good. Is there anyone who can verify what time you left for Sacramento, Suzanne?"

I avert my eyes. "No one I can think of. I went to the doctor earlier in the day."

"What for?" He's still grinning, but I can hear the suspicion in his voice.

"To renew a prescription."

"You've got to stay strong," he says. "Everything's going to work out, but the media is wild with this story. Don't talk to anyone unless it's arranged through me. No reporters, understand?"

"Of course not," I say.

We all drink more than we should. I'd run down the stairs, go home right now, but I know I couldn't begin to drive down the street, let alone the highway.

"There's no reason this has to hurt your reelection campaign," Denny tells Eric. "Continue to say you want to work with the police. You'll need to meet with them. You, too, Suzanne."

"I'll try," I say, praying it never goes that far. The thought of facing strangers right now is beyond me.

"What about the, ah, lie-detector test?" Eric asks.

"There are ways around that."

"What ways?"

"For one, you hire your own. It's been done before."

"Done before and criticized. There's no way I'd do that. It would ruin me politically."

"Then suck it up and volunteer to take one. You'll be under a lot more pressure that way."

"Why would he want to do that?" I ask.

"He's not a suspect. Shit, there isn't even a crime. If he lets the cops give him a polygraph, he's a fucking Boy Scout. He's a hero. And it's strictly voluntary. He does it to get the media off his back."

In the dim light, I can see my husband nod.

Denny goes out and brings back Chinese food, which Eric and I pick at on the patio. Denny is a different story. This is a man who doesn't miss meals. He wipes out the rest of the lemon chicken straight from the carton without apology and insists that we open our fortune cookies.

"I don't want to see my fortune," I say.

Eric's mirthless laugh bears no resemblance to the one I'm used to hearing. "And my cookie probably doesn't even have a fortune."

Denny reads his, crunches down the cookie and casts covetous glances at ours. I start to offer it to him, then stop. I've given enough tonight. I don't have even a fortune cookie's worth of generosity left in me.

After polishing off the rest of the rice, Denny settles back, rests his laced fingers on his stomach.

"The ag vote is the big problem right now, Suzanne."

He says it as if I don't understand anything about politics or agriculture.

"I know," I reply, "but if the budget is approved, the farmers will back Eric and cross party lines to do it. They know he's on their side."

"And they're on his side, in spite of this mess." Denny smiles, and I realize why at first he looks almost harmless. His dark eyes literally sparkle as if lit from within. With the candlelight reflecting from them now, he looks friendly, avuncular. I want to trust him, want to believe he possesses the wisdom to chase away this nightmare we are living.

"Agriculture has always been loyal, and it has a long memory," I say. "My father was a farmer. I know how it works."

"The farmers are also paranoid," Eric says. "If you don't vote for them, you're against them. Your father was that way, too."

"He was a wonderful man." I dare him with my tone to challenge that. When he remains silent, I turn to Denny. "The farmers know Eric voted for the relief benefits. They know he'll support them."

"And they want to support him," he says. "They want to show their gratitude."

I whirl to face Eric. "You wouldn't have a fund-raiser, not now with everything that's happened?"

"Not a traditional fund-raiser," Denny puts in. "Just a show of support, a dinner in Fresno at the McBride Ranch." His twinkling eyes turn on me, and I know now the reason for this meeting.

"I can't go," I say, looking from him to Eric. "Not even to Jerry McBride's. I can't go out and face people. The press will be all over us. We won't be able to get away from them."

"You won't be alone," Denny says. "We'll whisk you in and out. This invitation is the first positive break we've had. We can't turn it down."

"Positive break?" I say. "A positive break would be if they found that girl."

"That, too."

"This is just PR. That's all it is."

"I could use some good PR right now," Eric says. "Jerry Mac carries a lot of weight. He was your father's best friend. It's a fitting place."

"It will be a low-key event," Denny puts in.

"Right," I say.

"As low-key as it can be under the circumstances. We'll make it a lunch, so you two can get out in a hurry, say you're stopping on your way to somewhere else."

"So wait a second," I say. "You've already told them we'll do it?"

Denny drums his fingers on his stomach, glances over at Eric.

"Come on, Suzanne. It's a couple of hours out of your life, that's all."

I get up without another word to either of them, leave them out there on the patio staring at each other.

The condo has two bedrooms, a master and a back bedroom Eric uses as an office for himself and whatever staff member happens to be dropping by. I pause in the hall; I can't walk into the master bedroom with its king-size bed.

I go into the office with its functional futon and computer furniture. I walk to the desk, pick up a frame. My daughters and me, years ago on a visit to San Francisco, our arms around each other, hair flying. It's difficult to recognize myself tangled in that light, young and laughing. I'm touched that he still keeps the photo on his desk, one of two.

The other is his college graduation photo, Eric and his mother, their stoic smiles so similar it's frightening. His mother's strawberry-blond hair is pulled straight back, nothing but face between her and the camera. She never wore makeup, not even lipstick, which she considered a sin. Vanity made allowance for hair color, though. By the time she died, she had made the Miss Clairol metamorphosis from light red to carrot to flaming redhead.

I try to get comfortable on the futon, pulling up the afghan stretched over one arm. Eric says he sleeps in here sometimes when he works. The afghan smells of something fresh, soap maybe, the ocean. As it sinks into my senses, I feel safer here with it than I would in the other bed.

"Are you asleep?"

I open my eyes, see his shadow in the doorway.

"I don't know. Is it morning?"

"Almost." I see that he is wearing his shorts, nothing else. "I was going to leave you there, but you cried out."

"I did?"

"A bad dream maybe. Do you need anything?"

"No."

"Want any company?" His voice softens. Although I can't see his face, I imagine a smile there.

"I'm fine, really."

"Okay. I'm going to try to sleep a little more. You, too. Lord knows, we need the rest."

I lie here after he leaves, feeling the room, realizing how ridiculous this is, that I'm trying to shape myself to the futon in the office of my own husband's condominium while he sleeps in the bedroom. I took a vow thirty-one years ago, and whatever the problems, I can't solve them huddled in here.

I get up, tiptoe into the tiny bath next to the office to wash my face. Mascara smudges give me a hollow-eyed, ghostlike look. There's nothing but a dried-up bar of glycerin soap in the metal dish. I make it lather in my hands and let the warm water run down my face.

The mauve hand towel has seen better days. It hangs stiffly, and I know Eric has used it to wipe out the sink, probably weeks before, as he always does at home.

With my eyes shut, I open the cabinet beneath the sink and feel around. My fingers connect, and I bury my face in a fresh towel.

I start to hang up the towel, then study it. It's large, what's marketed as a bath sheet these days, pale pink, a loopy, chenillelike surface on one side, expensive. It's been wadded up, shoved behind the garbage pail in the back of the otherwise empty cabinet. My fingertips tingle as I touch it. There's something wrong. It doesn't belong here.

I run my fingers over the surface, the damp section where my face has been and down. A smear of what looks like makeup darkens the shell-pink tone. As I see that, I also glimpse several hairs. I pull one out—curly and copper—drop it as suddenly as I picked it up. But there are more. This thing is full of short, reddish hair. And now, touching it and trying not to, seeing the images in my mind of that girl on television, what the hell am I going to do?

I begin to fold it up to return it to its hiding place. The bottom ends are stuck together. I pull them apart, and then I see it, a large, rusty colored smear. Makeup, I think. It's surely makeup. Let it be makeup. But makeup doesn't look like this. Only one substance looks like this. Only blood.

"What are you doing in there?"

I whirl around to face him.

"Washing my face," I say.

"What's the matter?" He spots the towel. "What's this?"

I shove it into his hands. "You tell me. It's in your bathroom."

"You know I never use this room." He glances down at it, makes a disgusted face. "Damned aides are pigs, like all young women these days. Luigi says the ladies' room is the filthiest bathroom in his restaurant. Tampons clogging the toilets, makeup all over the place. Suzanne, what's wrong?"

I'm backing away from him, into the narrow room, knowing that I can be cornered, looking past him, like an animal, planning an escape out the door.

"I just need some sleep."

His hand reaches out, grazes my bare arm. "Alone? Maybe you need something to relax you."

"I need sleep," I say once more. "I need time."

He steps back. He's always sensed rejection in a tone, a gesture. Nothing can make him retreat faster than the possibility that someone he wants doesn't want him. He's misread me in the past, but not now.

"Then perhaps we should try to sleep just a little bit more." He squares his shoulders and waits for my response. I nod, try to smile and hold my breath until he leaves me alone in this room once more.

"By the way," he says, as he exits, "don't use this bathroom. There's something wrong with the drain."

"Okay," I say. Then slowly, I creep back to my new bedroom, lock the door and stare at the ceiling from the futon.

31 days

The Senator

Damn women. On the worst day a political aide could quit, Nancy Vasquez did just that.

"I don't believe in you anymore," she said, stringing out the word "believe" like lyrics in one of the mindless songs she played all day in his Pleasant View office she was supposed to be running. Typical PR major. No wonder she didn't care about him.

He had two vacancies—April's, in Sacramento, which he didn't dare fill, and now, Nancy's in Pleasant View. Suzanne insisted that they bring Melinda down from Mendocino. She'd already proven her loyalty by getting them away from the press that night in Noyo Harbor. He didn't want to interrupt her studies, but Suzanne reminded him Melinda was on summer vacation, and working for him was better than hanging around her folks' motel.

"She can stay with me at the house," Suzanne said. "It will be good to have her, and you need someone you can trust at the Pleasant View office."

Calls were made, offers confirmed. Knowing the press would note Nancy's departure, Eric let it leak that she'd been replaced by a family friend and hoped no one would question further.

Today, however, someone might. Today someone might question anything and anyone. A month of harassment by the press, of seeing himself every time he turned on the television had made him crave anonymity. He still wasn't sure he should have done this, let alone in Fresno, so near his hometown of Pleasant View.

Although the investigation had blown way out of proportion, April still had not shown up. Thanks to the constant pressure from the Waynes and the prick of a reporter from the *Valley Voice*, the police wouldn't leave him alone. As if taking a break from the real news of the economy and the war, the media were having a field day. Just as bad, Suzanne seemed to be fraying. She'd declined since that night in the condo, declined. He was worried about her, about them. Today, she wore a short, sleek dress she couldn't carry off the way she had in the old days when they'd been a team. She'd lost weight, which made her look better from a distance, but at close range her face was drawn, her eyes too wide and frightened, even in casual conversation.

Of all her faults, he would have never guessed Suze would be weak when the chips were down, but then, the chips had never been down, had they? He'd always made sure their bets were safe ones. He'd been able to take care of both of them, until now.

Her choice of clothes was still excellent. Her sleeveless linen dress was the innocuous, classy type that impressed the farmers' wives without threatening them. There was always a vixen in the crowd, all carats and cleavage, always a grand old, dowdy white-haired girl. Piss off either one, and you were finished before you started.

The event took place at McBride's, the restaurant Jerry Mac and his brothers ran, a place where they showcased the beef they raised and the grapes that had made their family wealthy. At least it would be a friendly group.

Tom and Melinda rode with them, and Denny had declined his invitation to come along. An attorney would convey the wrong message, he'd said, like walking in with a cardiologist when you'd been accused of having heart problems. He'd suggested Anne Ashley, the PR woman, and she turned out to be a good choice.

Her sleek dark hair, pale skin and spotless white suit conveyed a squeaky-clean message that suggested she would not represent anyone who wasn't as pure as she. As she blanketed the room with goodwill, he smiled at well-wishers and tried to ignore his constricted clothing.

His tie felt as if he were hanging from it instead of wearing it. In spite of the one-hundred-plus-degree weather, he had put on a jacket out of respect for his host and guests.

Jerry Mac's introduction was effusive by farmer standards.

"A good man," he said. "One of us. And he proved that by his courageous vote in these times that are so difficult for all of us."

The applause soothed Eric and eased away the edgy nervousness he kept telling himself was natural. Some of the most powerful people in the Valley sat out there today in the banquet hall, supporting him with their applause. Hell, he might have a chance at the governor's job, after all.

As he rose to speak, he spotted the reporters in the back of the room, dressed only a step up from street people, the women as bad as the men. His gaze rested on the arrogant, red-faced one, whose angry eyes registered even this far away. But the eyes weren't looking at him. They were focused to his right, on Suzanne.

He gripped the podium and began to speak. "I'm here today at the gracious request of Jerry McBride and all of you who have demonstrated what I've always believed—that what's right for the people I serve is more important than anything, including what's right for the party."

He mentioned the important players in the room by name. They loved that. And he reiterated his commitment to agriculture.

"Finally, I want to thank you all for your support," he said. Applause drowned out his words. "And." He put up his hand until the noise subsided, then turned to look at Suzanne. "I want to thank my wife, Suzanne Loomis Barry, for her support, her faith, and most of all, her love." More applause. Suzanne straightened beside him. She wiped a finger under her eyes. Good. She was still with him.

This time, it was standing-ovation applause that died only when he put his arm around Suzanne's shoulder and sat down beside her.

"You're amazing," she whispered.

"Just smile as if I love you, because I do."

She nodded, did as she was asked, looked at him with a glow he'd almost forgotten.

He couldn't even taste the prime rib, his ears still ringing with the acceptance in this room. Denny was right. They needed this trip, even if it had been a risk.

"Mr. Barry?"

He looked up into the ruddy face of the reporter.

"Could I ask you a question, Mr. Barry?"

"Sorry, Eric's off-limits to the press today," Jerry Mac said pleasantly. He stood as if to show he meant it. "This is a social gathering."

"Would you like to make a statement about April Wayne, Mr. Barry?"

He wanted to shove the bastard's face in, but this rudeness, this intrusion was part of his life now. Clowns like this could ask him anything, anyplace, anytime.

"Jerry," he said, looking up at McBride. "Perhaps we should leave."

"No need for that," Jerry Mac said. Then to the reporter. "Let me get someone to refund your money, sir, because you're the one who's leaving here."

Tom and Melinda hurried up from one of the front tables. Tom was burly enough to be a bouncer, which was how he'd worked his way through college. Although Melinda looked fragile, she was no wimp, either. They both charged the red-faced stranger.

"Ryder," Tom said. "Who let you in?"

"Your apolitical friends of agriculture," he said. "I'm on my way out. Wanted to give my best to the senator and Mrs. Barry." He turned back so that he and Suzanne were eye to eye. "This must have been an ordeal for you, Mrs. Barry. Did you know April Wayne long?"

"What?"

"April Wayne and you were good friends, weren't you?" Past tense, the bastard.

"No, I don't even know her. I—"

"Suzanne." Eric gripped her shoulder to shut her up. "You don't have to talk to him."

"Out, Ryder," Tom put in.

"Odd," Ryder said, as if oblivious of Tom's hand on his arm. "I thought the senator said April was a family friend."

"How dare you."

Suzanne's expression didn't change, but he could tell by her still, cold voice that something had snapped. "How dare you come here and harass me like this so that you can sell a few newspapers."

"That's not my purpose, Mrs. Barry." Ryder moved closer to her, and his complexion flushed a deeper shade of purple.

"Your purpose is to dig dirt. You don't care anything about that girl."

"You're wrong about that." He dropped his reserve. Suzanne had pushed some button she didn't even know existed. Now, the reporter was on the defensive. "You're really wrong, lady."

"Get him out of here," Jerry Mac ordered. Tom stepped in, and Ryder was subtly escorted from the room as if he'd just stopped by the head table to say a friendly hello.

Suzanne glared at him all the way out the door, her fork still in her hand. He paused before stepping out, looked back at her, his eyes confused, haunted. Although relieved, Eric couldn't figure it out. This wasn't the Suzanne he knew.

"We need to go out for a smoke," Jerry Mac whispered to him.

He started to say he didn't smoke anymore, then realized what that meant. Picking up his glass of iced tea, he whispered to Suzanne, "Be right back. Don't kill any reporters while I'm gone."

All he got was an icy, wild-eyed stare.

"Suzie's gotten a little spunky," Jerry Mac said, once they were out of earshot.

"The media's been really unfair."

"That guy especially. He got some kind of grudge against you?"

"None that I'm aware of, but you know how liberals are." They stepped out on a balcony overlooking the fields of grapes that were served on every plate at McBride's. In spite of the sun that baked down on them, the field looked fresh and green as a spring morning. "You must be very proud of all this," Eric said.

"As if it were my own kid." Then, taking a sip of his whiskey. "I'm worried about Suzie, Eric."

"She's a trouper." At least she used to be, he thought.

Jerry Mac squinted into the sun, not looking at him. "She needs to know the truth, no matter how bad it is."

"I've told the truth," Eric said. "I—"

McBride sliced his hand through the thick air. "So has the press."

"Mac," he began.

His eyes still squeezed shut from the sun, Jerry Mac turned on him full force. "We're behind you, all of us, but you got to go public with this story. You're getting bad advice, Eric, real bad."

"I've got the best attorney in Sacramento."

"I don't care who you have. You got to put that girl's welfare first, and you got to do something to keep that wife of yours from going crazy."

"Suzanne's not going crazy."

"I've known her all her life," Jerry Mac said. "Guess there's not much more for me and you to talk about right now."

"I'd say there's a lot more," Eric said.

McBride cut his sun-freckled hand through the hot air again. "Not right now there isn't."

The Parlor Game
Barry Admits Affair With Intern

It was a regular occurrence now. The group met every night after work at the bar, watched the news, Larry King, and spun out the rest of each evening with alcohol and speculation.

Harold almost missed them on the weekends when the boring, boorish couples showed up for their one or two drinks before dinner, their proper chardonnays, their spritzers.

Kent and Whitey arrived first tonight, Whitey carrying the newspaper under his arm. Harold always brought his to the bar. It got conversation started, even with customers as tight-lipped as Whitey. Tonight the guy wore a T-shirt, obviously new, with an illustration of a 1960s Beach Boys' station wagon. Above the design, were the words, Woody It Be Nice? and below, Santa Cruz, California.

Harold wedged the pieces of lime in the tops of the two bottles and served the Coronas.

"Nice shirt," he said to Whitey. "You been to Santa Cruz lately, trying to see some of our state?"

"No, I bought this in town."

"That Whitey's a regular fashion statement." Kent arched an eyebrow at Harold. His own shirt wasn't much better, an oversize wild print of oranges and greens, the kind of design these youngsters thought people actually wore in the sixties. Kent was what Harold called a lummox, good-looking when young but lacking any firepower. His jaw would drop over the years. His eyes would fade, and no one, least of all him, would ever remember that women had ever looked at him with interest.

Before the two guys had finished their first beer, Janie Stuart and Heather Garabedian joined them. Harold plugged in the blender.

It'd be a margarita, for sure, Harold Bear. Lots of ice, Harold Bear. Like a big, fat snow cone, and yours are just the best, Harold Bear, the best.

Just as he predicted, almost word for word, pretty Janie demanded her margarita. Once Janie had it before her and paid him, she took the newspaper from Whitey, studying the headline.

"You see, I knew it all the time," she said. "He was having an affair with her. Bet he killed her, too."

"No way." Kent Dishman looked from his beer to Janie. "I wish you wouldn't talk that way."

"Or maybe she was pregnant," Heather Garabedian put in, "like I told you guys in the first place."

"Or the wife herself," Janie said. "She was there that weekend. Why didn't that come out right away? Could have been an alibi for him."

Her black dress was cut low, showing off her suntan and more than Harold wanted to think about. He wondered if she were that soft, golden color all over, and if so, how she did it.

Probably one of those suntan places, "fake and bake," he'd heard them called. God, she was beautiful. How could any woman bleach her hair down to white-blond, pull it all straight back in a knot, and look so fucking good that even a decent man had to watch his thoughts, his own stupid longings?

"Ought to be ashamed," he said in a louder voice than he meant. "A girl young enough to be his own daughter."

"Damn right." Janie slapped her empty glass on the bar like a dice cup, smiled at Kent to her left and Whitey to her right, then beamed at Harold. "Another margarita, Harold Bear. I'm going to slam nonstop margaritas the night I win the lottery."

"The night April Wayne's body is found?" Heather Garabedian's soft sorority-girl voice dug deeper than usual. Janie had a way of doing that to people, making them lose control. Harold had seen it before.

"That's not what I meant," Janie said. "You shouldn't be so literal, Heather, not to mention so hostile."

"It's not right."

For a moment, they all sat there, looking at each other. Then Whitey spoke again, his voice rough with anger.

"All of those missing girls, and only April Wayne getting the attention."

Janie leaned over and glared at him. "Hello? Does it occur to you that her family has enough money to get the attention?"

"It's still not fair. She wasn't any better than the others. She wasn't anything special."

"*Wasn't*, Whitey? Past tense? You know something we don't?"

"Only that the system really sucks, you know? The rules are different for senators and their women."

Harold had worked the bar business a lot of years, and he knew how to spot the problems. Whitey had all the makings. Harold decided he'd better keep an eye on him.

33 days

The Wife

Did I just break? Denial, disgust, feigned indifference, an unexpected voice on the telephone, a young woman calling me a bitch. Did I just snap? Maybe that's what happened to me. Maybe I could no longer pretend. That's what I told Dr. Kellogg today, Dr. Kellogg, better than the drug-supplying sadist of that first awful week. He listened well, let me draw my own conclusions. He is the only one to whom I have spoken anything close to the truth. A small beginning, perhaps, but a beginning.

I can't drive across town without jumping every time I have to make a left turn. I don't know what it is about people with this problem and left turns. I'll have to ask Kellogg. I read once that J. Edgar Hoover was that way. He'd been in an accident once, his car had been hit by another when he was making a left turn. After that, he suffered panic attacks and would make his driver take only right turns, sometimes going around for blocks. Nice to think that I share an illness with that psycho. What does that make me?

I have one plan today—going to Berta's for a touch-up, nothing more. The future's unraveling fast enough without any help from her. The authorities want to speak to me now. The requests are polite and firm. Rich Ryder is the only one who hounds me. He's even obtained my e-mail address. The message today said, "Considering that a young woman's life is at stake, I'm sure you'll want to cooperate."

I know enough about this disability of mine to understand that I must go out now, if I am ever to leave the house again. Kellogg asked today how I felt about it.

"I'm only safe when I feel the carpet in my house under my feet," I said. "I don't even want to go pick up the newspaper from the curb."

"And when you don't, what happens?"

"It gets more difficult. The safe place gets smaller and smaller. Pretty soon I'd have to live under the bed, and it wouldn't be safe for long. Whatever's after me would get there, too."

He leaned forward. "What is after you, Suzanne?"

"I don't know."

I started to say I wish I did, but I'm not sure that would be the truth.

I am still numb about the headlines and the fact that Eric won't discuss what happened between April and him. He said only that he was meeting with the police, that he had something to tell them that would prove hurtful to both of us and to our daughters. Hurtful, that was the word he used. Not shattering, annihilating. Hurtful.

I barely got the call in to my daughters before it hit the papers. Joy wants me to leave him. Jill, to whom all those Sundays at church stuck better than to the rest of us, is talking of forgiveness.

Berta doesn't ask, just hugs me, drapes me, paints the color on, humming something that's combination lullaby and spiritual. Once the color's on my head, "cooking," as she calls it, she sets the timer, crosses her arms and says, "Want to talk or read?"

"Read," I say. "I just can't—"

"It's okay." She pats my shoulder, picks up a pile of magazines. Eric's photo is on the cover of one. She flips it facedown on her table. "Sorry," she says.

"It's not your fault."

"You don't need it shoved in your face."

"But that's what happens. It's shoved in my face every single day, and there's nothing I can do about it."

"Here. Some pretty food in this one. Summer barbecue. Good way to save on the power bills. That kind of thing."

"Thanks," I say and gratefully take the one magazine that won't carry news of the philandering senator, the missing intern, and the silent wife whose neighbors say is such a nice person.

The perfumed smell of the hair color comforts me. I feel like I'm being cared for. I relax a little, tilt my head to look into Berta's eyes.

"I know that woman hired you," I say, "Gloria Wayne."

"She's been in for a couple of readings is all. I'm not working with the police on this one. Not much I can tell them."

I look down at the magazines, not sure how to ask. "Is she? Were you able to tell if the girl is alive?" That last word sticks in my throat. I swallow hard. Berta's face is indecipherable. Her eyes close, as if she is singing.

"Only God can say that," she recites. "You relax now. Let me get you a glass of water."

In that look, I see more than I want to know. As she goes to the water cooler in the back, to erase the truth from her face, I think again about April Wayne and wonder if we'll ever get our lives back.

* * *

The Girl

She spread the pink towel out over the beige carpeting. She'd brought the towels from her place. Men were so dumb about that kind of thing. Once they lived here together, she'd slowly get rid of the boring browns and soften the rooms with color. The towels were just the first step.

They were also insurance. Just in case the wife ever came here, she'd spot the towel and know at once that he had someone. She might even do what she'd been promising to all these years and divorce him. It's not as if they had to worry about the kids anymore, and divorce was no longer a kiss of death. In fact, a young, beautiful wife would be an asset. She could help Eric so much more.

Glorious Gloria couldn't grasp that, but her mother was just worried that she'd get hurt. She'd calm down once she got used to the idea, once she saw how much Eric loved her.

"I'll kill the son of a bitch," she'd shouted into the phone.

"You'll have to kill me first, Mama," she'd said. "And in case you didn't understand, I'm not phoning you for permission."

Glorious had started calling her names. She'd covered spoiled, foolish and headstrong before April said goodbye and hung up on her. That would piss her off almost as much as the fact that her daughter was going to marry Senator Eric Barry. Glorious hated letting anyone else get the last word.

She sat on the towel, her legs spread, carefully maneuvering the scissors through her pubic hair. The metal crunch through the wiry hair thrilled her. She had no idea it would feel this freeing. It looked pretty good. He'd said he wanted her to shave it, but she couldn't bring herself to do that. Still holding the scissors, she looked down to admire her handiwork. A perfect heart shape. She couldn't wait to see his face.

She had to call and tell him about it, give him something to think about on the way in. Her hand was almost on the phone when it started to ring. ESP, that's how it was with them. They were so connected they even finished each other's sentences.

"Hello?" A pause. Damn. She should have waited, let the machine pick up.

"Is Eric there?" Her voice. Oh, shit. He had said he'd leave April if anyone ever found out about them.

"Who?"

"Eric Barry. Who is this?" That voice, that demand. Who is this, as if she were the damned cleaning woman. It was too late. Eric would never leave her now. Couldn't.

"Who the hell do you think it is, you crazy bitch." She heard the gasp on the other end, then clicked off the phone, threw it across the bar.

Oh, God. What now? She could never tell Eric, never, never, never. The wife was crazy. She could have made it up. April poured another drink. Damn, she'd better think of something fast. What if Eric found out? What if he really did dump her? She picked up the scissors again. She'd have to kill herself if he did. She couldn't bear living without him.

The thought brought her to tears. She cried out all the pain, unable to stop herself except to sip the tepid gin. "Oh God," she sobbed to the empty room. "What am I going to do?"

She heard the answer clearly in her mind. "You are going to lie."

She didn't want to start their life together with deceit, but she had no choice. She walked to the answering machine and studied it carefully. Beneath its chrome lid were diagrams for saving, playing and deleting messages. She had only to push down two buttons, Play and Save, at the same time, and the messages would be destroyed. Crazy Suzanne must have gotten the wrong number, she'd tell him. No one called for him all the time she was here. He'd believe her, too, he would.

She placed the index finger of each hand on one of the two buttons, and pushed. The blinking light went clear. No messages. April wiped the tears from her eyes. No turning back. It was done.

40 days

The Senator

The budget was approved. In spite of the maelstrom sur-rounding his personal life, he'd pulled it off. There'd be per-manent elimination of the state portion of the sales tax on farm equipment beginning in two months, as well as permanent elimination of the state portion of the sales tax on propane. A year's suspension of the state portion of the sales tax on diesel fuel would start at once. He'd argued well that California was the only state in the nation to fully tax farmers for buying or leasing farm equipment. At least thirty-eight states did not even have any sales tax, he'd pointed out.

Getting rid of certain sales taxes wouldn't save the farmers, but it would help. Say what they wanted to about him, he did take care of his constituents, even when they weren't the peo-ple who elected him. Why wasn't anyone printing that? Why had the budget article ended up on the first page of the business section, while reheated information about his second talk with the police went above the fold on A-1? Because the media was made up of liberal, hypocritical assholes, that was why.

He'd tell Anne Ashley to get that story out. She'd done a good job of promoting the meeting at Jerry Mac's. As women went, she was too tall, too thin, and way too proper for his tastes, but she did what she said she'd do, and she required little hand-holding.

The story about his relationship with April had devastated Suzanne, but a broken fingernail devastated Suzanne. After he'd spoken with the police, admitted what everyone already suspected anyway, he'd flown to Fresno, visited with Jerry Mac again, over gin and rare steak in a local restaurant. One thing about farmers, you could eat the way you wanted to without having to impress them by ordering rare ahi or polenta or black bean sauce.

"It was the right thing to do," Jerry Mac said.

"You might reconsider that if you had to bare your soul to the police the way I did."

Jerry Mac nodded as if he'd been there. "You made a lot of friends by doing that. Our guys are behind you all the way."

"One of my daughters isn't speaking to me. Suzanne tell you that one?"

"I'm sorry," he said in a voice that sounded as if he meant it.

"And Suzanne's not saying much, either. You were right about her. She's having a rough time."

Jerry nodded. "That's what I was afraid of."

"I don't know." The gin's courage sharpened his response. "Will you look in on her while I'm gone, Mac? I'm so concerned for her welfare that I just don't know what she'll do alone in that house right now."

Jerry Mac's tight jaw stiffened. "She's always been on the fragile side. Ginny and I'll keep an eye on her."

"Thanks," he said.

Jerry Mac cleared his throat. "About that lie-detector test."

"I've volunteered to take one."

"Damn, that was the right decision." He nodded his approval across the table. "Can't be easy what you're doing."

"It isn't." He could feel his proper clothes squeezing the life from him. He wished he could wear boots, jeans, a short-sleeved plaid shirt the way Jerry Mac did, but the pecking order didn't work that way, never had. Clothes made the difference between people, and right now, he needed all the layers he could pile on.

"The election's just a few months away," he said. "Jenine Durison didn't stand a chance against you before. Now, she's stepping up her campaign."

"This will be over by November."

"I hope so," he said. "Either way, the party might try something funny. You know how rigid this district is."

"And how agricultural."

Jerry Mac's broad, ruddy face widened even more with a smile. "You crossed party lines for us. Think we won't cross them for you?"

Of course, that was what he wanted to hear, what he'd come to this Stepford town of farmers to hear, but he didn't dare let the victory show. "It could be a tough election," he said, "especially if April Wayne doesn't turn up."

Jerry Mac sat silent, staring at the amber pool of steak sauce bleeding into his fries. "She should turn up by then, don't you think?"

Eric shrugged. "How should I know? The longer it goes on, the less chance we have. What if she hasn't? Will you still back me? Will the rest of the farmers?"

Jerry Mac considered it, looking down at his darkening fries, then up at Eric. Finally he lifted the glass and swallowed the last of his drink. "You know Suzanne is like my daughter."

"She feels the same, Mac."

"Can you promise me you'll take that lie-detector test, prove to all those fools what we already know about you?"

"I already said I would. My lawyer's already scheduled the polygraph with the police."

"Then you can count on our support."

"You mean it?"

"Hell, yes." Jerry Mac pushed back his over-gelled strands of remaining gray hair.

"You aren't doubting my word?"

"Not at all."

"Just doubting my bad press, I suppose."

"Press, schmess. I'm a simple man, Eric. Take that damn polygraph, vote the right way on ag issues, take care of Suzanne and the twins, and in November, I'll pull you over the finish line if I have to."

"You won't have to," Eric said. "No one will, if you get behind me right now."

Jerry Mac's face reddened. "Consider us behind you," he said. "No matter what."

This was one amazing man. Although he came on like a Levi's-wearing shit-kicker, he exuded power, and in one short meal, he'd given Eric his strength back. The farmers would back him. Jerry Mac would see to it. All Eric had to do was pass one stupid polygraph. And there was a bonus. Jerry and Ginny McBride would check in on Suzanne—translated, watch her every move. Although he could barely admit it to himself, she might need to be watched now.

Although he'd expected more from the Santa Fe Depot in Fresno, he felt comfortable in the tiny train station that hadn't aged an inch since the sixties. Outside, dried, pink fruit clustered on the pepper trees. Train travel—the only civilized way to move from one point, and often one person, to another. Fresno was just the beginning. At Madera, Holly would join him. They would slide into adjacent seats, share cocktails, microwaved dinners, and sail north, momentarily stripped of their names, destinations and realities. He wanted to see her, to placate her as he always did, to love her back to his side of the court. And he would, of course. He always did.

Although it was already heating up that Saturday, he wore a baseball cap and windbreaker. It was an easy trip. They'd be in San Francisco by eleven-thirty, and if it all went well, who knew? Maybe they could risk one last time together. San Francisco always made him horny. Oakland was just a jump across the bay. No way would he risk trying to talk Holly into any of that tonight. What he needed was a guarantee she'd keep quiet about everything they'd done in Oakland.

The train arrived on time, at five to seven. The early morning air already radiated heat. He thought of San Francisco—the ocean, the breeze, the coastal chill—and had to smile.

As he walked faster with the small crowd moving toward the boarding platform, he became aware of a man slightly ahead of him and to his right. A younger guy in a T-shirt, he had the blank, flat stare of someone watching television. No, it was more personal than that, maybe just someone who'd recognized him and wasn't sure who he was.

"Morning." He nodded at the man, then walked briskly ahead onto the train.

"Morning, Senator."

Eric whirled around to glance at him. Not a reporter, not a lawyer, no one with a rational connection to him. Probably a weirdo who'd seen him on the news and would entertain all of his friends with how he'd met the infamous senator at the depot.

Eric boarded the train and headed up the narrow metal steps to what used to be called the club car. You were supposed to pick a seat first, but this train was never that busy. As it pulled out of the station, he looked out at the scattered crowd breaking away from each other, trailing back to their lives after having seen off loved ones. The man who'd greeted him hadn't moved. He watched each car, as if flipping stations on a television set. Looking for something. An iciness settled into Eric's bones, an odd feeling that the towheaded guy wasn't there to see anybody off, nor greet anybody, either. The guy knew Eric would be on this train.

As it turned out, the Valley suffered a power outage that weekend. How nice for him to be on the train. He overheard a mother, whose kids ran up and down the aisle while she called on her cell phone for weather reports. Not exactly the restful ride he'd planned. Another woman, thirty, thirty-five maybe, sitting across from him but two seats down, hadn't stopped sobbing since she'd gotten on. Damn women. As if she were the only one in the world who had problems. If she only knew.

Holly got on in Madera. He spotted her on the platform at once when the train pulled into the station. Large dark glasses hid most of her face, but the short, fluffy hair stood out among the bland bodies in the crowd. Whoever said redheads couldn't wear red had never seen Holly. The short suit exactly matched her glossy lip color. He wanted to take her in his arms on the spot. Instead he forced himself to look out the window as she settled across from him on the other side of the table.

Once they were moving slowly out of the station, he said, "Power outage in the Valley today. Going to be another hot one."

"Oh?"

"Lucky for me. I'll be in San Francisco."

"No one's listening, Eric. You can stop playing games."

"Just trying to take every precaution."

"I know all about that." She pressed her lips into a straight, hard line. He knew the look, knew what it took to erase it.

"Holly, please."

"You said I was the only one."

"You were. You are. The only one I love."

"And that girl, what was she? What did you do to her, Eric? Did you take her to Oakland, too?"

Her voice was rising. No one seemed to notice. The woman down from them continued to sob into her tissue. The dumpy man across the aisle continued reading his *San Francisco Chronicle*. The cell-phone woman's kids dashed up and down the space between them. Holly put her head in her hands.

"Calm down, baby," he said. "I never took anyone there but you. Take it easy. Let me get you an iced tea."

She shook her head. "I don't want anything. I just want you to tell me the truth."

"I'm trying," he said. "That's why I agreed to meet you, in spite of the danger."

"Danger? A girl is missing, maybe dead, and all you can think about is the media seeing you with me."

"Holly, please. Don't make it worse than it is."

"How could it be any worse?"

"You could say you don't love me. That would be the worst."

"The terrible thing is I do love you, Eric."

"Then we'll get through it."

"No, we won't."

"How can you say that?"

She took off her dark glasses, looking directly at him with red-rimmed eyes. "Because you're a married man who has every intention of staying that way. Because you had an affair with your intern while you were having an affair with me, probably slept with her in that same bed where we slept together, probably tied her to the same freaking bedposts. How many other women have you had in that bed, Eric? How many *people?*"

"No one. Holly, listen to me. You're the only one I love."

"Liar. Did you do the funny stuff with April, too?" The little-girl voice that had once aroused him now sounded irritating and spoiled. He already knew he'd spend the night alone in San Francisco, and that was fine with him. What he had to do was convince this little brat to keep her mouth shut.

"I'm not lying to you, I wouldn't."

"I asked you about that girl when it first happened, the last time I saw you in Sacramento. You said nothing had gone on."

"I apologize," he said. "I didn't want to risk losing you. That's my biggest crime, my only one."

She hesitated, then, subdued, laid her sunglasses on the table between them. That was more like it. "That weekend she disappeared, you called me just like always."

"Why wouldn't I? I didn't have anything to do with it."

"And you weren't worried about her?"

"Not at all. She's young, headstrong. I figured she'd turn up."

"Where was your wife when you were calling me?"

"I used my cell phone. You know about my marriage. You know everything, honey."

"She's the one I feel sorry for. Being married to you all of these years—no wonder she's crazy."

"She's not crazy. She—" He felt himself sputter. Should he defend Suzanne, or would that just anger Holly more? He had to say something to stop the way this morning was playing out. He no longer cared about San Francisco or even Oakland. He just needed to convince Holly that they should part friends. Silent friends. "I think I told you that she wasn't well."

"Wasn't mentally well."

"Yes, something like that."

"Disturbed. You said she was disturbed."

Her mouth twisted, and he realized she was not all that attractive after all. That hair dazzled anyone who looked at her, promising a beauty she couldn't deliver.

"Yes. She's had serious problems since before we were married."

"It couldn't have helped her to hear about your relationship with April," she said. "It hurt me more than I can say."

Yes, Holly, it's always about you, Holly. How did he ever stand this selfish narcissist? "I'm sorry," he said. "I never dreamed any of this would happen. I'll do my best to keep your name out of it. I'll never mention you to anyone, I promise."

"Oh, I believe you. That's one thing I do believe for sure."

"You can't believe I had anything to do with it?"

"Why not? You lied about it to her parents, to the police and to me."

"Clinton lied about Monica. People in my position don't relish having their private lives exposed."

"Monica wasn't missing. All Clinton lied about was a blow job."

"Please," he said. "Quiet down. How can I make up for what you've been through? I don't want you to hate me. I want to make it right."

"How?" Was that a gleam of avarice in her eyes? He grabbed at the possibility.

"I don't have a lot of money. The legal and PR expenses are draining me, but we could work out something."

"You'd give me money? To stay quiet?"

"No, Holly. God, I'm not trying to pay you off. I just want to help." He leaned forward, placed his hands on the table, palms up. "You mean too much to me to let this end in anger."

The gleam in her eyes burned now with full-bore hatred. "You don't know the meaning of the word. You don't care about that girl. If I were the missing one, you wouldn't care about me either." She slid across the seat, pulling her shoulder bag with her.

"Wait." His stomach knotted with desperation. "Holly, you're totally wrong."

"Not this time." Her voice was a low whisper. "Maybe something I know will help them find that girl. If nothing else, it will show them the kind of man you are."

"You vindictive bitch." The words sprang from his lips before he could stop himself. Her pale face flushed with anger, and for a moment, he thought she would strike him. Instead she pulled herself from the seat, her chest rising and falling rapidly.

"Those are the last words you'll ever speak to me," she said. "I'll remember them every time I start to miss you or wonder if I did the right thing." She hooked the bag over her shoulder and collected her sunglasses, holding on to the table to steady herself. He had to stop her before it was too late.

He moved over to the outside seat, but before he could get up, the man with the newspaper appeared beside Holly. "Better stay where you are, Senator," he said.

He was burly and balding with hooded goat eyes that appeared incapable of a direct gaze. She'd betrayed him, the bitch. From the moment she'd gotten on this train, she'd betrayed him. He hadn't stood a chance.

"You didn't have to hire a private detective," he said to her. "I wouldn't have hurt you."

"He's not a private detective." Holly's confidence returned, her eyes steely before she covered them with the glasses. "He's my attorney, and that's his tape recorder."

He sank back into his seat as the two of them walked down the aisle—the sexy redhead in the red suit, and the overweight attorney in his linen jacket, their bodies moving back and forth with the swaying of the train.

48 days

The Mother

Gloria Wayne wanted to kill Eric Barry. That's all there was to it. This Holly woman made it even worse, more terrifying. It wasn't as April had said, that they were in love and ready to buck all odds to be together. He was a predator. He'd let her daughter remain missing, lied to all of them, to protect himself. Hating him was the only thing that got her out of bed—that and Rich Ryder's daily calls. Together they planned new stories, always true, to keep April's name in the news and keep Eric Barry on the defensive.

Gloria and Jack walked back inside their home, their arms around each other, in the pathetic, choreographed way they'd become used to doing. A pose, a stance that photographed well, that elicited prayers, that kept the story alive. The hot lights of the television crew followed them down the driveway, in through the side entrance to the garage.

The door leading to the house clicked shut behind them.

"Are they gone?"

"No, but they can't see you in here."

"Thank God." The tension in her shoulders softened slightly. She crossed the tile entry and settled before the fireplace.

"Drink?"

"No, thanks. You have one, though." The polite give and take of two strangers going slowly crazy.

"Let's leave tonight," he said. "Go away."

She jumped, not realizing he had moved behind the chair in which she had settled. She turned, looked up at his drained face. "Like where? Paris?"

"Not that far. We need to stay close in case—"

"I know."

"I was thinking of the coast, maybe Monterey. Or we can head the other direction, have dinner in Santa Barbara. We could get there in, say, five hours."

"What about the new development? Aren't you starting construction?"

"I've cleared my schedule. The foreman can handle it."

"I shouldn't leave Karen alone."

"For one weekend? You think she'd mind?"

She could have asked more questions, could have made excuses, but something told her to lighten up just this once. The sadness in his thin face cut so deep that she couldn't bear to turn him away.

"Let's go," she said.

They took the Saab, his toy car, an odd-looking, silver-gray vehicle that got more appealing, as some people did, the more time she spent around it.

They opted for an easy two and a half hours to Shell Beach.

"It's the way to make something happen," he told her as they drove. "If we sit around here, nothing will change."

"Like if you wash your car, it will rain?"

"Something like that."

Although he'd never been handsome, he'd had a wild-eyed allure that had charmed her back in 1970 whatever. Jack, the crazy man. Tell him he couldn't do something, and he did it. Say he'd lose his ass, and he'd double his investment, sweating around the clock with his men until a subdivision was completed.

He'd wanted to be an artist, but was too practical for that. After his father died, he'd taken over his construction company and grown it. His moderately priced homes changed the landscape of the Valley. They made it possible for many young families to go from renting to buying, and had made him rich in the process.

Wealth was just a byproduct of Jack's passion for his work. Unlike other developers, he never tried to buy off politicians. He talked to them, respected responsible city planning, and before he was finished stating his case, he could usually get even the diehards to acknowledge that Jack Wayne might be a developer, but he was a hell of a nice guy.

She searched through his curly hair, his battered flesh for a semblance of that man she remembered. Someone different sat in his place. She studied him. His face swallowed by hollow cheeks. His desperate eyes. Human hurt personified. Her husband.

They'd been over the questions since April had disappeared. Had she been angry enough to run away? Had she said anything that might be a clue they'd overlooked? Today, they just drove.

The air changed the moment they came over the pass. Gloria lowered her window.

"Feel the change?"

He flashed her a smile of acquiescence. "Someone should paint those colors, the way they go from dried-up yellow to green like this."

"You could," she said.

"Not anymore, maybe never."

She leaned back in her bucket seat, looked at him. "So tell me, Jackson Pollock, what are we going to do this weekend to keep from losing our minds?"

"I don't know, sweetheart." He didn't turn his head this time, but she could tell that his eyes had filled with tears.

"Jack?"

"What, sweetheart?"

"Did she ever call me Glorious Gloria?"

"She didn't mean anything by it."

"So she did. She really did call me that?"

"Yes, sometimes, when you were on your high horse." He stopped and checked her face to see if she'd taken offense. "You know how she is."

She bit her lip, unable to speak. Finally she said, "Yes. I know."

They traveled on in silence, the CD player as quiet as they. Two people, she thought, people who had conceived a daughter together, unable to talk to each other as their car sped over the hills and the darkening ocean swallowed what was left of the sun.

49 days

The Wife

Melinda arrives around five, just as I am going to try to force myself to eat. I singed the bread for my BLT, forgetting that our toaster has to be watched and coddled if it's to perform. Barry's Wife Lost Mind Growing Tomatoes In Valley Heat the next headline will read.

It's an unexpected visit. I thought Melinda would work later, as the other aides always do, but I'm glad to see her. She's curled her flyaway hair and put on a long, shapeless dress of a crinkled blue fabric printed with blue dots, her attempt at business attire. There's something wrong with her face, though. Her skin's too pale, her eyes ashen.

"Don't turn on the TV," she says.

"Oh, God, what's happened? Have they found her?"

"No, but there's a rally going on." She joins me at the sink, places the burned bread onto a plate, as if time can repair the damage. "Pretty lame, but we didn't plan it. We'll probably get blamed for it, though."

"A rally? For Eric or against?"

"For. It's a few blocks from here." She looks from me to the television as if to assess how much I could take. "Larry King's got it on."

I'm not hungry anyway. Motioning toward the wraparound sofa in the den, I pick up the remote control, clutch it in both hands.

Larry King leans forward, large face hunched through his shoulders. To Larry's right, in the upper quadrant of the screen, a sweaty-faced man with an evangelical topknot above his shiny forehead addresses the crowd. As he looks toward the monitor, the man's words break through, a once-soft Southern accent hardened by years in the San Joaquin.

"Senator Barry's staff helped me when no one would. They helped me get the right form to fill out so that I could save my business." He pronounces it binness. "Thank you, God, for Eric Barry. He helped me save my business."

"Stay, Eric.

"Stay, Eric.

"Stay, Eric."

The crowd's chant reminds me of "Free Willie" or "Go Raiders" maybe. Substitute any phrase as long as it isn't too complicated. This group of protestors with their sweat and their florid complexions wouldn't know the difference.

"Told you it was lame," Melinda says, leaning over the back of the black leather chair I think of as Eric's because no one else ever sits in it.

"An embarrassment." I've seen real protestors in the late sixties, not that I'd ever dared take part in anything more political than a governor's luncheon. "How low did they have to troll in our community to pull out this element?"

"Anne Ashley didn't even know about it," she says. "I think

the farmers started it. The word spread, and everyone else crawled out of the woodwork."

Even King's most obnoxious talking heads look stunned as they debate Eric's chances for reelection in November.

"No way," says the attorney with the shimmering eyes that look more drug induced than enthusiastic.

"He could pull it off," says Lindy Squire, the magazine editor. "Suppose his wife came forward, forgave him? If he publicly apologized to the Waynes and Mrs. Barry for the problems he's caused, perhaps he could do it."

"What are you smoking, Lindy?" the attorney interrupts. "The guy's finished."

"The police admit he's not a suspect, Doug."

"The police aren't telling us what they know. Contrary to what you might think, they're not accountable to the media."

"What are your feelings about Suzanne Barry?" King's voice cuts through the strident debate.

"My heart goes out to her," Lindy Squire says. "She must be in terrible pain."

"Shut it off, Suze," Melinda whispers. "Don't do this to yourself."

But I can't turn away.

"According to Holly Yost, the meeting planner who says she also had an affair with Eric Barry, Mrs. Barry has severe emotional problems."

"That's what he says, and while he's trying to justify an affair at that."

My legs melt. I sink into the sofa, turn to Melinda. "They really think I'm crazy, don't they?"

"They're the crazy ones. They don't even know you."

The camera sweeps over the crowd again. The faces of the protestors, their features flattened by the glare of the sun, gaze back. In the corner of the sign-carriers, I glimpse a tall man in the slouched stance of an outsider. He wears a black shirt, in this heat yet, and his face shines with sweat and whatever he had to drink last night.

"Ryder," Melinda says.

"It's his fault. He ran the story." I jump up from the sofa, knowing what I have to do. "Come on, we're going down there right now."

"Suze, we can't."

"Stay here then, but I'm going. I have to defend myself."

Melinda's driving her old station wagon, not the white van Eric keeps at the Pleasant Valley office for his staff.

The ancient air conditioner doesn't touch the heat-crammed car.

"Sorry about this thing," she says. "I never needed A/C at home."

For a moment I wonder what I've done to this child whose diapers I used to change, this little girl who wanted to grow up, get involved in politics, change the world. "I shouldn't have suggested you start working for him," I say.

"I'm glad you did. I've already learned more than I have in all my poli-sci classes put together. It's a better summer job than the motel."

"There were so many strangers, all of a sudden," I say.

She looks to me for more, but I can't finish the thought, about what it's like to have people stare in my windows, ring my doorbell, about how I needed to see someone I know, someone who knows me, who knows I'm not crazy.

Sweat trickles down my neck, and my underarms itch as if I haven't bathed in weeks. She takes a corner fast, and I feel a tug of anxiety. No, I'm too angry for that. Dr. Kellogg told me that once. When you're sick, when you're really angry, the panic attacks stay away. They don't stand a chance against the real thing. They're cowards.

This is all I need. Wife Killed In A Wreck After A Wild Ride To Rally Of Misfits. Ryder would probably say Eric killed me, too, tampered with the brakes or something.

"Damn, maybe I am crazy," I say.

Melinda glances away from the road. "Want to go back?" Tendrils of the hair she pinned up this morning cling to her neck. Her words make sense. I'm ashamed of my anger.

"I just want to see. Please. Maybe we can just sit in the car."

We pull into the parking lot, crawl along the outside of the cameras, windows down.

A man in a three-piece suit is passing out something to the people in the first row.

"Don't they feel the heat?" I say.

"Too rabid," she says. "This is their moment."

"I'm proud to say this here's a picture of my son," the man announces as if accepting an academy award. "He was six pounds when he was born and sixteen pounds when he died."

Several women in the audience sigh in unison. *"Oooh,"* they say. *"Oooh."*

"That's why they're here, to exhibit their flaws," I tell Melinda. "It's about them, their pain."

"I just want to say that without God and Eric Barry, I never would have made it," the man continues. "My prayers go out to him and the missus."

"They mean well," Melinda says, and I can hear the lie in her voice.

"They're freaks. This is just an excuse to tell their stories. It's *Queen For A Day* mentality."

"What's that?"

"A TV show before you were born. Never mind. It doesn't matter."

"Want to go home now, Suze?" Her complexion is blotched, her pale hair in kinks at her neck. I do, but my hand reaches for the door, the hot handle.

"Suze, wait."

"You."

I approach him from behind. I can tell him from the stance, the black shirt with its large stain of sweat.

111

He turns, and something flickers for a moment in his eyes, the kind of look he might give a rattlesnake he'd just spotted in his path.

"What's the matter? You think I came to do you in?"

"I'm just surprised. Are you here to make a statement?"

"Suze?" Melinda's gentle voice. I ignore it.

"Do I look crazy to you?" I put a hand on each hip, stare into his eyes. I'm rolling on adrenaline, unable to stop, the way I was that night, when that girl called me a bitch. "I said, do I look crazy? That's what you told your readers."

"I never said that, Mrs. Barry. The tabloids ran those head-lines."

"But you started it."

"I quoted Holly Yost, what she said the senator told her about you."

"My husband would never say that." I feel tears, am not sure how I'll ever hold them back. "Do you know what you're doing to my life?"

"I'm sorry." His blue eyes send me mixed messages, part guilt, part concern, part delight at having a new piece of news to print.

"Eric, stay.

"Eric, stay.

"Eric, stay."

The chant brings me back to reality, makes me realize I can't sacrifice my husband to satisfy my vindictiveness.

Melinda steps forward between us, introduces herself to Ryder.

"You're the spokesperson for the family?" he asks.

"For Senator Barry's local office only. I'd like to say that we had nothing to do with the organization of this rally today, al-though, of course, the senator appreciates the support of the people he has represented so long and so well."

She sounds polished, prepared. A kid. I need to get out of here. I'll follow Melinda.

"Mrs. Barry," he says. "I'd like to talk to you."

"She's not making any statements today," Melinda says. "Come on, Suze."

"Don't you agree that finding April Wayne is what matters, Mrs. Barry?"

I turn from the ambivalent eyes. It takes all the strength I possess to do so.

"Why hasn't your husband made a statement?"

Just keep walking. Don't pay any attention to him. The car is right ahead.

"God bless Eric.

"God bless Eric.

"God bless Eric."

Melinda opens the door, scoots inside. I hurry to the other door.

"God bless.

"God bless.

"God bless."

"Mrs. Barry, Suzanne?"

I turn in spite of myself. My gaze meets his across the car, a man with a mission, at least as much as those people in front of the television cameras.

"What?" I ask, although I know I've already said too much.

"We're coming out with an editorial in Sunday's *Voice*," he says. "We're asking for the senator's resignation."

I gasp inwardly. On the outside, I'm cool again. I climb in the car, slam the door, and Melinda takes off.

"Did you hear that? They're calling for Eric's resignation."

"Doesn't make any difference," she says. "He won't resign. Look at the support he has."

I glance back at the grocery store parking lot, the sad little group and their megaphones.

"Yes," I say. "He'll be fine."

113

* * *

Later, I can't believe that I had the audacity to confront Rich Ryder like that. I fight the fear I've seen in Eric's eyes, the fear that I might be getting worse.

"Because you're changing the way you deal with people?" Dr. Kellogg asks. He doesn't mention that I haven't been able to sit down since I entered his office today, that I stand at the door, my arms crossed, pressed against my chest.

"The way I deal with some people, not everyone."

"This reporter, Rich Ryder?"

"Yes. He has no right to pry into my life."

"And Eric?"

"I try to be a good wife."

I glance at him as I pace before his office door. His eyes don't leave my face. "You're changing the way you deal with Eric?"

I itch all over, the sweat of anxiety trying to break through my calm, pharmaceutical shell. "I don't know."

He looks down at his notebook, then up at me, his expression so concerned that I want to throw my arms around him and tell him I'll be all right. "What makes you think you're getting worse?"

"Because if it weren't for those little pills I take, I'd be a walking panic attack." I try to say it like a joke.

"You aren't a walking panic attack," he says. "That's an oxymoron."

I realize it's his lame attempt at humor and laugh. Then something hits me, something that never occurred to me before. "Would this have happened to me anyway? If Eric's intern hadn't disappeared, would I still be dealing with this?"

He starts to nod, then, as if by will, forces his head to remain still. "Sometimes it takes an event."

"But I've been having various types of panic attacks for a long time."

"And we've talked about that before. You know why they started."

I shut the image out of my mind. I can't bear to remember, especially not now. "You're the only person in the world who knows that," I say. "Besides, it may not even be the reason."

"And if it is the reason, maybe it's not as horrible as you think."

Now I'm pissed. I came in here seeking help, and this old man in his ratty sweater in the middle of summer, no less, dares to question my past, my pain.

"I think it's the reason, and I think it's horrible. It ruined my life."

"Do you think your life's ruined?"

"Now it is. My daughters are at war. My husband's being crucified by the press. And the whole damn world thinks I'm nuts."

"Do you think you're nuts, Suzanne?" The question darts out before I can think about it.

"Hell no. I mean, I have a problem, but I live with it. I've always lived with it."

"Does Eric know?"

It's the first time he's ever asked me. I lean back against the wall of his office and uncross my arms. Our hour is almost over. I have nothing more to say, no more demons I can bear to pull out and examine right now. Tears fight their way to the surface. I blame Kellogg for that.

"I am a good wife," I tell him. "I was a good daughter."

"Suzanne." His voice is thin and strained, a tiny breeze of hope I can barely feel.

"I'm sorry. I have to leave now. The *Voice* is going to run an editorial. They're going to try to destroy Eric's career. I need to fix that. I can't spend my time like this."

As I burst into the hall, I hear his voice behind me, stronger now. "I'll see you next week, Suzanne."

59 days

The Parlor Game

April's Medical Records Sought

The *Valley Voice* editorial demanding Senator Barry's resignation caused a stir. Barry ignored it, meeting with the farmers, spending time with his family, waiting for the Senate to meet again.

The group at the Hofbrau had become regulars, just like the faces on *Larry King Live*. Harold began to anticipate their visits. Tonight, they were cranky, sniping at each other as if they—and not the faces before them—were the television show. He turned on the blender, buzzing away the rest of their words. Summer continued to burn itself out. Although it had been almost two months, April Wayne's disappearance dictated the mood of the town. Years later, Harold knew, he'd remember this summer in terms of her face in the newspaper, on the television, and these conversations that drifted in and out of his bar.

"Jeez," Kent said. "Why don't they leave it alone?"

Janie sniffed her Brandy Alexander as if it were wine. "When there's no news, they have to make it up, right, Harold Bear?"

"Right. What are you having tonight, Whitey?"

"Thought you said the blender was broke," he said through clenched teeth.

"I fixed it."

Janie grinned. "Plugged it in, you mean. Harold Bear hates using the blender, except for me."

"Hell, I don't care," Whitey said. "Give me a beer then. Bud Light."

"Sure thing, Whitey."

"I want what Janie's having," the Garabedian girl said. She'd always want what Janie was having her whole damned life, but she wouldn't get any closer than the blond tips she bleached into her coarse black hair.

"Sure thing, Heath," he said. "What do you think about them going after her medical records?"

"I think they're important. Really important. Maybe they can find out if she was pregnant."

"Or had VD," Janie said happily.

Kent shook his head. "Damn, you have a dirty mind, girl."

"And Eric Barry has a dirty life. With all of those women, you know he's got something."

"Then maybe they ought to check out his medical records," Kent said.

Harold cranked nutmeg over the top of the Alexander and served it to the Garabedian girl.

"Me, I don't think Suzanne Barry's crazy," he said.

They all stopped, looked at him.

"Why not?" Janie demanded.

"We would of known it, right?" Harold said. "We shop in the same grocery store. I can't tell you how many times she's come in here for dinner."

117

"He's right," Heather said. "We would have known something."

"Unless she was mildly crazy all the time," Janie said. "Maybe she just flipped out after her husband got involved with April."

Kent sighed his disgust. He usually didn't argue with Janie, but Harold could tell he'd just about had a craw full.

"You've been reading too many tabloids," he told her.

"Don't knock it. They might be sleazy, but that doesn't mean they don't get some decent tips."

Harold could sense it when conversation overheated, and that's what was happening here tonight. "You're awful quiet tonight, Whitey," he said.

"Just thinking." The guy had kept his glasses on after looking at the newspaper. They were the tinted kind that were supposed to get darker outside and lighter inside, only inside they never got light enough. Whitey looked as if he were staring at him though a smoke-gray film.

"What do you think, Whitey?" Janie asked. "Should the senator resign?"

"Damn straight he should."

"Think they'll find April?" she said.

He shrugged. "Even if they did, and even if the senator had something to do with it, he'd go scot-free. That's the way you people look at things in the Valley. The whole place is just all fucked up."

"Please," Heather said. "Could you show the ladies here a little respect?"

Kent shot him a frown. "Cool it, man. I know what you're saying, but this ain't the place for it."

Janie nodded as if her honor had been avenged. "If you don't like it here, perhaps you should move back to Albuquerque."

When Whitey didn't answer, she pressed it. "Well?"

"Well, what?"

"Maybe you ought to head on back to New Mexico. Why'd you come here in the first place if you hate it so much?"

Whitey gave her a look Harold wouldn't have wanted to be on the receiving end of. "Personal business. When I finish it, I will go back."

Something in his tone shut her up. A jarring silence fell over the bar. Even the magpies in the back got quiet. Harold clattered glasses to fill the sudden void.

"'Nother Bud, Whitey?" he asked. "Hey, how about those Giants?"

The Girl

She climbed into her clothes so fast she barely knew what she was putting on. Get dressed, she told herself. Put on makeup. Look respectable, and lie, lie, lie. She understood now something she'd refused to admit before. If Eric knew what she said to his wife, if he found out that she'd told her mother, he would drop her in two seconds.

She was not going to let that happen. She couldn't handle any more hurt. When he got here, she'd suggest they go out for a drink, complain about how bored she was hanging around the condo. They'd visited a couple of neighborhood bars before. He'd certainly agree if she said she wanted to go. He'd take her a lot more places than he did if she didn't always jump his bones the minute he walked in the front door.

Her mouth tasted like turpentine, and Eric was out of bottled water. She tried to chase the taste away with another icy swallow of gin. An acquired taste, people said, and they were right. Her first martini, at the Hofbrau at home when she was still underage, tasted so much like cologne that she'd spit it all over the shirt of the guy she was with. Now her tastebuds were conditioned. Not that she'd ever have a drinking problem; she was too disciplined for that. She had too many goals to kill her brain cells with a lot of booze.

119

Tonight, though, she needed all the courage she could get, artificial or otherwise.

She closed the doors to the balcony. It had stopped raining and the sky was shot with color, and in spite of the muggy air, it was going to be a beautiful night.

The phone rang again, and she gasped. Please be Eric, she begged the caller. Please don't be that bitch. Please.

"I know you're there." The bitch's throaty voice broke, then paused. Hovering over the phone, April held her breath, waiting for the rest. "I know you can hear me, and I'm coming there right now."

"No," she said out loud, truly frightened now. "No. God, no."

She held the martini glass in both hands and gulped. The gin burned its way down. Her goal wasn't to feel good anymore; it was to not feel anything. Just stop this trembling and not feel anything.

Etta James continued to sing. This must have been the hundredth time she'd heard "At Last" tonight. It no longer brought her joy, no longer sounded like the beginning of anything. There were no beginnings in this room.

As April started to take another swallow, she felt the glass slip out of her hand, felt it before she heard the crash on the tile floor. Oh, no. She couldn't do anything right tonight. She bent down, picked up a chunky piece of glass. Suddenly a red stain covered her hand. Drops of blood trickled through her fingers to the floor.

"Shit."

She hadn't even felt the cut. Now blood leaked from it. She nudged on the faucet over the sink with her left hand, held her right one under the cool stream. Cold water and pressure. That was what she needed. The pink towel on which she'd sat while trimming her pubic hair still lay folded on the drainboard. She wrapped it around the leaking cut and squeezed.

Broken glass, blood, a crazy wife on her way. It was out of control. Erase the message. Erase the message. But she couldn't fight the tears anymore. They ran down her face onto her chin as she sobbed, leaning against the bar, her face buried in the towel that wrapped her throbbing right hand. She cried so hard she didn't hear anything until the lock clicked and the front door opened.

She jumped, clutching the pink towel to her chest.

"April." Eric closed the door behind him and gave her a quizzical look. "What is it, April? Honey, what's wrong?"

62 days

The Senator

The room could have been any office in any type of business, an insurance company, maybe, the conference room of a bank. There was no reason to feel nervous, Shig Yakamoto, the technician, had told him. Just ignore the equipment connecting him to the machine that could determine his fate. They could do this more than once if they had to. Eric assured him they wouldn't have to.

He faced a blank wall, his arm banded as if to determine something as simple as his blood pressure and not his future. A smaller similar device fit around his finger, and a larger band of gray, elastic material surrounded his chest. From the beginning, he could tell that Shig knew his way around the equipment and the procedure. He shared the universal lawman trait of making the most horrible business sound as normal as talking football with a friend in a bar. That's what happened when you lived this stuff twenty-four hours a day, when you earned a living hooking people to machines and asking them if they were murderers.

He sat to Eric's right, at an angle, his laptop flipped open. Eric hadn't expected the computer, but now that he thought about it, what should they use? A truth-or-consequences bell that clanged every time he got the wrong answer?

The questions started out easy, as he'd been told they would. His name, his job, his address. That threw him for a moment. He felt himself falter, then stated his address in Pleasant View, the house where he and Suzanne lived. Just think about the house where he lived, his daughters. Picture them as children, his beautiful family.

"Were you involved in a personal relationship with April Wayne?"

"Yes."

"To your knowledge, is April Wayne pregnant?"

"Not to my knowledge. No."

"Do you know where April Wayne is?"

"No."

"Did you do anything to harm April Wayne?"

"No." He'd never harm April. He let the questions buzz past like pesky mosquitoes.

"Are you withholding any information about April Wayne?"

"No."

"Okay, Senator, that'll do it. Let's start again."

"I thought you said just once."

The man flashed him dazzling capped teeth. He'd had something put on them to make them this white. Eric wished he had the nerve to ask what. "Two more times."

He asked the questions again, rearranging the words slightly. Eric retreated into the safety of the past, putting himself far away from this invasive process, the way he did at the dentist's office, trying to ignore the probing, distancing himself from the pain.

123

That night, he went back to the condo and flipped the stations until he saw Holly's face, her pouf of red hair, and had to stop. How she could do this was beyond him. Her attorney, the goat-eyed man from the train, sat beside her, ever the wise mentor in search of the fast buck. He knew the type.

As Holly lisped out her version of their affair, Eric cursed her silently. "He lied to me," she said. "I thought I was the only one."

That's what it was really about—old-fashioned female jealousy. That was Suzanne's problem, too. That whole thing in her head—fragile, fragile, fragile—was for effect, just to make him feel guilty.

At least Holly wasn't mentioning Oakland. She wouldn't dare. Falling for a married man was one thing. She could still elicit sympathy from part of the public. If the other stuff got out, it would wipe away that sympathy for good.

Holly and the goat were after something, probably a fat book deal. He'd just managed to force himself to click them into silence when the phone rang.

"Clean as a whistle," Denny announced. "You passed the polygraph, partner."

Thank God. "Of course I did," he said. Then, "Hey, Denny, I've been sitting here watching Holly Yost tell the world what a bastard I am. Any chance we might have a drink, maybe catch a late bite somewhere?"

"Life's a bitch, isn't it?" Denny always got philosophical when he drank.

"Mine sure is right now. It will get better, though. If I didn't have faith, I'd jump off that fake grass on the roof out there."

They'd burned through wine and appetizers in Brother Luigi's back room, and now, they drank straight whiskey at the bar on the top floor of his condo.

When the barmaid returned, Eric hesitated. "This had better be my last one," he said.

"Why's that, partner? You're not driving."

"But I'm starting to feel it. Guess the appetizers weren't enough."

"I think I ate more than my share," Denny said. "I forget my manners when there's food on the table."

"I had plenty."

Denny shook his head and peered into Eric's eyes as if addressing one of the ubiquitous television cameras that had been following him around since the story broke. "All the years I've known you, and I've never seen you drunk."

Eric looked out over the patio at the stars blurring into the lights of the city, a pretty city from this far away. "Thought I owed it to the office and the public. Seldom get as much as tipsy. Never take a bribe. Always vote my conscience. Hardly even swear. And now this."

Denny nodded his sympathy. "Let's go out on the roof," he said. "Less chance anybody recognizing either one of us."

"That's right. I'm making you famous, man. Every time I turn on the TV, there you are."

"Someone's got to speak for you."

"Don't cry on my shoulder. For what I'm paying, it's the least you can do."

Denny's eyes twinkled. "We get out there, I'll show you what you're paying for."

Imitation grass covered the rooftop balcony, and green wrought-iron tables and chairs clustered around the black, kiosk-shaped heating units no one would need for many months yet. The air had cooled, and for the first time all night, Eric felt as if he weren't drowning in sweat.

The heat and the late hour had taken their toll. Only one couple remained on the roof, and they were so engrossed in each other that they hadn't noticed or cared that anyone was sharing their space.

"Think they're married?" Denny asked.

"No."

"Sorry. Guess that was an inconsiderate question."

"Don't apologize. The question's fine. Contrary to what you might think of me, I believe in marriage and commitment. Always have."

"Make that apology number two then. You know, you're really different from the person they talk about."

"I'd say that's an understatement."

"Speaking of married." He pulled out a green wrought-iron chair and sat. "How's Suzanne doing?"

"Not as well as she has been. Pressure's getting to her, all that stuff about her illness."

Denny gave him an unfathomable look. "She's a wonderful woman. That's got to be tearing her up."

"It's not my fault what Holly tells the press. She's after financial gain."

"A book deal?"

"Or a centerfold spread, whatever. Wait and see."

"Wish you'd told me about her," Denny said.

"I didn't think she mattered. She was in the past."

"The very recent past."

"Okay, Denny. I didn't think she'd talk."

"They all talk, my friend. In a case like this, they all talk sooner or later, and very, very publicly." He looked down into his glass then back up at Eric with bleary, impatient eyes. "If you have anything else you want to talk about, clue me in before someone else comes forward, okay?"

"Nothing else," Eric said. "The polygraph ought to tell you that."

"Lily-white." Denny shrugged and raised his thick eyebrows. Since his frequent television appearances, his gestures had taken on a cartoon quality.

"Lily-white is good."

"The media will point out that these things aren't absolute, but the end result will be positive." He reached down into his briefcase and came up with a bag. "Pretzels," he said, digging in. "Chocolate covered. Help yourself, and I'll get us another drink. While I'm gone, take a look at this." He slid an unmarked manila file across the table.

"What's this?" Eric asked.

"The reason you pay me what you do." He grinned in the dark. "A list of missing women."

"How's that going to help me?"

"They're all in April Wayne's age range. They all lived in the general vicinity of her neighborhood." He leaned across the table, his head so close that Eric could smell his pungent chocolate breath. "Most important, they're all murdered or missing in the last five years. Suggest anything to you?"

"Lousy police work?"

"Maybe that's all. Or possibly we're dealing with a serial killer. Maybe one crazy killed all these women, and maybe the same crazy killed April, too."

It took a minute to unscramble what Denny was trying to say. What a mind—working outside and around the problem, instead of from the inside out. It seemed almost unsavory to be able to think that way, to go in one leap from protecting a client to tracking five years' worth of murdered young women.

"You missed your calling," he said. "You should have been a screenwriter. Science fiction."

Denny stuffed his pudgy fingers into the bag. "Lucky for you I studied law instead."

Eric felt pretty bleary himself by the time they boarded the elevator for his floor.

"Think you better sleep it off on the futon," he said. "Don't want you taking any chances."

"I'll be okay, partner."

Telling obstinate Denny he'd had too much to drink wouldn't work, but Eric knew what would. "I could order a pizza. It'd be here in ten minutes."

Denny perked up. "You like pepperoni?"

"You know I do."

At the moment, the thought of food nauseated him, but he didn't want to let his most important ally risk his life after drinking all of that booze. It wasn't responsible behavior.

When they got off at his floor, Denny's step seemed more lively, probably because he was contemplating lifting a juicy slice of pepperoni pizza to his mouth. As they turned the corner, they saw the crowd assembled outside the door of the condo.

"Back to the elevator," Denny ordered.

"It's him," a male voice shouted.

They ran, Eric imagining the worst as he dashed down the hall in the direction they'd come just moments before.

"Senator Barry, do you have any comments? Senator Barry, Eric, wait."

The elevator doors slammed shut in front of them. Eric leaned against the wall.

"They'll be waiting downstairs. You know they will."

"We're getting off before then." Denny had taken a swift trip to the land of the sober. He jabbed the button for the fourth floor. "We can use the stairs from there," he said. "Get to my car before they figure out what we've done."

"Where'll we go?"

"Brother Luigi's. Back door. What fucking news broke?"

They took the stairs as fast as they could, Denny in the lead, his plump body bouncing like a round, tight ball. A dangerous man to tangle with, Eric thought, faster than he looked, and tough.

They made it out the side door, into the garage and Denny's car without anyone spotting them. TV cameras cast their lights outside the building, but by then, they were safely pulling into the street.

"Assholes," Denny said.

"Jackals."

He turned the corner and sped up. "They'll sit there all night, their lights shining on your window. Next stop, Brother Luigi's. That work for you?"

Eric nodded. He had nowhere else to go. "You think they found her?" he asked.

"Never know. They don't usually find people in the middle of the night, though." He pulled off the street at the next light. "I'm going to call ahead," he explained. "Find out what Brother Luigi knows, order us a pizza."

Not necessarily in that order, Eric thought.

He was wrong. The first two words out of Denny's mouth after identifying himself over the phone to Brother Luigi were, "Holy shit."

"What is it?" Eric asked as Denny put away the phone.

"Oh, partner, I'm sorry." Denny looked sober as the judge he hoped to be one day. For one moment they sat there as the passing headlights and the night noises filled the car. "It's Suzanne," he said, his tone suddenly professional. "They had to take her to emergency. It's all over the news."

"What happened to her. Did someone—"

Denny shook his head. "Nobody did anything. They're calling it a possible suicide attempt. We better get you home."

62 days

The Wife

I'm still woozy when I open my eyes and swim toward the eyes peering down on me, eyes the color of a beer bottle held to the sun. Their light blinds me. I try to move away, back into the safe fog.

"Suze? Honey?"

"Go away." The distortion hurts my ears, my throat. "I want to go home."

Someone takes my arms, turns the touch into a grip. "That's why we're here, Suze. We're going to take you home."

"Who's we?"

"Denny and I. Come on, honey. Let's get you up now, and when you feel less groggy, we'll go."

My eyes fly open. The face comes into focus. I take a deep breath, expel it in a rush of words. "I'm not going anyplace with you. Help, someone."

The grip tightens. "Suzanne, damn it."

"Help, please. Please help."

The drive home is a quiet one. I regain my voice, but my husband's accusing eyes follow me everywhere. Finally we settle in the kitchen, across the table from each other, watching the drawn blinds that separate us from the reporters and their camera people.

"Why is he here?" I ask.

"Denny? Don't be rude. It's not as if he's in our faces. He's watching TV, for christ sake."

"That's not the point. He's here, in our house. Do you think we need an attorney?"

"Frankly, after what happened, we need some kind of damage control."

I think about picking up my teacup but realize my hands are trembling too badly. Instead, I place them around it for warmth. Odd, the ceiling fan around me is whirling. The air conditioner is on. PG&E has been threatening power outages for three days, and I'm freezing.

"There's something I need to ask you," I say.

He cocks his head, gives me that TV quizzical look, as if demanding what I could possibly ask of him.

"The girls are coming in tonight."

"That's right."

"We need to sit down and talk to them."

"You know I talk to them all the time."

"You talk to Jill all the time."

"Only because Joy's being difficult." He picks up his teacup, tries a taste. "But then when hasn't she been difficult?"

I try again. "They'll both be here tonight. We need to talk to them, and you need to tell them the truth."

"*I* need to tell them the truth." He slams back his chair from the table, stands as if addressing a group. "I'm not the one who took an overdose."

"And I'm not the one who broke my marriage vows."

His face darkens. "If you expect me to go into all of that with the twins, you're on more drugs than I thought. I told you all you need to know. They're my daughters, not my wife."

"They're your family, Eric."

"And yours. And they wouldn't be here if you hadn't almost killed yourself." I gasp involuntarily. "It's true," he says. "You're the one who got hysterical, and if anyone needs to explain anything to the kids, it's you."

I stare at his set, determined face, and for a moment, I see his father—that self-righteous look we both hated—in his eyes.

"There's only one thing we can do then," I say.

He leans on the back of his chair, cocky, not about to back down. "And what's that?"

"I need to talk to the girls, and you need to go back to Sacramento, to that apartment of yours."

"Are you trying to punish me?"

"No, I'm trying to get you to talk, to me, to your daughters."

"You're amazing, Suzanne," he says, "the only woman I know who attempts suicide, then tries to get her husband to take responsibility for it. You need to go back to that old shrink you like so much."

"I have," I say.

"Oh, that's wonderful. I can imagine what you told him."

Somehow this horrible conversation is making me stronger. My voice is coming back to me now. "Only the truth," I say. "Now, I'd like you to leave."

"You mean that?" His eyes flare. The old rejection anger tenses every muscle in his body. "You really want me out of this house?"

I nod. "I'll support you publicly. I'm not going to break my vows, but until you're willing to talk to me and to our kids, I think you'd better stay in Sacramento."

"Fine," he says. "I'll call you later."

And without further discussion, he is gone.

* * *

"I didn't try to kill myself."

I've talked to Eric, the girls, but the sound of my voice still scares me. I can feel the scrape of the tube in my throat. Oh, God, I had tubes in my throat.

Dr. Kellogg sits across from me in his office in one of the gray, plushy chairs intended to make this feel more like a friendly visit than a session. He's an old man with vein-splattered pale skin and watery blue eyes that don't miss anything. In spite of the hundred-plus weather outside, he wears a beige cardigan that looks as old as he. I wonder how cold-blooded one must be to wear a sweater in this heat.

Since I've had my panic attacks, I've seen several therapists on and off. It's required for renewing my prescription. Some bring their own hostile agendas with them. Some simply prescribe the meds and stay out of my psyche. Others try to help. A few make a difference. Kellogg is one of those.

"How did it happen?" he asks.

"I watched one too many of those TV shows, listened to that Holly woman one too many times. I know I shouldn't have, but I did. Melinda, our intern, was in the next room."

"She's the one who brought you in?"

"Yes. I guess she found me after I lost consciousness."

Kellogg nods. "And what medication had you taken, Suzanne?"

"Valium, more than I should have. Things had gotten so bad that I couldn't get in the car without having a panic attack."

"Your prescription?"

"My husband's. He uses them to sleep when he's home."

"That's all you took?"

I'm ashamed, but lying is fruitless. He probably already knows. He just wants to hear me say it.

"Alcohol."

"What type?"

"Wine. You know I'm not a drinker. It just all hit me at once, sitting there, hearing that woman continue to talk about sleeping with my husband."

"You never guessed something like that was going on?"

"None. We never even argued. We had great sex."

"Great?"

"A good sex life. Nothing to complain about."

"Even though you live almost three hours apart."

"We're together most weekends. How many husbands and wives spend quality time together during the week, anyway? I had no idea he was having an affair, let alone that he—" I feel the tears start and reach for the tissues. "I'm sorry."

He nods, moves rhythmically in the chair as if rocking a child lost in the folds of his sweater.

"He lied to you about the other women, even after April Wayne was missing?"

"Yes, he denied everything. But I knew when that Holly woman talked, that she was telling the truth. She knows too much about what he's like sexually."

"And how is that?"

I lick my lips, realizing my mouth has gone dry. I wasn't brought up to discuss these matters with anyone. "She called him kinky," I say.

"And what do you say?"

"I think he could be a little on the kinky side," I reply. "I don't really know, though. I've been with only one other man and no one since we've been married. He always said I wasn't adventurous enough. Maybe that's why he had to go to other women."

"You know that you can't make him behave or not behave in a certain way," he says.

I look out the window at the parking lot to keep from crying. "I keep thinking it must be my fault. Because I wouldn't do the things he wants to do."

"What things?"

"Kinky things. Please, I don't want to think about it any-more."

Dr. Kellogg leans forward, squints his watery eyes as if try-ing to come up with an answer for me.

"Do you have any idea what you can do to keep something like this from happening again? What will make you feel stronger?"

"For him to stay away. He and his attorney came when they heard what happened that night. When I saw him, I burst into tears. I can't stand being near him. It reminds me of everything he's done, how he's humiliated me, made a mockery of our marriage."

"Do you have any friends, anyone you can have come stay with you?"

"Melinda. She's running his office here, but she's really as much my friend as she is his."

"Anyone else?"

The sadness of the answer depresses me. "The other wives have pretty much dropped me. There's Berta, who cuts my hair. She's a little strange, but I consider her a friend. I trust her."

"You need to be able to call these people when you need them," he says. "I don't want you taking any medication for a while."

"What about the panic attacks?" I ask. "I can't even walk through a grocery store without having to hang on to my cart. I'm that shaky."

"Legs of jelly?" It's a term we've explored in the past.

I nod. "As bad as they've ever been."

"Then lean on your cart, if you have to. Remember what we talked about before. Legs of jelly will still get you there."

The thought, maybe the way it's wrapped in his voice, gives me comfort. At least I have legs. They aren't working well right now, but they will get me there. I look into his kind face, won-der how many crazies he's seen today, how much pain he's witnessed. "Is there anything else that will help me right now?" I ask. "Anything?"

"Just remember you're not alone."

"I feel that way."

"But you say you feel better without your husband around. Do you feel more alone or less alone?"

"Without him there? Neither. I do feel stronger, though."

"How is he reacting?"

I can still see his face. "He's very angry," I reply. "That's how he is when he doesn't get his way. My husband is a very controlling man."

It's difficult to say. Eric and I have always agreed that talking about each other to someone else is a betrayal. Considering what he's done, I shouldn't feel guilty. It's the truth. All I've done is tell the truth.

I rise to leave, barely able to find my feet. As is our custom, we hug at Dr. Kellogg's office door. "Good session," he says. "You worked hard. I want to see you in two days."

"Not a week from today?"

"Twice a week for now."

The unspoken prognosis flattens me. "Am I going to get better?" I ask him.

"Yes," he says. "I think you're already getting better. See you in two days."

I think of his words all the way to the car. *Legs of jelly will still get me there. I am not alone. And I'm not responsible for my husband's actions.*

One of the oddities of therapy is that, as horribly invasive as it feels while I'm going through it, only a few minutes after I leave Kellogg's office, relief floods through me. I feel freer than I have since that horrible moment in front of the television picture of Eric's other mistress. I let myself revisit it in my mind, testing my own strength. An attractive woman, younger than I, blithely saying on every talk show on television that she'd slept with my husband, that his sexual habits verged on kinky.

That was what sent me to the pills, what made me forget every-thing that happened afterward. It was like the night when April Wayne called me a bitch or that other night so many years ago when these attacks first began. I know it happened, but I can't remember it moment by moment. I don't want to try.

Kellogg's right. I've worked hard. That's enough for now. I have the rest of the day to myself, and conversation with Melinda and the girls tonight if I want it. Joy will be proud of me. As I get in the car, I see Holly Yost's smiling face again, and I wonder just how kinky Eric gets when I'm not around.

67 days

The Mother

Gloria Wayne still wanted to kill Eric Barry, but now she wanted to kill his attorney, as well. The fat creep didn't care anything about justice. It was all about saving his client's hide and promoting himself in the process. He smirked from every talk show, his pudgy face glowing with self-importance. He was convinced, he said, that April had fallen victim to a serial killer. "Fallen victim." It was the way he talked. He wove in just enough facts to make people question suspects other than Eric Barry. His red herring intrigued even Rich Ryder.

Ryder had taken to meeting her at the gym in the morning when she put in her forty minutes on the treadmill, the only activity that seemed to calm her. Good practice for her, she told him. If she could talk and run, her heart was behaving.

She didn't care if Rich Ryder saw her sloppily dressed and sweating, probably because it wouldn't register with him. He wouldn't notice if she were barefoot, but he could spot a lie with those unflinching bloodshot eyes, and he was more committed than anyone outside the family to finding April.

She hooked herself to the treadmill and turned it on, walking slowly to warm up. "You ought to join me one of these mornings," she said, acknowledging his paunch with a nod of her head.

"When my jeans get too tight, I drink light beer. That's my fitness regimen." He leaned on the treadmill next to hers, notebook in hand. "Don't let it get out, but I'd never been in one of these places until I met you."

"Crusader Rabbit in a gym. It could ruin your reputation."

"Is that what you think I am?"

"Nothing wrong with that." She felt the treadmill kick into the next level and tried to pace herself. "I had a social conscience once myself."

"I can believe that," he said.

"And I wasn't protesting the prevalence of acid-green sofas or shabby-chic decor, believe it or not."

"Now I'm curious. From activist to interior designer. What happened?"

"Maybe I'll tell you about it sometime."

A cold-hot stream broke out along her forehead. They always started this way, harmless bantering as she warmed up, then the heavy stuff after she broke a sweat.

"Will you hate me if I find myself some coffee" he asked.

"Not at all. Rough night?"

He grimaced back. "Let's just say it wasn't a light-beer night."

By the time he returned with his coffee, she was into it, feeling the sheen on her skin, the endorphins that helped her relax under the burden she felt every minute of the day. His hands shook a little as he lifted the plastic-foam cup to his lips. It made her feel sorry for him.

"Add some cream to that?" she asked.

139

"I like it black," he said, "with a cigarette."

"Not in here."

"Not for a long time. Still think about 'em, though." Half lost in her now-strenuous run, she heard him sip. "I got a call from Denny Petroni yesterday."

"On the serial-killer theory? I almost feel sorry for Barry having Petroni for an attorney. All he cares about is promoting himself. I'll bet he's the first one out with a book."

"He's not stupid," Ryder said. "Young women have disappeared in Sacto and in the Valley, for that matter."

Across the way, she could hear an aerobics class gear up, all loud music and husky voices. Somehow when she hadn't noticed, the treadmill had changed gears again, and she'd started running. She could smell her own sweat, feel her legs fly up behind her, and she imagined that he could see the bottoms of her feet. She could say anything to Ryder, and did.

"Unless every one of those young women had an affair with Eric Barry—unless he promised to leave his wife for every one of them—I'm not interested."

"Good point."

He walked in front of her treadmill as she spoke, watching her face. It was his intensity, not his features, that made him attractive—not attractive as in sexy, just passionate, alive. His pale eyes were on fire, and although he wore only a black T-shirt and jeans, he conveyed more power than that hog Denny Petroni could ever dream to.

"If it's such a good point, why are you staring at me?" she asked.

"Just checking. It doesn't matter as long as we find April. You know that, don't you?"

"Of course I know it. I also know, I believe, that we won't find April if we let Eric Barry get away."

"I'd hate him, too, if he'd taken advantage of my daughter."

"This isn't about hate. He's reprehensible."

"That doesn't make him guilty of a crime."

"He's at least guilty of not telling all he knows," she said. "Even if April were the victim of a serial killer." She paused. It was too horrible to put into words. "Even if she were, he might know something about her habits that would lead us to the person who was responsible."

"You're right," Ryder said, giving her his first real smile of the day. "Let's keep hammering him."

She felt herself smile as well, feeling free, the way you did when you could finally yawn, even if you'd forgotten how, once you saw another person do it. "That's what I wanted to hear," she said.

He turned away, and now she had only his voice blending with the soft motor of the treadmill. At least she could hear through it, not like her noisy contraption at home. "Got an idea for you, Gloria."

"What's that?"

"You'll think it's corny, but it might help."

Not being able to see him made her feel as if they were speaking on the phone, less intimate, fewer rules. "I've already tried light beer," she said. "Can't drink enough of it to get high."

"I'm talking about a support group."

She shut off the treadmill, turned to look at him. "A bunch of losers crying about their dead kids? You can't be serious."

He walked around to join her, still holding his cup. "When do you go into work? Eight? Maybe we could get some coffee on the way, not here, of course."

"At one of your support groups, perhaps?" She was sure the contempt reflected on her face said the rest. He seemed to draw back from it.

"It was just a suggestion."

"One that doesn't work for me, I'm afraid."

Before he could say another word, she threw her towel over her shoulder and left the room, walking into the early morning sun that was already too hot and too damned bright.

72 days

The Mother

She couldn't believe she was really doing this, entering a room full of strangers, holding her husband's hand.

"We just use first names," the woman, who introduced herself as Rose, told her at the door. "If you're uncomfortable, we don't even need that."

As if they didn't know who she was. As if they didn't recognize Jack and her from every newscast since April's disappearance. Looking at him, at their intertwined hands, she felt as if he were a prop—Howdy Doody to her Princess Summer Fall Winter Spring.

"You sure you want to stay?" she whispered to him.

"Might as well give it a try." He squeezed her hand, nodded at this Rose person. "My wife and I, we're pretty private people," he said.

"We understand that, Jack."

Rose wore a long, black dress. She was short, heavy and, except for her wide innocent-kid smile, looked close to sixty, sixty-five maybe. "This meeting's about grief," she said, as they reached the room at the top the stairs. "Missing children, miscarriage, suicide." It seemed a lot to cover in one group.

About twenty-five people gathered around a horseshoe of three long tables. She and Jack settled in the back; Rose went to the space in middle of the horseshoe.

Gloria allowed herself a quick look around. Most of the women wore T-shirts with slogans or photographs. She prayed it would never come to this for her. She was just observing, and only because Ryder insisted. She was not a victim, nor was April. Just visiting. God, she missed her April.

"We have some guests tonight," Rose said, kicking back her right foot as she spoke. The self-conscious gesture endeared her to Gloria. Although she hadn't planned on it, she stood up when Rose said, "Please welcome Gloria and Jack."

The applause felt genuine, warm. Damn. The tears rolled down again, unbidden. Jack, too. Poor baby, he'd risen with her. Now his face caved in with grief.

"Gloria and Jack, you're in our prayers," Rose said. "Now, we need yours as we update one another. Who'd like to begin? George, would you start?"

A heavy black man raised himself up from the table. "Guess you know they found Jenna," he said. "No trace of who did it." His voice choked in his throat. The woman beside him touched his arm, whispered a song of words Gloria could not identify. "I'm here, though," he said. "I'm here for all the girls they haven't found, good girls like Jenna, girls who need their families and their prayers. We're their families now. We're all they got."

Rose wiped her eyes. "God bless you and your family," she said. "Maurice? How are you tonight?"

"Sad." The wiry old man sprang from the chair like a marionette. "I miss my Betty every day, but I know she's in a better

143

place." Tears squeezed out of his eyes, as if the puppeteer controlling this tiny man had pressed a secret button. Gloria didn't know how much more she could take. There was too much grief in this grief group.

She endured more, as Jack shuddered beside her. The emotion-drained father of a raped daughter, an angry widow, a hollow-eyed gay man mourning a life partner who'd died from AIDs. His story was the most depressing. The man couldn't even be with his lover in the final days at the hospital, because he wasn't recognized as a bona fide relative. His lover's brother, who hated them both, had inherited what was left of the estate. "I've lost everything," the man said. "But I haven't lost my memories. No one can take away the years we shared."

Two more people spoke, but Gloria could barely follow what they said. She couldn't take her eyes from the face of this soft-spoken man fighting for his life, unable to claim recognition for his union.

"Gloria, would you like to add anything tonight?" Rose asked.

Heads turned. Gloria realized she was looking back at a group that had become an audience. If only Jack could help. He couldn't. She knew that. He was a smart man, a successful man, but what had happened had robbed him of his strength. She'd come to terms with his strengths and limitations long before they married; he'd probably done the same.

"We lost our daughter, our only child, more than two months ago," she said. "We want her back." Applause drowned out her words, gave her the courage to continue. She stood, leaned against the table. Damn Ryder. How did he know this? How could he have predicted this was where she belonged?

"We've all had losses," she said. "We can't give up. We can't stop hounding the press. We can't stop talking about our loved ones. We've done nothing wrong. They have done nothing wrong. Only by keeping their stories alive can we honor them, maybe even save them and ourselves in the process."

Applause again. She felt more words ready to spill out of her lips. But this was enough—enough for now. She slipped down next to Jack. When had he sat down? Oh, God, they'd listened.

Rose moved back into the horseshoe. "Jack, would you like to add anything to that?"

He ducked his head, looked up at her. "My wife just spoke for both of us. She's better than I am at this type of thing."

"No one's judging you," Rose said. "If you'd like to speak later on, let us know."

Gloria felt the heat of his gaze, knew what she felt was his pride in her breaking through all the other walls. She'd done it, by God, and would continue to.

After all these years, it was almost enough. Still, a tiny tug inside of her suggested that it would be nice if Rich Ryder could have seen it, too.

The people in this group had nothing in common, although an uncomfortable percentage were minorities—African-Americans, Latinos. The few white faces in the room appeared outraged, as if they'd been promised exclusion from such pain. Gloria knew the feeling. She thought she'd joined the club years ago. Never paid her dues, though, not until now.

She stood again, without being asked to. She didn't care anymore.

"I want to increase the reward," she said. "For our daughter, April, by ten thousand."

They applauded before she could finish speaking. Jack bobbed his head. It was the first time he'd looked able to handle anything said in this room.

"And," she said, "I'd like to contribute a matching amount for anyone else here tonight who is trying to locate a missing loved one. Use it where you see fit, Rose."

Stunned silence, then more applause.

She loved these people. She loved them as much as she'd loved actual family members. She could help them with money, help them with support. And they'd help her, too. Somehow they'd find her April. Oh, please, someone help her find her daughter.

"Hear you're a star."

Ryder lounged on his treadmill as he watched her work out.

"The support group?" she asked.

"You know what I'm talking about. I'm just trying to give you a compliment. A thank-you would be nice."

"Thank you," she said. "I don't know exactly how to react. It's pretty weird."

"Not that weird. You've been through enough that you can help others. You know that, don't you?"

"I'm not sure." She shot him a quick glance. "How'd you know it would be such a good place?"

"Give me credit for a little experience."

She tried to find his eyes again, but he'd bent his head, looked down at the invisible figures on the treadmill. She pushed a button, cranked hers up.

"Hey, Ryder?"

He glanced up. "We on a last-name basis now?"

"Thought you wanted to buy me a cup of coffee."

His expression shifted; his watery blue eyes narrowed, as if trying to sniff out a lie. "You want coffee? With me?"

She turned off the treadmill. "One condition," she said.

"What's that?"

"We go somewhere where no one will recognize us."

"Alaska okay with you?" he asked.

"I'm on a short leash. Know of anywhere closer?"

"There's a newspaper, not far from here. Last I heard they still served coffee."

Once they settled at the corner table on the *Valley Voice* patio, she looked at his face, ruddier in the sunlight, and said, "You can smoke if you like."

"Told you I quit."

"Why do you still smell like it?"

"I don't know, but it's a scary thought."

"Maybe it's just me. I smell smoke all the time now, especially in my car. It's as if it's coming out of the air conditioner." Now, why had she told him that?

"Air quality," he said. "Some days here are like standing over a barbecue. Gloria—?"

"Yes?"

"Why'd you come here with me?"

She put her elbows on the table. "I don't know. I don't even like coffee."

"Is it because of the group?"

She tried to reason it out, couldn't. "Maybe. They weren't what I expected."

"Everybody who loses someone isn't a loser," he said.

"I know that. You have to remember I haven't lost anyone, not for good. Those people. Most of them were there because someone they loved is dead."

"I know. Either way, you have something in common."

"But it's so painful."

"It's painful anyway."

"But not hopeless." His eyes were so light in the sunlight that she could barely read the mood there. "It's not hopeless, Ryder, not for any of us."

"For some of us," he said. "But we still go on. We have to."

"I remember reading back in college, some Zen koan, the only way out is through. You believe that?"

"Too heavy for me and too early in the morning." He leaned back in the white, plastic chair and said, "Maybe I shouldn't have sent you to the group. It's just that you're hurting too much, and it's the best group of its kind around."

"Tried them all?" she asked.

"Yeah."

He kept his eyes on her as if to dare her to ask more.

"Why weren't you there last night?"

"Thought I'd let you do it on your own the first time."

The first time. The phrase reverberated through her. Oh, God, she couldn't take it a second time. Please, God, don't make her need a second time with those poor people. She didn't want to be with them, didn't want to be like them.

"You've been my support group," she said. "You're the only one who really understands how it feels, and you're the only one who's helped."

His eyes softened. "We'll have our own support group, then, you and I."

"I think we already do," she said.

He nodded, lifted his coffee cup to her. "So do I," he said. "Partners?"

She lifted her own cup. "Partners in finding my daughter and keeping that slime's name in the newspaper until we do."

They clinked cafeteria faux china. "'Til Barry do us part," he said.

It was the first time since they'd met that she'd seen him smile with more than his lips. The sight of it warmed her as nothing had since that last awful conversation with April and the silent emptiness of the days that followed.

An embarrassed moving of cups followed. She could sense his need for a cigarette, smell it. "There's more I'd like to ask you," he said, "but it better wait."

She understood that, too. "We'll talk again. Thanks for the coffee. I'd better go."

"Think you'll return to the group?"

"It's not the solution to anything, not for me," she said. "You understand that, don't you?"

"Didn't say it was. I just wanted you to know there's a place to get help when you can't find it anywhere else."

She didn't want to think about what that meant. "Not the kind of help I need."

He shrugged. "Sometimes anything's better than nothing."

And to that, she had no answer.

81 days

The Wife

What's happened to our family is bringing out the best in people and the worst. I've received letters conveying so much kindness I can't bear to read them, and from people I've never met. I've also watched strangers point me out on the street as if I were an historical monument, without hearing or feelings.

And today, almost three months since April Wayne's disappearance, I see a familiar face next to mine inside a tabloid someone placed against my front door while I slept.

Psychiatrist Says Barry's Wife Capable of Murder.

The nervous-looking shrink who toyed with me when I went to renew my Xanax peers from the newsprint, glasses catching the glare of a camera flash. One look at his face, and I remember his nasty remark about couples counseling when I desperately needed to believe that the stories about my husband's infidelity were lies.

According to the article, a janitor in his office stole his notes about me. I know the shrink himself is behind it. In the purloined notes, he says that Suzanne Barry was hysterical the day he met with her. He repeats my curse, which the tabloid has cleaned up, for the sake of its family audience: "F—— you."

From there, the doctor, whose name is Wainwright, goes on to describe me in unflattering, probably accurate terms: "fidgeted with her jewelry," "tore at her clothing," "said she was afraid her medication had stopped working." And finally, "When asked about her husband's infidelities, she became violent and disoriented, threatening to get even with me, then before I could respond, running, sobbing, from my office."

That part is a lie. I would remember that. I force myself to look at the article again.

A layperson's description of anxiety disorder follows, as if to add some credibility to Wainwright's hatchet job. What makes me feel worse is the tiny photo of me in the upper right-hand corner of the page. "The Barrys during happier times," it reads. Happier, indeed.

I'm standing with too much hair and not enough skirt next to Eric the day we announced our engagement. My face is open as a flower. It breaks my heart to remember how I felt that day.

Except for his longer, flatter hair, Eric doesn't look that much different than he does today. Years later, when instructing me on how to behave at political events, he told me it wasn't enough to smile with your lips. You have to learn to smile with your eyes. Although I didn't know it then, that's what he was doing when this photograph was taken. So, I think, did the deception go back this far? Did I ever know how he felt?

I don't want to answer that. Better to stay upset at the shrink. I call the local office just in case Melinda hasn't seen the article. She has and is furious that I have.

"Why can't they leave you alone?" she says.

"It doesn't hurt anymore," I say. "I'm just angry now. I'm going to call the medical center."

"I already did. Dr. Wainwright's long gone. We'll find him, and if he hasn't already lost his license, he will."

Her friendship is another gift that's come with this tragedy. I'll miss her when she returns to school at the end of September, but I wouldn't inflict this town, this Valley, on anyone who has other options.

We chat a few minutes more, and she says, "By the way, Eric would like you to call him."

"Maybe tomorrow," I say.

"I know how you feel," she says. "Anne Ashley's releasing another story to the papers. I think he'd like to talk to you before then."

"What kind of story?" I ask. "Another woman from his checkered past turn up?"

"Suze."

"Well?"

I hate myself for being sharp with her.

"A public statement. He's going to release an explanation to the voters in the district. We're putting it together right now."

"You and...?"

"Tom. We're working by phone and e-mail—with Eric's input, of course."

"That's probably a smart move," I say. "I'll be home tonight," I say. "Ask him to call me if he wants to talk about it."

He calls. I agree to his request, although I can't believe he thinks the case will be solved by the election in November.

"Whatever our personal problems," he says. "I need you with me for the election."

Personal problems, as in two mistresses he still denies—one who knows too much for me to be able to convince myself she's lying, the other who told her mother he was leaving me for her.

"Our personal problems will never be solved until you tell me what really happened," I say.

"I will when I can, Suze. Then you'll understand. I love you."

151

"Goodbye," I say. I was raised not to hang up on people, but that's what I'd like to do. I'd like to throw the damned phone through the window.

Dr. Kellogg says I can come at once, so against my better judgment, I take the freeway. It's changed since the last time I drove it, and change is not good when you have the problem I do.

The pavement reflects the white light of the sun. My fingers sweat. They're slipping off the wheel. I have to get off. I take a right exit, expecting it will lead back to the main street. But it doesn't. It's taking me up, narrowing. I'm heading for this arterial bypass high up in the air.

My foot leaves the gas pedal. Cars behind me honk and pass in a rush. I can't move. I stop right there, at the last possible moment before entering the ramp, pull as far to the side of the road as I can. A honk blasts, another. I sit shaking, look in the rearview mirror, see a truck bearing down on me. God, this isn't safe. I could be killed. I reach for the door handle, force my legs to work. I manage to get out, lean against the hot metal as vehicles speed past.

"Help," I whisper, but the wind swallows my words. "Help," I repeat in my pathetic, thin voice. "Help."

It's almost five o'clock, blazing hot in the Valley, everyone in a rush to get home to their beer, Larry King, the ongoing saga of our lives. I force my legs to take me to the other side of the car. At least I can get my purse, my Xanax. I reach in, pull out the shoulder bag. My fingers shake as I locate the container of pills. The panic has such a grip I wonder if I should swallow two, but remember what happened the last time. I can't take that chance.

A large truck seems to slow. "Help," I yell, waving this time. It lumbers past like an elephant.

A smaller car slows down. "Help." I wave frantically now. It backs up until it is directly in front of my car.

"Get in," the driver calls out, and I scramble inside.

She's young, Hispanic, wearing a blue shirt, an ID clipped to it. She must work for a hospital. I'm safe.

"Thank you," I say with what voice I have left. I can barely hear myself above the oldies station playing on her radio.

She reaches out, turns it down. "I always stop for women alone. What happened?" she asks as we drive off up the very ramp I feared. "Car trouble?"

"Yes," I say. "The car just stopped."

"You have a three-A card?"

I nod, fresh out of voice. The tiny car speeds easily along the new overpass. I manage to look down, and I know I couldn't have driven this alone.

"Good. You can use my cell phone to call three A. Where can I drop you?"

"I live on the other side of town," I say. "The tow-truck driver will want me to stay with the car."

"But that place isn't safe. What about the shopping center down on Chavez Avenue, where that Office Depot is?"

I tell her that will be fine. I call the automobile club. I tell another lie.

The Girl

Almost instantly, she was herself again. Eric tended to the cut on her hand with deft fingers, wiped away her tears. She'd been melodramatic getting so upset about crazy Suzanne. He wouldn't believe an hysterical wife with a history of mental problems over her. As he held her, she promised herself that if she got away with this, she'd never lie to him again, as long as she lived.

They sat on the patio, breathing the night. Eric made himself a drink and pulled her close to him on the chaise. It had been her gift to him, something Glorious Gloria had given her from her studio, because, she said, the beachy look doesn't work in the Valley.

"You smell like cigarettes," she said, snuggling next to him.

"Been with some friends. I'm the only one who doesn't smoke."

"I smoke sometimes," she confessed. "Not very often, though."

"You shouldn't. My generation had an excuse. We didn't know better. We paid the price, too."

She touched his lips. "You ever smoke?

"You kidding? My mother would have killed me."

"She was really strict?"

"Yeah, but a piece of cake compared to my dad. He was a cop, but that was just an excuse for his brutality."

"Tell me about Sergeant Barry," she said.

"Some other time." He stroked the silky sleeve of her kimono. "It's too nice a night, and you are way too sexy to talk about that boring stuff."

"But it's you, it's your past, Eric. I like hearing about it." She also liked the mention of how sexy she was. She stretched her legs out, resting her bare feet on the glass-topped coffee table. This was the way she could wrest him from what remained of his marriage. After all those restrictive years with Suzanne, he had found a partner who would grant him any fantasy, and he couldn't get enough of her body.

"How would you like it tonight?" she whispered in his ear. "How would you like me?"

"Wild." His mouth tasted sharp and cold from the drink. It aroused her even more. Soon those cold lips, those teeth, would be all over her.

Sex was a menu of possibilities with him. Sometimes he wanted the little girl, sometimes the wild woman, sometimes the hired whore. She'd give it all to him, anything to make herself indispensable. At first his appetites had frightened her, but she'd learned that like martinis, they were an acquired taste. Tonight he wanted wild. He wanted to conquer. She liked it that way, too, especially after, when he held her so tightly she knew he could never let her go.

She pulled away from the kiss, touched her tongue to his ear, relished the moan that followed. "I can be as wild as you want. I already carved a new heart for you."

"Where? On the trunk of a tree?"

"The tree between my legs." She flipped open her kimono, showed him the trim job.

"God." He reached for it, but she pulled away, panting now, want-

154

ing him on the spot. That was not the way he liked it, though. He didn't like it too easy. He liked it rough.

"Have to catch me if you want the heart." She moved around the table to the door. He rose from the couch, his pants jutting out in front. "Mr. Politician have a hard-on?" she taunted. "Where does he want to put it?"

"Come here, damn it." He crouched and moved slowly toward the door. Her breath came rapidly. She could smell the heat emanating from her. So savage was his expression that she believed, in that moment of their fantasy, that he was indeed the predator she feared. She screamed, and he lunged for her.

"No." She slammed shut the patio door just as he got there, ran through the kitchen, down the hall, with him behind her. "You have to catch me," she shrieked, "have to catch me if you want me."

"I'll catch you, all right." He slammed her against the end of the hall, knocked the wind out of her. She almost dropped with the surge, but he caught her with his arms, pulled her against him.

"No."

"Yes, damn it." He yanked harder. Pain shot through her arm. She heard the loud tear of the fabric, and pulled away, the sleeve dangling. She knew she must look as fierce as he, her hair bushed out, her chest heaving. She tried to sidestep to the bedroom, but he grabbed her again.

"I've got you now, you little slut. You won't get away this time."

He bit her neck, and she screamed again. He belonged to her now. He'd never get anything this wild from his wife. Buttery sweat ran down her forehead, her chest.

"Tell me what you're going to do to me, Eric."

"I'm going to fuck you until you beg me to stop, then I'm going to fuck you more. I'll make you swallow every inch of me."

"Yeah? Then you better tie me up," she whispered. "Tie me to the bed again, so I don't get away."

He brought his face, distorted with passion, close to hers, breathed her own breath out of her, pressed her against the wall. "I am going to tie you up," he said, "but not here."

That confused her. Suddenly she was aware of her body, her naked limbs. "Where, Eric?"

"Friend of mine has a place where we can do what we want to do. I've told you about him before."

She leaned against the wall, remembering the stories he'd told her during their lovemaking, her boastful comments in return. "Your friend from Oakland?" she asked.

"Yes," he said, "Alfonso. He's in town. Why don't we have a drink somewhere, then go see him?"

A drink, in public. He was taking her out in public, introducing her to his friend. She could take whatever Eric dished out, Alfonso or no Alfonso. In fact, the idea of having his friend watch them intrigued her. Afterward, they could come home, and if Suzanne were there, he could make his choice on the spot. She hoped the psycho did show up.

"Where would you like to go for a drink?" she asked.

"A place I know, probably not the kind of bar you frequent. Better wear something sexy."

"And no underwear?"

The grin spread across his face. He pressed her against the wall, kissed her deeply. "I won't be thinking about anything else," he said. "I can't think of anything else but you."

She put on a short black skirt and a see-through top. Her nipples brushed the fabric, pointing through the rust-colored flowers.

He changed into a pair of jeans and baseball cap that made him look years younger. That's what she did. She brought out the boy in him. Soon they'd be in his convertible, the wind whipping her hair, nothing to stop them.

He went ahead of her to the car. April broke out into the night, happy and full of this wonderful body she'd been blessed with. The time had arrived. She'd done everything right, and now she was finally going to get a commitment from Eric Barry. She could just feel it.

90 Days

The Wife

I stand next to my husband in the photography studio, unable to believe I've consented to this. Ironically it once would have been Eric's dream—the cover of a national magazine. Princess Di. Liz Taylor. Clinton and Monica in that embrace, the pitiful beret. Tragedy covers, I think. You seldom appear there because of your happy life. Eric would have wanted it, anyway, at any cost. He hungered to be something, somebody, and no victory he ever achieved satisfied that craving for long.

I glance over at him to see if there's anything in his face to indicate he's enjoying this. One look assures me that he's as miserable as I am. The matte powder the makeup woman applied has given his skin a poreless, cadaver cast. His eyes are a dull brown, his expression grim.

Anne Ashley arranged this session as well as the interview

following it. She's picked out the dress I'm wearing, the coordinating tie for Eric.

"Isn't this a little hot for August?" I ask.

"Not in other parts of the country." Her frosty voice conveys the rest of the message. California is gauche, the San Joaquin Valley especially so, and the wives of senators in trouble should know better than to question the professionals.

"But if we're doing this for the election, why does it matter what they think in other parts of the country?"

She sighs and explains, with kindergarten enunciation, how the business of politics works. That, combined with her large face, animated with makeup and dark hair, gives her the look of a doll.

I am certain she believes the rumors about my mental stability or lack of it. Further, she must assume that disability affects my intelligence. Those other people I see in Dr. Kellogg's waiting room, the ones who turn their eyes away from me and from each other, must also live this way, just less publicly.

We do as we are directed. Eric puts his arm around my waist, and mine goes automatically around him. He's lost weight. I can feel his muscles tense at my touch.

We flew here separately, and I am to go back immediately following the photograph. We both agreed that I shouldn't participate in the interview.

I look into the lights, then at Eric, see only white-brightness where his features should be. The photographer coaxes us to smile at each other. I try.

"There," the man says when it's over. "That wasn't so bad, was it?"

"Not at all," Eric replies, but his face looks whitewashed. Anne Ashley pauses at the door.

"Let me know when you're ready for the interview," she says.

Eric turns to me. "Well?"

"Well?"

"Thanks for coming, Suze. I didn't want to fight fire with fire, but the media will destroy me if I don't strike back."

"You think the interview will do it?"

"I hope so."

"Will there be anything in it you haven't told me?"

Color floods back to his face. "Of course not. I've told you everything."

"No, you haven't."

"We could talk more if you let me come home."

"Do you really want to?" I ask.

He nods. "I want our marriage to work as much as I want this election. I love you, Suze. I want to be with you." He reaches for my arm, must feel me cringe. He lets go of me in exasperation. "Damn it, are you afraid of me, too? Can you, after what's been said about you, believe a word of those stories in the tabloids?"

I wish I could say something to ease the pain in his eyes, but I hurt, too. "I don't believe the tabloids," I say. "It's just going to take time for me to trust you again."

"Eric," Anne calls from the door. "They're ready for you."

Eric will join me for his first fund-raiser in early September. He's told me repeatedly how much he needs me for this election, how much he wants to save our marriage, and I'm trying. I don't want to do anything I'll regret. Still, I don't want to end up stranded on the freeway again, metaphorically or otherwise. I don't want to end up having my stomach pumped again. I don't want to die.

I tell all this to Dr. Kellogg the day after the article comes out. I look at the photograph on the cover and see another woman. This can't be how I look now, this haunted, hateful face.

"What would you like?" Dr. Kellogg asks.

"For all of this to be over, of course. For Eric to be elected, if that's what he still wants, for my marriage to go back to normal."

"Back to the way it was?"

I jerk my head up, look into his eyes to see if he knows something I don't. "I'm not sure. I don't really know what my marriage was."

"What did you want before the marriage?" The question stops me. I feel as if I'm on a quiz show.

"I wanted to be a good wife. That's the way I was raised."

"Before you were married?"

"I wanted to be a good person, to make a difference."

"How? What did you want to be other than Eric's wife?"

"A teacher," I say, breathing out the truth in those two words.

"You have the education. Why didn't you pursue it?"

I feel the heat in my cheeks. After all of these years, I'm still embarrassed. I'm not sure how to break the feelings and failures down into a few words. Finally I say, "My problem. I tried student teaching, couldn't stand in front of a classroom. My advisor told me I wouldn't be able to teach."

"That had to hurt."

"It wasn't meant to. He was a nice person, but he could see there was something wrong with me. I was really bad in those days."

Kellogg leans forward. "Why not try it again?"

"Now?"

"Teachers are in demand, and age isn't the barrier it once was."

We sit staring at each other, his watery eyes trying to coach the right answer out of me. I know from experience that he won't speak until I do. "I think I would be a good teacher," I say.

It's the best I can do.

I leave the office and feel a flood of relief. An elderly woman sits on the waiting-room sofa holding a magazine and staring straight ahead. When I enter the room, she looks away out the window. I remember how I felt as the object of Anne Ashley's scrutiny, the way she slowed down the pace of her sentences and exaggerated her doll-face features as she spoke to me.

"Hello," I say to the woman. As she turns to look at me, I meet her eyes and smile.

"Hi," she says, and smiles back.

The Parlor Game
Barry Breaks Silence, Grants Exclusive Interview

The three of them got there within minutes of each other that night.

"Where's Whitey?" Harold asked.

"That asshole?" Janie said. "Who cares?"

"Can't you be nice for five minutes?" Kent said. "Whitey went to see his grandmother in Livermore, who happens to be ill, by the way."

She sighed, trying to look bored by his criticism. If Harold were making bets, he'd wager these two weren't going to have a summer fling, after all. They looked like a cute couple, but cute ended when Janie opened her mouth.

"Only someone like Whitey would have a grandmother in Livermore," she said. "Hey, Harold Bear, is the blender broken again tonight, or did you decide to plug it in?"

He lifted the cord. "It's always working for you, darlin'."

"If it's working for her, it ought to be working for me." Over the summer, Heather had perfected whining to an art. "I'm a paying customer, too."

"What's the matter, Heath?" he said. "You got a gripe tonight? Don't love old Harold anymore?"

"I'm just upset," she said, blushing. "Can you believe that Eric Barry has the gall to stay in the election?"

"He says he hasn't made up his mind yet," Kent told her.

"And he did pose for that hideous magazine cover."

"Did you see what a pissed-off mama that wife of his looks like?" Janie said. "I wouldn't want her after me."

Heather glared at her. "You've always had it in for her. The poor woman just looks sick."

"She's sick all right." Janie tapped her head with her index finger. "Up here."

"I don't know," Harold said. "I've watched the woman. I don't believe there's anything wrong with her."

A thin young woman in a long, flowered dress leaned against the door listening to them. Harold watched her cross the room and move up behind the others. She stood there poised for a moment, then she burst out, "You're damned right there's nothing wrong with her. Suzanne Barry is as sane as anyone in this room. More so."

Janie whirled around, ready to take her on. "Who the hell are you?" she said.

The girl met her eye to eye. "My name's Melinda. I work in Senator Barry's office here." Damn. That's all Harold needed tonight. The girl turned to him. "I ordered two tri-tip sandwiches."

"To go?" Harold asked.

"I sure as hell don't want to eat them here."

He nodded toward the door to the restaurant. "Right through there. We didn't mean anything about your boss's wife. We were just talking."

"That's the problem," she shot back. "There are too many of you people talking and not enough of you thinking."

Janie slid down from her stool and went around to face the girl. "Now, wait a minute," she said. "Suzanne Barry's got to be hiding something. Why's she afraid to go out in public?"

"She's not afraid to go out," the girl said.

"How come she's sending you to do all her errands then?"

"Janie, please," Heather said.

Janie didn't even bother to look at her. "I have a right to ask. Doesn't she work for the senator? Aren't our tax dollars paying for those sandwiches she just ordered?"

"I'm a family friend," the girl said. "I'm *her* friend. We're having dinner together, and she's not crazy. She has better sense than any of you. If you really care about what happened to

April Wayne, why aren't you out trying to find out what happened to her?"

"That's what cops are for," Janie said. "That's what boyfriends are for. Why isn't Eric Barry telling all he knows?"

"You don't know what he's told the police," she said. "Just because he doesn't feel it necessary to talk to the press doesn't make him a criminal, and it certainly doesn't make Suzanne one."

Janie's laugh was about the same temperature as the walk-in refrigerator. "Spoken like a true politician, which I'm sure is your lamer little goal in life. That's the only reason they posed for that magazine cover. The creep actually thinks he can get reelected."

"And why shouldn't he?" the girl said. "He hasn't done anything."

"Sleeping with his intern isn't anything?"

"He didn't do that."

"He admitted it to the cops, didn't he?" Heather said. "That's what the papers said."

"Since when can you believe what the papers say? Senator Barry hasn't done anything immoral. He's not that kind of man."

Janie made a sound of disgust. "I can't believe how naive you are."

"Fortunately I don't have to explain myself to you," the girl said.

"And neither does your boss's wife, lucky for her." Janie smiled. "I'll bet she's the one who killed April, and she and the senator covered it up."

Before Harold knew what was happening, Kent had jumped off his bar stool to confront Janie. Startled, she moved back against the bar as if trying to fend off an attack.

"Shut up about Suzanne Barry, will you?" he said, grabbing her wrist. "I'm sick of hearing the way you put her down every time you open your mouth. She never did a damn thing to you."

"Let go of me," she shrieked, wresting her arm away from him.

"Stop calling her crazy, and stop acting like you know what happened to April," he said, spacing out his words. "Because you don't."

Janie rubbed her wrist, still taken aback. "Pardon the hell out of me. I was just speculating."

"Character assassination is more like it," the girl said, and to Kent, "Thanks."

"I don't want to hear anymore," he said, his gaze still fixed on Janie.

"You've made your point," she said. "Mind if I get back to my margarita?"

"Just remember what I told you. No more knocking Suzanne Barry or April either."

The heat. That had to be the problem. These guys were all nuts tonight. Good thing crazy Whitey was taking a breather.

"Come on," Harold said. "Let's all be friends. Sit down, darlin', and I'll buy you a drink."

Melinda gave a short laugh. "There's not enough booze in the world to make me sit for five minutes at this bar full of losers."

"Hey, watch who you're insulting," Heather said.

"I mean it. Is this all you people have to do? Sit around and speculate about somebody else's life? You disgust me."

She turned for the door.

"Hey," Harold called over the bar. "What about your tri-tip?"

"Keep it," she said. "Or feed it to the barfly here. Maybe it will help sober her up."

With that, the girl disappeared, the group at the bar staring through the open door at the empty hole she had left in the night.

"What a bitch," Janie said long after the fact.

"Can't win 'em all," Harold told her. "Come on, Kent. How about another round?

Kent shook his head. He hadn't smiled since his exchange with Janie and didn't look ready to start now.

"No, thanks," he said. "I've got to get going. Guess I'm just not in a drinking mood tonight."

104 days

The Senator

His condo would never be the same. They'd vandalized it with their investigation, scraping the paint off the walls, yanking out drains, ripping up his carpet. Eric sank down on the bed next to his half-packed suitcase and surveyed his surroundings. He'd never feel the same about the place, never be comfortable here again.

All his years of public service had been reduced to this, a torn beige carpet that no matter how he repaired it, would always remind him of the humiliation he'd suffered in the last three-plus months. He'd have to move, not now when everything he did was front-page news. After the election when the press quieted down, he'd have to find another place, that's all.

Nothing he did satisfied the media. Nothing would. He didn't care what they thought, but he did care about the election, and the jackals could swing that one way or the other.

They were his quickest route to the voters. He had no choice but to agree to the magazine article, another exercise in degradation. And now this. A television interview that put him into such a rage to think about that he shut his mind every time he realized he'd actually consented to it.

Got to pack, to get going, to stop feeling sorry for himself. He'd need to gargle again before he caught the plane. His throat ached, and his voice made him sound like a three-pack-a-day smoker. Anne Ashley had coached him around the clock, feeding him the questions they would ask, making him memorize answers. Her directives pounded into his head. *Look directly at the camera. Show remorse. Apologize to the family.*

That would be a cold day in hell. No one would tell him what to say, not even now. On some of the points, he made it clear to her that he wouldn't violate his integrity just to titillate the viewers. No, he'd agreed to the interview because he had no choice, but he wasn't going to compromise himself or his family.

Anne had wanted to give the first interview to one of the nationals, Barbara Walters or Larry King. He'd nixed that in favor of a panel of local journalists. Where he gave his interview, the big cats would come, and his district was what mattered. This was one way to show that, to show them—his constituents.

He flew to Pleasant View that Monday morning. He and Suzanne had reached a truce of sorts. She agreed to be photographed with the twins, but refused to be questioned herself. He wouldn't have allowed it, anyway. His family had been put through enough.

Regardless of her initial reaction, he knew he could count on Suze. And he could count on the twins, too.

Heat still hung in the air as he dressed that evening. What he'd give to be able to be himself, without a tie and coat. The filming took place in the public television station. The building felt friendly, maybe because of the countless fund drives in which he'd participated over the years. The manager and board of directors respected him. They must know how important it was that he had chosen this for his venue.

Everyone greeted him when he came into the station. The manager—Judy, Julie, maybe—a diminutive woman with short, gray hair, threw her arms around him. "We're with you all the way," she said.

"Thanks," he told her. "I'm going to give it my best shot."

Three local reporters were to interview him: Nora Barrett, the local radio talk-show host, Mary Lou Recendez, a news anchor he'd always considered a lightweight and Rich Ryder, the one bad apple, who wore his usual scowl from the minute Eric sat down at the table facing them. Ryder's olive-green suit looked too heavy for the weather, and his florid face reflected the lights.

Eric looked down to escape Ryder's annoying gaze. He'd refused a manicure, not wanting to look what his mother would have called "dandied up" for such a solemn occasion. Odd what one remembered sometimes.

He liked his fingernails, a minor vanity he allowed himself. Short and rounded, they ended with a blunt edge that conveyed strength. Sometimes lately, at his moments of greatest doubt, he could look at his hands and know that he would be okay.

The moderator, the editor of the *Valley Voice*, introduced them. Eric started to glance around, to see how many people had begged, borrowed or bought their way in to witness this, and then remembered what Anne Ashley said. *Look directly into the camera.*

Mary Lou went first. Her tiny chin jutted out from her heavy face, and he could see she intended to base her career on this evening.

"Senator, what was your relationship with April Wayne?"

"It was and is a close personal friendship."

"Where do you think she is?"

"I don't know. I just hope she hasn't fallen prey to the individual who seems to be responsible for the disappearance of other young women in this area."

"The serial killer concept," Nora Barrett interrupted. Her red hair and green contacts concealed many flaws, except for the fact that she was too old for television now. That, and not her damned good journalistic skills, must explain her move to radio.

He looked from her to the camera again. "It's not a concept, Nora. It's fact. A number of young women have turned up missing or dead in the last five years."

"And you think April might be one of them?"

"I pray that she isn't."

"Senator." Ryder's voice boomed out, causing him to turn involuntarily. "Did you have an affair with April Wayne?"

He could have leaped to his feet and grabbed this bastard by the lapels of his ridiculous green suit. Eric forced himself to settle back down, take a breath before he found what was left of his voice. "I explained my relationship with April Wayne to the police. I don't think I need to go into details with you, and for the sake of my wife and daughters, I won't."

"It's my understanding that you didn't tell the police, that until Gloria Wayne came forward, you denied any sexual involvement."

He forced all expression from his face. *Don't react emotionally, whatever you do,* Anne had said. *React intellectually. Be proactive, not reactive. Don't let them forget that you volunteered for the polygraph. Repeat it until you're sick of hearing yourself say it. Make them acknowledge it.*

"What you've heard is incorrect, Mr. Ryder. We told the police everything they needed to know. We volunteered information, took a polygraph."

"What questions did Mr. Yakamoto ask you?" Pushy Mary Lou led with her chin again.

"The important ones, the only ones that matter. I answered

169

negative to each. Again, may I point out, it was a voluntary action. The police did not require it."

"During this voluntary polygraph," Ryder said, "were you
asked about Holly Yost?"

"I don't see any reason to answer that question here."

"To clear the air, Senator. You're viewed as not forthcoming.
Holly Yost says that she had an affair with you."

"She's lying." The words slipped out, and he couldn't pull
them back. Screw Ryder and Holly. It wasn't an affair, anyway.
She was nothing but a slut.

"You didn't have an affair with Holly Yost?" Mary Lou
asked.

"I barely knew the woman. We had dinner a couple of times
when I was a speaker at a meeting she set up. It was strictly professional."

"Why would she lie?" Ryder cut in. "She hasn't benefited
from this."

"Not yet." He let Ryder know with his eyes exactly what he
thought of him. "More important, she has nothing whatsoever
to do with the disappearance of April Wayne."

Nora cleared her throat and leaned forward, speaking in her
tired drawl. "What do you think happened to April, Senator?"

"I don't have a clue. I can only speculate."

"What do you think of the Waynes' assertion that you
haven't told all you know?"

He bit back the quick retort, remembered what Anne had
drilled into him. *Go for empathy, sympathy. Do not insult the
Waynes.*

"They have to say what they can to keep their daughter in
the public eye. I'd do the same thing if I were in their position
and it were one of my own children. When their actions involve
and damage my family, however, I have to draw the line."

"Oh, come on, Senator." That asshole Ryder again. "Don't
you think you might have contributed to your own problems
by not being forthcoming?"

"Because I wasn't forthcoming, as you might call it, with the media, doesn't mean I wasn't with the police. I told them everything."

"Everything they needed to know, or everything you thought they needed to know?"

With that, Eric threw out Anne Ashley's script. He knew how to deal with this bastard. "You're not interested in my answer, sir," he said. "You're interested in maligning me."

"That's ridiculous."

Good. He'd pissed him off, caused him to lose balance for a moment. "No, it's not. You know the police are looking elsewhere. You know we volunteered for the polygraph."

"Senator," Ryder said, his face grim. "Would you mind explaining to us, who is *we*?"

"I beg your pardon?"

"*We* took the polygraph. *We* told the police everything they needed to know. With all due respect, Senator, how many people are you?"

"I'm a family, Mr. Ryder. Every decision I make is based on a consensus of my family, my staff. We're a unit, all for one. You'll soon realize that if you haven't already."

Ryder pressed on. "That's all fine and good, but why did you agree to the interview if you refuse to talk about your relationship with April Wayne?"

Deep breath. "I agreed to talk because it's time to talk," he said. "Because the police have made it clear they're looking in other areas."

It was working, without any coaching. He knew what to say, and this was the time to say it. The cameras drank him in, and he stared into the vortex of their lights.

"Where?" fat Mary Lou asked.

"That's not for me to say. I wouldn't want to cause April's parents any more pain."

"Other areas of the country?" drawled Nora, intrigue evident in her tone.

171

He looked into the camera. "Other areas of the investigation, other suspects."

"Tell us," Ryder said, "who are these mysterious other suspects?"

"I know of only one." Denny would be screaming at him for leaking this theory, but Denny didn't know how it felt to take shit from this smug asshole.

"And who is that?" Ryder asked.

"I'm not going to give you his name," he said. "But I'll tell you this. She had a boyfriend, and the police are checking him out." Screw Denny. It was the truth, and it would draw attention away from him for a while.

Nora gasped. "April was seeing someone else?"

"That's not what I said." His voice sounded harsh, dictatorial, but he didn't care. "April was seeing *someone*. She had a boyfriend. The police are aware of all of this. I've given them all the information they need."

The questions swarmed at him like bees now, but he'd made the points he wanted to. No reason to answer right away. The interview was over. He looked down at his hands, his fine, strong fingers, his short, square nails, as he waited for the camera to leave his face.

He'd won. The commercial breaks would be interwoven with shots of him with his arms around his wife and girls. Besides, once he'd gone off Anne Ashley's script and told the truth about the boyfriend, he'd blown the whole scandal wide open. Without such an aggressive action, the Waynes would always be the victims. He'd never have a chance. Now, he had one. Now, people would know that April wasn't the perfect virgin they'd visualized. Why did everyone expect the victim to be perfect? Why did they always side with the damned woman?

Anne Ashley's face was stark. Denny just patted his arm. Maybe they didn't like the turn he'd taken, but he'd shaken it up in a way their safe strategy never would have. The investigation would take a different turn now, and all people would remember was that April had a boyfriend.

Now he could relax a little. Suzanne had said he could come home. Joy wouldn't be there, but Jill would, and Melinda. They'd have dinner, talk about their next move. They would not turn on the TV.

Denny walked out with him, through the back parking lot. "Better get going," he said. "Anne's keeping the reporters at bay."

"You understand why I had to say it?"

He nodded. "We'll talk about it later. I think your timing was pretty damned good, though."

Eric removed his jacket, loosened his tie and started to get into his car.

"Evening, Senator."

He looked in the direction of the voice, saw the silver-haired cameraman or whatever he was in his Beach Boys T-shirt. The guy's face, his stupid shirt, stuck with him, even after he reached his car. Something about him looked familiar. Eric had seen him before, but when?

The Parlor Game
Barry Says April Had "Boyfriend"; Parents Respond To Attack

Janie watched the beginning of a news broadcast, waved away the talking heads on the screen. Harold kept the show on but shut off the sound.

"April had another lover all along," she said. "See, I told you."

Heather continued watching the soundless screen. "No, you said the wife did it. I said she was pregnant. I still say I'm right. Maybe she was pregnant by this other guy. Maybe that's what drove Eric to do what he did."

"If he did it," Janie said. "I'm still betting on Suzanne Barry."

Kent cut a glance at her. "What did I tell you about that?"

"I have a right to my opinion," she said. "That's all I'm saying."

Heather turned away from the screen. "So, who do you think this other guy is? Do you think he'll come forward?"

Janie shrugged. "I don't know? Whitey?"

He placed his fingers to his lips as if trying to shush himself before he finished speaking. "I just think it sucks. Asshole senator can get away with screwing around, maybe get away with murder, and no one cares."

Janie ignored him, turning to Kent. "What about you? Think this boyfriend will come forward?"

He took a swallow of beer. "No."

"Why not?" Heather asked.

"He just wouldn't, that's all. Why would he come forward now?"

"To save April?" Heather suggested.

"Maybe April doesn't need saving," he said.

"You really believe that?" Janie asked.

"Yes," Kent said. "I do."

108 days

The Mother

Gloria forced herself to go to the studio the day after the interview. She had to. After Eric Barry's angry response the night before, she felt deflated. He wasn't just withholding information anymore. He was trying to ruin her daughter's name.

Karen had kept the business going. That morning she'd actually hand-delivered a sofa so that a client would be able to get it before the furniture store's scheduled delivery. She and the client's husband had carried it in and positioned it two hours before the woman's luncheon guests were due to arrive.

Karen still wore her jeans and T-shirt, her hair damp from the exertion and the heat. She took a long swallow from her glass of iced tea and set it down with a noisy clinking of ice at her desk.

"Why don't you go home? You know your heart's not in this."

Gloria sat on the edge of her own desk next to Karen's. "I have paperwork to do."

"I've kept it up pretty well."

"What would I do without you?"

"You don't have to worry about that. Just worry about taking care of yourself."

"Did you watch that bastard last night?"

She nodded, her face grim. "The papers have panned him, not just the *Valley Voice* either. Can you believe what a loser of a PR person he must have?"

"Fuck PR," she said. "He's trying to ruin my daughter's reputation."

"No one believes what he said about this mysterious other guy," Karen said. "Men have been doing that to women for years. What he said just makes him look worse."

Gloria crumpled a piece of paper in her hand, squeezed it into her palm until it hurt. "You can't imagine what I'd like to do to him."

"I feel the same way. Regardless of what happens." She paused. Pain registered in her eyes, and Gloria felt the familiar internal stab of dread. "Regardless," she said, "nothing that happens to him, no punishment, will be as terrible as what he deserves."

"I'd like to do him in myself," Gloria said. "I was a pacifist in college, didn't even believe in the death penalty. I'd kill him right now if I could."

Karen nodded. "I know. You need to take care of yourself, though. Eat now and then, for starters. I brought some bagels. Could you go for one?"

"Not right now. I need to get to work. I've got to do something, or I really will hunt that bastard down and kill him."

"In that case," Karen said, "I think maybe you should stay in the office today."

She couldn't concentrate, but Karen's presence and the absence of Jack's helplessness calmed the fury that had claimed her since she'd heard the bastard's vicious comments about her daughter the night before.

She liked the showroom, which was like a cross-section of lives—tableaus of cherry wood and distressed pine and the clean lines of black lacquer—not all her taste, but all tasteful for what they were. Housed in one of Jack's shopping centers beside a bookstore on one side and a bagel and coffee house on the other, it felt more like home than home did.

She stayed at the office until close to four, forcing herself to focus on the paperwork, trying to tune out the static of dread that continued to sputter in her mind.

Karen and her partner, Trish, had tickets to the philharmonic, and Gloria insisted that they close up early.

"I'll be fine," she said.

"Jack at home tonight?"

"He's meeting with builders out at the new center, so I really will be fine. I can have the house to myself. I want to stay here a little longer, though."

"At least you'll have company." Karen was looking at something, past her shoulder, through the window. "Rich Ryder just drove up."

Gloria felt a flush of joy. This was what she needed, time with Ryder to brainstorm the case, try to come up with new angles.

"Am I glad to see you," she said, when he entered the showroom.

His tan shirt gave him a subdued look and toned down his complexion. His hair was tan, too, longer at the sides and pushed back the way a child would do. Yes, with the exception of the thinning place on top where his scalp was starting to show, he had the hair of a young boy.

"I tried you at home this morning," he said. "Came by earlier, but you were closed."

"I was making a delivery," Karen said.

177

After Karen left, Rich settled in the chair across from Gloria's desk. "Iced tea?" she asked.

"You have anything stronger?"

"Let me check. I could use something, too." The refrigerator had four bottles of Heineken. She opened two of them. "Hope you don't mind drinking out of the bottle," she said. "I didn't think you'd want your beer in a paper cup."

"This is fine." He took the beer, making himself at home in the showroom with its schizophrenic variety of room settings. He had that quality, the ability to blend into his surroundings, probably an essential trait for a reporter. She wondered which came first, the trait or the career choice.

"I was just telling Karen I want to kill Eric Barry," she said.

"Just don't be quoted saying it." In spite of the gruff voice, his eyes were kind. "What he said last night was unconscionable. I felt for you when I heard it."

"I almost called you."

"You should have. I wouldn't give you my home number if I didn't want you to use it."

"I would if I needed to, but I didn't think bitching about how much I hate Eric Barry would qualify."

"Anything qualifies at this point."

"Thank you." She took a swallow of beer to choke back the tears.

"His PR people really screwed up to allow him to say all of that," he said. "Poll results of the interview are still coming in, but they're terrible. More than seventy-five percent think he's hiding something. Almost the same number say they wouldn't vote for him."

"What will he do next?"

"Probably a national interview, try to correct the damage he's already done. And if he's smart, fire Anne Ashley. She's called this one wrong from day one."

"He said terrible things about Holly Yost, too."

"At least she's around to defend herself. And she will. She

kept quiet after she revealed the affair, but expect her to come right back at him. That'll be good for another week or so on the front page."

"Good. Whatever it takes. We just have to keep putting the pressure on them."

"We will." He finished his beer and replaced it on the napkin.

"I may have a lead."

"What kind of lead?"

"It's unprofessional for me to discuss it with you. You know that, don't you?"

"But you are going to discuss it with me. You're going to tell me?"

"Yes. I want to. I feel you're more than a source on this story."

"You know I am, Ryder. What do you know? Something about Eric?"

"About his wife. I don't think she was with him that Friday night the way she claims."

His words made her shiver. Countless scenarios played out in unison in her head. "How do you know?"

"Talked to her housekeeper. She was supposed to clean the house Saturday morning about eight. She arrived at seven-thirty, which she'd done in the past. Saw Suzanne pulling out of the driveway."

Chills streaked down her neck, her arms. "So she lied about spending the night in Sacramento. Does she know the housekeeper saw her?"

"I don't think so. The woman said she hasn't mentioned it to her, and from the looks of the house that morning, she was in pretty bad shape when she left. The housekeeper found an unpacked suitcase on a chair, and the television was on. She'd smashed a couple of china plates against the drain board, left the pieces all over the place."

Gloria's mind fought its way through the facts, trying to figure out what this meant for April.

"You're amazing, Rich. You're just amazing."

He tried to look solemn, but a small smile broke through. "Not yet. All I've managed to find out so far is that Suzanne lied about spending the night with Eric."

"That means he doesn't have an alibi, after all."

Ryder nodded. "And neither does she."

"I still say you're amazing. Are you going to print the story?"

"Not yet," he said. "First I'm going to let her know what I know. See what I can get out of her."

They drank the remaining beer, taking their time with it. Gloria's animation had little to do with alcohol, she knew. Finally a hole in the lies Eric and his wife had constructed. Ryder had broken through. If he played Suzanne Barry right, their entire fabricated story might fall apart. They might still have a chance to find April, and right away.

She watched Ryder across the room, the certainty of his movements and speech, the way he could put seemingly unrelated facts together and come up with a common denominator. If Suzanne Barry really were in delicate emotional health, Gloria didn't envy her when she had to tangle with Ryder.

She locked up the showroom. Theirs were the only two remaining cars in the lot. They walked slowly to hers.

"I'm glad you came by," she said. "I needed to vent."

"So did I. And I wanted to talk to you about Suzanne. You know you can't say a word to anyone except your husband."

"Jack's not up for it right now. Besides, the day-to-day dealing with the case is extremely frustrating for him. He just wants April to walk in the front door."

"That's what we all want. Don't tell anyone about my talk with the housekeeper then, okay?"

"I won't. You'll let me know what happens, won't you?"

"Of course." He paused. This was an awkward parting. They still had much left to say. For a moment, she considered inviting him to the house, but that didn't feel right, either.

"I'd better get going," she said.

"Have you thought any more about the group?"

"I can't go back, Ryder."

"You liked them, though?"

"I did. There's just so much pain there."

"I know."

In the dusk, she could see the pain in his own eyes and wished she could ask him about it. She was afraid to, though. She'd already heard too many dead-kid stories.

"I'm lucky to have you," she said. "You and Karen."

"And your husband?"

"It's hard to explain."

"You don't have to. It's part of what happens. The one person who should be able to help can't because they're wrapped up in their own grief."

She felt the truth of his words like an ache. "You understand it all, don't you?"

"Yeah," he said. "It's a shitty thing to have to understand, but I guess I do."

She looked up into his eyes, the closest she'd ever been to the pain of another human. Yet she didn't feel she'd be consumed by it the way she did with Jack.

"Gloria." His voice sounded like a warning. She waited, sensing without thinking what was happening, as he lowered his lips to hers. The kiss was as harsh as his voice had been, deep and hard. She wrapped her arms around his neck, let it happen.

At once, they parted. Gloria leaned against her car touching her lips. They felt bruised. Ryder looked as stunned as she felt. He stepped back from her like a sleepwalker.

"You all right?"

"Yes, fine. I—"

"I'd better go now."

"Me, too. Good night."

She stood against the car watching him drive out of the lot.

What in the hell had she been thinking to let that happen?
What had she done?

The Girl

They sat together in the bar. April let her shoe drop and slid her
bare foot up his leg.

"I told you you'd like jalapeño martinis," she said.

He lifted his glass. "Love them. Bet it's the first time anyone ever
ordered one in here."

She looked down the bar at the various beer bottles, the occasional
straight shot glass. Some of the women wore strapless tops, and almost everyone was in jeans, T-shirts, talking above the rhythmic
smacking of bar cups.

"That's one of the benefits of being with a young woman," she said.
"We're still not afraid to try something new."

He rested his hand on her leg. "One of the many benefits. The problem with you is you're so damned habit-forming. You know I can't
let you go."

That was what she wanted to hear. She slid a leg over his. She
wanted to ask if he really meant it, if he really wanted her forever, but
that was her need, not his. She had to focus on his needs if she were
going to make this work out right.

"I'd let you take me right here if you wanted to," she whispered.

"Don't tempt me. I just might."

His jeans felt rough on her leg. Good-rough, like their sex.

She touched her tongue to his ear. "Hope your friend gets here soon.
I don't think I can wait much longer."

"You won't have to," he said. "He just walked in."

The Wife

I can't believe I'm doing this. All of my life I've tried to avoid threatening situations. Now, here I am, walking next to Berta into a building with the shiniest halls I've seen in decades.

"You really think I need to do this today?" I ask her. "Wouldn't it be better once the fall term starts, and all of the employees are back at work?"

"Re-entry counselors don't get summers off no more than hairdressers." Her singsong voice calms me like exotic music as we walk slowly along the polished halls. "Angie was here last week when I came in to register."

"But you're a graduate student," I say. "Maybe I should have waited to come to you with this."

"Where else you going to turn? Those phonies who pretended to be your friends 'til you needed them?"

"I don't care about them," I say.

"You care. You wouldn't have done it to them."

I look at her tight, sure body, her calm face, its perfectly symmetrical features. "I don't think I would."

"You wouldn't. I know people. I always knew that I could trust you."

I have to turn away from the open honesty of her face. "But then you ought to know. You're the swami woman."

"Not with my friends, I ain't." She checks me out again, surveys the others lining this hall, their comfortable clothes, the careless postures of the young.

"That shrink doctor gave you good advice," she says. "This is a good time to look into teaching, if you think that's what you want to do."

"What I *wanted* to do," I correct her. "But that was a long time ago. I'm not sure I'll ever be suited for it."

"After what you been through? You kidding me?"

"I'm just not sure I could really stand in front of a classroom," I say, "and I'm not ready to find out right now. Really, I just wanted to talk to you, Berta. I didn't mean that we actually had to come here, I mean, on campus."

"Why not?"

"Because I'm not ready for anything yet. There are too many questions."

She nods, and I see the sympathy in her dark eyes. Something else, too, a determination to see this quixotic mission through.

"Here's the place," she says. "Angie's good people. She helped me when I went through re-entry. Just remember, you don't have to do one damned thing right now but listen."

"That's all I can do," I say.

The door's locked, with a lopsided second-grader clock stuck into the window, its long hand pointed to the twelve, and its short hand to the six. A reprieve.

"It shouldn't be long," I say. "I can wait on that chair over there."

She looks at me as if evaluating my ability to carry out that action. "Okay. Let me give you my cell phone number in case you need me."

"You mean I can't just send you ESP?"

"You could, but you're a little stressed out right now. I wouldn't be trusting that stuff if I were you."

"Are you still helping Gloria Wayne?" I ask.

She shakes her head. "Can't help that woman. Better for me to work with police, not the victim's family. Hurts too much."

Victim, I think. She called April Wayne a victim. "Do you think they'll find her?"

"I try not to think about it. I spent too many years going places I didn't have any business." She shrugs, taps her forehead. "Up here."

"You helped a lot of people, though, didn't you? That's what the papers said."

"I guess I helped, if finding out the truth helps anyone. What I didn't realize is that when you mess around with that stuff, you don't just walk out the same as you walked in. The residue, Suzanne. You got to deal with the residue." She sings the word in my face like a song.

College students, oblivious as only the young can be, pass as we stand there. "Are you going to quit?" I ask.

"Already have. From now on, I'm just a hairdresser."

"What changed your mind?"

"This case. April Wayne's mother. She's a good woman, Suzanne."

"She hasn't been good to my family."

"She's scared. She's looking for help, for hope, anywhere she can find it."

"By attacking my family?"

"And by coming to me for answers she doesn't know how to find anywhere else. But I've been messing where I shouldn't be messing too many years now. If I try to help that woman, it could be the end of me." She brushes her hands against each other as if getting rid of invisible dust.

"The end of you," I say. "Like—"

"Like death," she replies. "This one could kill me."

We stand there in silence for a moment, her brown eyes focused beyond me on something I can't see. I don't know what to say next. I can't make light of her statement. I know she meant every word.

"I'm glad you're staying out of it," I say.

"Doing my best to."

We chat a few more minutes, waiting for Angie, the re-entry director. Berta starts to leave, then returns to me. "You'll take the bus home, right? You know how to do that?"

"Of course. It won't be the first bus I've ever taken."

"All right then." She gives me a hug. "Just talk to Angie like you talk to me. You don't have to decide anything right now, not for a long time."

"I know that," I say. "Thank you, Berta. I love you for this." We hug again, and I think to myself how lucky I am to have this one strange woman for my friend—she who is worth any number of interchangeable Tinkertoy politician wives.

The moment she walks away, I begin to feel uneasy. What do I think I'm doing? I can barely get out of bed in the morning. I can't even get my husband to talk to me. Every person with a TV thinks I'm nuts, and now I'm trying this?

The chair feels too narrow. I can't look down. Instead I watch the students, how easily they move through the hall without considering their surroundings, without a thought as to what waits through the next door, adjusting their pace to carpet or tile. Perhaps that is the secret, to ignore the environment.

Kellogg and I discussed the concept of my car as a metaphor for my life. Before people owned cars, trains were the metaphor, he said. People used to dream about being on a train that was out of control. The dreams were the same, the anxieties. Only the metaphors changed. Somehow, it made me feel better to know that it's not my car that's endangering me but my thoughts. I can change my thoughts. I will.

A woman in her mid-forties approaches the office and unlocks the door. She's small, Hispanic and preoccupied, carrying a couple of bulging folders. She gives me an automatic smile, and I nod back, know that I should say something. But maybe she isn't Angie. Maybe she just works with her. My mouth goes dry. I should have taken a Xanax. She closes the door behind her, takes the paper clock from the window. I stand, feeling my legs begin to shake. Why today? Why can't I just cross this stupid hall and open the door? There will be chairs inside, the safety of carpet. If I can just get to the door, I will be okay.

My breathing quickens. I can't get enough oxygen. This one is going to be major. I've got to get out, into the fresh air, the grass, in case I fall. I walk, robotlike, taking large, uncertain steps, a drunk person. I'm sure I look like a drunk person. Finally I break through the front doors, swallow air like water, hanging on to the automated coffee machine. The rest will be easy. Just walk faster and faster toward the bus. I can do that, yes. Just get away from here. I am running by the time I reach the bus stop. And crying.

I know Joy is watching the video of the interview again when I come in. She quickly mutes the sound. Jill has gone to her boyfriend's family cabin at Bass Lake, but Joy has stayed for a few days, ostensibly to help Melinda at the office.

She had little to say to her father after the horrible television interview. "Why won't he answer?" she repeated again and again, as Jill, Melinda and I sat in silence. I hated Rich Ryder for his aggressive questions, yet I waited, as if watching a movie, wanting the answers. I hated myself, as well, the shot of the four of us, a daughter on each side of him, our arms around each other, the kids holding us together. I walked through it, though, smiling when Anne Ashley said to, watching Denny nod approval from the sidelines. After the filming and we all got to let go of each other, Eric had thanked us and taken off with Denny. "Disgusting," was all Joy had said, and although I remained silent, I agreed.

She's a good kid. Both of our girls are, but she's always been the most difficult. Every family has a truth-teller, Dr. Kellogg has told me, and the rest of the family punishes that person for it. Joy is ours. From the time she was small, she poked holes in the fantasies we created to make her life easier or just more fun. She wanted no part of Santa Claus or even the Tooth Fairy. She signed up for Spanish instead of Latin, saying anyone with roots in the Valley needed to speak the language of the people.

She publicly protested to name a street after farm worker organizer Cesar Chavez in spite of our farming background and Eric's refusal to commit. In her bedroom here, she still has the framed poster she put up when she was in high school. It's a black-and-white photograph of Chavez leading a group of picketing farm workers, and beneath it, the words, "*Si, se puede.*" *Yes, it can be done. Yes, we can do it.*

Although I said and truly believed I wanted Joy to be her own person, I know now that I really wanted her to be more like us.

She looks up when I walk into the living room from the garage.

"What's wrong?"

With her blond hair clipped at the top of her head, she could be a high school student. We had them late, so that we'd be properly settled, Eric said. Joy always said he planned it that way so that voters would think we were younger. Maybe it was a little of both.

"Nothing's wrong," I say, sitting across from her. "It's just been a long day."

"Not to mention a long four months."

"Yes, that, too."

"Where were you?"

"I met Berta for coffee." That's all I dare say.

She nods approval. "Good, you need to get out." Then she adds, "In more ways than one."

"Joy, please."

"I mean it, Mom. How long are you going to put up with his shit?"

"I don't have to explain my marriage to you," I say. "I'm sticking by your father. It's my job."

"Your job?" She waves the TV remote at me to make her point. "Who made you believe that, Grandpa Loomis? You want to be treated the way he treated Grandma?"

She's treading too close. She can't remember that much, can't know anything. "Times were different then," I say. "Grandma Loomis loved her life."

"Right. The slaves were happy, too."

"You're not being fair," I tell her. "Your grandparents were wonderful people."

"I know that," she says, "but you always told us from the time we were little that we could be anything we wanted to be. Did anyone ever tell you that?"

I bite my lip and look away. "I don't remember," I say.

She gets up from the sofa and comes over to my chair, wraps both arms around my neck from behind. Tears run down my cheeks, onto her bare arms. She rests her chin on my head, and I know that she is crying, too.

"You're strong, Mom," she says in a thin voice. "You're stronger than he is."

I want it to be true, for her as much as for me, for all of us. Instead, I pat her hand. "It will be okay, baby," I say.

We are still like that, holding on to each other when the doorbell rings. Joy bounds for it, as if it has freed her from this emotional vise.

"Wait," I try to warn her, but she's already there, opening up our home to Rich Ryder.

"I don't want to talk to you," I say.

"I think you might want to hear me out," he says. "I spoke with your housekeeper."

I stop halfway across the room, Joy still holding the door. I don't dare ask him in. I can't. And I'm afraid to let him leave.

"Why should that interest me?" I ask.

"I think you know. Do you mind if I come in?" He glances at Joy. "Perhaps we should talk alone."

"There's nothing I would say to you that my daughter can't hear," I say. "And no, you can't come in. So you talked to my housekeeper. That doesn't have anything to do with me."

"Yes, it does." His voice is a flat rasp. For a moment, looking into his icy-blue eyes, I sense a hunger, as if he needs this confrontation, feeds on it. "She arrived here seven-thirty the Saturday morning after April Wayne disappeared. You were just pulling out of the driveway."

"That's a lie."

"She saw you leave. Then she went inside. You'd left a bag behind, partially packed. You'd left the television set on, and you'd broken dishes. Pieces of china were scattered all over the drainboard and floor of your kitchen."

The images flash in front of me like color photographs as he speaks. Suitcase. Television. Dishes. I'd smashed dishes as Eric had smashed my dreams. Oh, my God, and then what had I done?

"Get out," I say. "Get out, or I'll call the police."

I move toward the door. I'll attack him physically if I have to. I'll beat his chest, scream until someone comes to help.

"I'm going," he says, backing up. "Don't you want to tell me what you were doing that Friday night? And what about your husband? What was he doing?"

"Leave this house right now."

"I'll find out," he said, his voice lowered. "I can promise you that."

Joy slams the door behind him. Her fair skin is a white mask, her eyes large. "Oh, Mom."

"It's okay," I say as I try to quiet my racing mind.

"No, it's not. Why do you always tell me it's okay when it isn't?" She fires more words at me. "I called that Friday, and you didn't pick up. It's true, isn't it, Mom? If you weren't with Dad, where did you go that night? Where were you?"

I can't fight anymore. I'm beaten, out of lies. I look into her frightened eyes, wish there were something, anything I could say, other than the truth.

"I don't know," I say.

119 days

The Senator

Eric had just backed the convertible out of the garage when he spied Denny's Mercedes. He stayed in the car as Denny approached. "What are you doing out in the boondocks?" he asked.

"Trying to see a client." Denny patted the black car as if it were a horse. "She's a beauty."

"I wanted red, but I'm glad now that I stayed with something more conservative," he said. "I thought I'd drive up to Humphrey Station for lunch, just to get away. Suzanne's crying. Joy's bitching."

Denny crossed his arms over his hefty chest. "It ain't gonna get much better, partner. Holly Yost is now claiming you made threats on her life."

"Shit." He sank back against his seat. "She's a lying bitch. I haven't even talked to her."

"Hey." Denny put up a hand. "I'm only the messenger. The media will feed on the story, though, especially your good friend, Mr. Ryder."

"What's my legal stance?"

"Zip. Yost doesn't actually say the threats are from you, just that an anonymous caller told her she'd better keep her mouth shut about her affair with you. The implication's clear."

"How're we going to respond?"

"I'm going on *King* again Monday. All we have to do is tell the truth. You're not threatening her. You haven't spoken to her in months and have no intention of speaking to her."

"Why's she doing this, Den?"

"My guess? She's pissed off, as well she should be." He leveled his gaze, gave him a schoolteacher look. "You shouldn't have said what you did in the interview, partner. You pissed her off, you pissed off the Waynes, and you pissed off Anne Ashley. She's threatening to quit."

"Let her," he said. "You know, it might be easy for you to Monday-morning quarterback the interview, but this is my life, not one of those TV talk shows you've grown so fond of."

"I know that."

"Do you? I've got a wonderful wife, whom I happen to love, by the way, and two daughters to consider. I couldn't just come out and say I had sex with that tramp Holly."

"No harm intended." Denny flashed him a good-natured grin. "I'm in no position to judge anyone. I just want to get you off the hot seat while there's still time to get an endorsement from the governor for the election. One way to do that is to show some remorse for April Wayne's family."

"Screw them. That mother of hers is half the reason I'm on the hot seat in the first place. When the governor called last week, she had the gall to tell me I needed to come forward, as if she has the right to dictate my behavior. That's Gloria Wayne's fault."

"Her behavior's excused. Her daughter's missing, remember? She's probably dead. At least that's the public's perception. When you show disrespect for the Waynes, you sway the public's support even more strongly in their direction, and away from you."

"I see your point. I was just so pissed off at Ryder that I wanted to shove that little tidbit about April's boyfriend down his throat."

Denny nodded. "That's all the talk-show hosts can ask me about. At least with Holly's trumped-up charge, we'll have a new topic."

"You really think April had a boyfriend?" Eric asked.

Denny stuck his jaw out, as if chewing the question. "I don't know for sure. She was seen with a guy on several occasions. He could have been a boyfriend or just a buddy. She ever mention anybody special to you?"

"No one. She didn't know many people in Sacramento."

"So maybe this guy wasn't from Sacramento." Denny shrugged, patted his middle. "I don't know about you, but I'm getting hungry. I'd go to Humphrey Station with you, but I have another lunch date."

As did he. At least Eric didn't have to make excuses. "I'll talk to you later then. We need to stop Holly."

"Nothing's going to stop Holly." Denny walked around the Jag, checking it out. "So, how much did this run you?"

"Not as much as your bill. It's worth every dime, too." He glanced at Denny's car. "It's the most freeing feeling in the world. Nothing can catch you when you're driving this baby."

"It still isn't the best for your image right now."

"Bullshit."

"I'm just talking about public perception—spending all that money for a car."

"A sports car, which happens to be made by Ford," he said. "Lots of decent people drive sports cars, people whose company I prefer to many of my colleagues, including our two-faced bitch governor."

"She hasn't made a public statement yet," Denny said. "You could still have a shot at the endorsement."

"I'd better," he said, "after everything I've done for her."

Located about a half hour out of town, Humphrey Station was a former stagecoach way station and mail drop that had survived the old west and continued as a watering hole and restaurant for those passing through, or like him, who wanted an out-of-the-way meeting place. The San Joaquin Valley was like that, a link to the sophistication of San Francisco and Los Angeles but less than thirty minutes from tangible evidence of sagebrush, pioneers and outlaws. He understood this dichotomy, always had, instinctively. And because he did, he had a deeper awareness of his constituents, the blood of wildness that still flowed through their veins. He knew who they thought they were and who they really were, a sum of all of these diverse parts. As was he.

The sun had burned the color from the hills. Brittle brown grass and strips of darker fences bordered the winding trail. The road breathed hot air into his face, fresh, though, the higher the hills climbed and the farther he got from town. He felt it strip off layer after layer of the anger, fear, humiliation that he'd been carrying for four months now, and he felt himself lighten as he released it all into the wind.

After a few minutes, he spotted a couple of police cars ahead, and his heart hammered as if he'd just gulped black coffee. That's what this whole damned thing had done to him, made him paranoid and weak. He wasn't going to allow it. Didn't have to put up with it. He hit the brakes, anyway. Something about a fast convertible pissed off everyone who couldn't afford one for himself, especially cops.

He glanced down at the gas tank. He'd have to fill up when he got there. He'd gotten so caught up in Denny's news about Holly Yost and hadn't wanted to make another stop. Besides, he was running late. The sound of the engine was sweet music urging him forward. He swung into the curve, his body arcing with the car, able to breathe again, able to smile.

He spotted Fonso's car the moment he neared the old wooden building. He pulled into the parking place beside it in a cloud of dust.

The Parlor Game
Barry's Alleged Lover Reveals Phone Threats

Janie allowed them to leave on the sound on the television that night. Holly Yost was making the rounds, and everyone wanted to hear what she had to say. She wore a blue-green suit with a high collar, and she'd had her reddish hair cut boyish and short since the first interviews with her.

"She's a little long in the tooth, if you ask me." Janie ran a hand over her sleek, blond hair as if age were a disease she could ward off indefinitely.

"I think she looks good," Kent said.

"You would." Janie's interest in him seemed to have dimmed since the night he grabbed her wrist.

"She's pretty," Heather said. "Besides, Janie, she's thirty years old. What do you expect?"

"I guess a guy like Barry doesn't care, anyway. He likes them young. He likes them old."

"He doesn't like them at all." Whitey looked up from his Corona. "He hates them. That's the whole problem."

Weird guy. Never a nice thing to say about anyone. Harold would be glad when Whitey's business with his grandmother or whatever was over and he moved back to New Mexico where he came from. He was one of those guys Harold had seen too many of in his day. No surprises, nothing new, just a lot of negativity that eventually could keep the regulars away. Too many Whiteys could ruin the bar of a less-experienced owner.

Harold turned on the blender, whirled another margarita for Janie.

"Quiet," Heather said. "She's talking."

Harold turned up the sound as the composed redhead on the screen described the threats she'd received.

"Did the caller sound like Eric Barry?" the interviewer asked.

"No, it wasn't Eric. I would have known."

"Have you ever heard the voice before?"

She shook her head. "I'm not sure. I don't think so."

"Who would have any reason to threaten you to keep quiet about your relationship with Eric?"

"He's the only one I can think of," she said. "He told me not to talk about it, he lied on that television interview about it. He called me a liar."

"You maintain you had a serious relationship with him?" the interviewer asked.

"Yes, I did. We talked every day, even when he was in Pleasant View with his family. I actually thought we had a future together."

"In spite of his marriage?"

"He said his wife had mental problems. He indicated they'd agreed to divorce once his daughters were out of school."

"Was the senator worried anyone would find out about your relationship?"

"He was terrified," she said. "Because of my job, we could stay anywhere we wanted. He always insisted on a different hotel every time, never wanted to stay at the same place twice. He even had what he called a D-Day plan."

Janie sighed. "She's rehearsed this a million times, hasn't she, Harold Bear? She's going to write a tell-all book once this is all over."

"Be quiet," Heather demanded.

"Yes, that's what he called it. A D-Day plan. He wanted to totally control our relationship right down to what might happen if he died."

"If he died?"

"Yes. I told him it was silly. He was in excellent health, but this was what he insisted on. If he had a heart attack or was taken ill, I was to call 911, then remove all traces that I'd ever been in the room and get out at once. If he died, I was to do the same thing. Just get out of the room and take everything with me that could prove I'd ever been there."

"What were you supposed to do about the senator? Just leave his body in the room?"

She nodded solemnly. "Yes, until I was out of there. Then I was supposed to call a special number and leave a message saying exactly what happened."

"Do you still have the number?" the interviewer asked.

"Yes, I gave it to the police."

"So, then. If the senator died suddenly, you were to leave his body, get out and call that number. Where would that mysterious call go?"

"To a friend of his," she said. "In Oakland."

"Turn it off, Harold Bear," Janie said at the commercial break after the interviewer had told Holly good-night and introduced Denny Petroni. "I can't stand listening to that attorney of his."

"He's so smart he's scary," Heather said. "Before you know it, you're almost agreeing with him."

"You, maybe. He doesn't care what happened to that girl. He just wants to get Eric and maybe his wife off the hook."

Denny Petroni faced the screen, expression eager, as if he could see all of the people watching them, and approved.

"You don't care about her any more than he does." Whitey's voice drowned out Denny's denial about the phone threats.

"Of course we do," Heather said. "What do we talk about every night?"

"That doesn't mean you care. You couldn't care less about her. It's like some sick sport for you."

Harold felt movement to the side, saw Kent swing his empty beer bottle over his head.

"Hey, wait." Harold rushed to the other side of the bar, grabbed Kent's hand from behind. "This isn't that kind of place. Cut it out." Kent's grip was too hard to break.

"I care," he shouted at Whitey. "I care what happened to her, and I'm sick of you thinking you're some fucking expert when it comes to other people's feelings. You're not even from here. You don't know anything about us."

"I know enough." Whitey got off his stool.

"Watch it," Harold said. "I'm too old to fight with you fellows, and I don't want to call the law."

"Then tell him to shut his mouth," Kent said, still holding the bottle.

Whitey slapped some bills on the bar. "I'll shut my mouth, all right, you prick. You can stick this stupid town, all of you. That goes for you bitches, too."

Heather gasped. Janie stared, mute, her eyes bright with something Harold couldn't name.

"Now, Whitey," Harold began.

"Get out of my way, you two-bit piss ant. You can stick this bar, too. That girl who came in that night, that one who works for the senator, she was right. You're nothing but a bunch of losers in here. Not one of you is going to change history."

Still swearing, he raged past Harold and out the door.

Kent's shoulders sagged. "Son of a bitch," he said.

Harold grabbed his shoulder. "He's gone," he said. "What's going on with you, anyway, man? You aren't like this."

Kent shook his head as if trying to get rid of whatever had triggered his outburst. "It won't happen again," he said. "I promise."

Harold could throw him out and be justified, but he'd known Kent Dishman all his life, and he wasn't like this. Something about Whitey, about what was happening on the television had set him off. The magpies on the other side of the bar began to chatter again. The night could have turned ugly, but it hadn't. This was his town, his bar, and everything was okay.

"Keep me that promise, okay, Kent?" Harold looked at the women's silent faces. "Hey, let's see some smiles, pretty ladies. The next round's on me."

121 days

The Mother

Gloria turned off the television. She'd gotten to where she couldn't look at Eric's attorney, and he'd been on every night this week, responding with glib platitudes to Holly Yost's charges. Gloria had talked to Holly once on the phone, to thank her and to tell her that she had their support.

If she hadn't come forward, it would have been only Gloria's word against Barry's that he had been involved in any extramarital affair. Without attention focused on him, April's disappearance would have been old news by now. Gloria couldn't let that happen.

Jack came into the room, carrying a glass of ice water. He still had on the khakis he'd worn all day, and he hadn't showered.

"I take it you're going back out on the site," she said.

"Got to do something." He raked his fingers through his

curly hair. "This is driving me nuts. I thought it would get better."

"I know. It's the opposite, though."

"What can we do?" His eyes gleamed with tears. She couldn't take this tonight. She just couldn't.

"We're doing it all. As long as we can keep Barry's name before the public, the police will be forced to keep looking for April."

"But where is she?" The question required no answer. There was no answer. Jack went over to the table, picked up the green leather scrapbook she'd seen there earlier. "I went through this today," he said. "I looked at her photos, the ones from the drama club, every single one. Have you looked at them?"

"I've seen them a hundred times," she said. "I don't want to look now. I can't."

"Why not?"

She stared right back into his accusatory gaze. "Why the hell do you think? Because I need every ounce of strength I have to keep going, to make them find her, that's why. Because if I let my mind drift off for one minute where it wants to go, I'll cave in, and that won't do any of us any good."

"She's dead isn't she?" His voice came out in a thin, high stream.

"Shut up." She backed away from him and the book. "I won't let you talk that way in this house. We have to believe she's all right, have to have faith that they'll find her. If we don't, we'll all be lost. She'll be."

Tears streamed down his weathered cheeks. He made no sound, no attempt to hide them, as if forcing her to witness his pain was his only hope of relief.

"I'm going to work," he said. "It's the only place I can keep myself together."

His work, his passion, and she had none, no one, except her daughter. After he left, she turned on the television again, standing before it, daring it to tell her something she didn't already know.

"I think what Eric Barry said about her is terrible," one of the ubiquitous blondes on one of the ubiquitous panels interjected. "We have a girl who's missing, who's probably dead. She can't be here to defend herself."

Gloria snapped it to another station, let it skip over the faces talking about her daughter, the strained features of Eric Barry, the smirk of that disgusting, fat attorney, talking about her daughter, all of them talking about her daughter. Who was missing. Who was probably dead. No, please not that. Not dead.

"I'm sorry to bother you so late," she said when Rich Ryder answered the phone.

"It's not late."

"Maybe it just feels that way then. You told me to call if I needed you."

"Of course."

"Well, I do."

She felt guilty leaving her home, the yellow ribbons that told the world they were waiting for April. She also felt relieved. Whatever happened had to be better than staying there.

Ryder handed her a bottle of beer as she walked in the door. His apartment was neater than she'd anticipated. One slightly old brown leather sofa, a couple of chairs, a stereo playing Van Morrison far too loudly—a comfortable life that she'd just interrupted.

"Thanks," she said.

"Thought it might take the edge off." He lifted the bottle. "My edge, I mean."

He looked solemn, as frightened as she. Yet he was cleanly shaven. The blue shirt he wore looked freshly pressed. He'd combed his hair, wet it, she could see, tried to wave it on the right side, probably the way he'd done since he was a little boy.

The gesture endeared him to her. She stood before him, holding the bottle.

"This might not be the smartest thing I've ever done."

"Probably not."

"My daughter..." She couldn't finish, damn it, couldn't even say it.

"I know."

"No one else understands."

He set down his beer, opened his arms to her. "I understand, Gloria."

She went to him, handed him her beer. He set it on the table then kissed her with those fierce, hard lips, the way he had the night in the parking lot, the night she could still remember, still taste even now. He slid the dress from her shoulders, stroking her neck the way one might stroke a cat. She didn't have to do anything, only needed to move to his rhythm. He would take care of her. He would take care of everything.

His body was tight and wiry, except for the paunch, thick with fragrant hair. She leaned down, pressed her face against it.

"You showered for me," she whispered.

"Every night. Just in case."

He kissed her as they undressed, his mouth fresh with beer. She could taste his hunger there. "I didn't take a shower," she said.

"Good."

He knelt before her, speaking against her flesh as if there were another woman within her only he could reach, whispering, tasting, churning her into another substance, spinning her out like silk. Yes, her body felt like silk.

He pulled her down to the floor, on top of him, penetrated her, lying still and silent for a moment. It had happened. They were joined. She touched her fingers to his lips, met his sorrowful eyes with hers and took him in. Oh, God, she needed this, to be held so close to him that she couldn't tell whose perspiration, his or hers, trickled between her breasts.

Afterward she felt nothing but peace. She looked down at him. The sorrow had been replaced with a soft blue calm. Naked with Rich Ryder. Having sex with the reporter who was trying to solve her daughter's disappearance. She should apologize, but that would be dishonest. She'd figure another way out of this moment of awkwardness. She placed her fingers to his lips once more. "I could use that beer now," she said.

He laughed, reached out for the bottle, handed it to her. "There you go. Bet it's still cold."

It was. "I didn't want to get drunk first," she said. "Didn't want an excuse."

He traced a trail of perspiration down her chest. "I feel the same way. That would have been too easy."

She handed him the bottle. "I know how this is going to sound, but I've never cheated on my husband before."

"No?"

"Honest. My marriage has been pretty miserable, but he's a decent man, and I owed him that."

"And now?"

"I couldn't help myself. Didn't want to help myself."

"Neither did I." He stared at the bottle, took another drink and handed it back to her. "There hasn't been anyone in my life for a long time."

"Why not?"

"I'm not sure you're ready to hear that one."

"I'm ready." She leaned up and kissed him. "I know you lost someone. I didn't want to hear it before because I was afraid it would be too sad."

"It's pretty sad, all right, a tragedy."

"A child?" The words burst out of her mouth. "I'm sorry," she said. "I don't mean to pry." But she did, of course. She wanted to know everything about him.

He shook his head. "Not a child. A lover."

"Oh, no."

"She was killed by a drunken driver," Ryder said. "Me. Wouldn't Eric Barry love to get hold of that story?"

"I don't know what you did, but you would never keep silent when a young girl's life was at stake," she said. "You wouldn't do that."

"I don't think I would. What I did do was as bad as it gets. Barry is about the only one who can top it."

"What happened?" she said.

"I was working for the *Chronicle* in San Francisco. Had the career I wanted, living in a city I loved. Pretty full of myself."

"I always wondered why someone with your talent was working here."

"It's a good paper," he said. "I'm from the Valley originally. My folks are here. After what happened, my wife divorced me, took the kids. I came back here to heal, I guess. That was almost seven years ago."

"Your wife?" She hadn't counted on that, saw that he had heard the distrust in her voice. "You were married?"

He nodded, and the shadows returned to his eyes. "You don't want to hear the rest of this."

"No, I do. You've just never mentioned having a wife."

"We got married when we were still in college," he said. "Had a son and a daughter who just last year started speaking to me again. You've got to understand I didn't think I was doing anything wrong. That's part of the reason I hate Barry so much. He has the same attitude, doesn't care who he hurts."

"I can't picture you hurting anyone on purpose," she said.

"I didn't, but it happened, anyway. I drank, I played and I thought it was okay because, in my mind, I was someone special, a writer."

"So this wasn't your only lover?"

"The only one at the time. Unlike Barry, I was always faithful to my other women."

"Oh, that's lovely."

"It gets worse," he said. "This woman was good, smart, too, young. It was her first job. She wanted to be just like me, she said. How seductive is that? I fell for her because she fell for me, thought I could balance the woman at home and the woman at work."

"And could you?"

"I never had a chance to find out. We'd been together two months when it happened. We were in her car. I was driving. It was late, coming home from the coast. We'd hit a bunch of winery tasting rooms, and I shouldn't have been driving. A car was passing in a single lane, hit us as we came around the curve."

He spoke shotgun style, firing the words at her as if reading a telegram, his voice devoid of emotion.

"That could have happened if you hadn't been drinking."

"I'll never know that for sure. My wife did the smart thing. The day I got out of the hospital, she left me. She's married again. Husband seems like a nice guy. She told me the last time I saw her that leaving me was the best thing she ever did."

"So she's still bitter."

"That's one way of looking at it. Maybe just relieved. I try not to think about Wendy much anymore. That's my ex-wife's name. Wendy."

"And your lover? What was her name?"

He shook his head. "If you don't mind, I think I'll stop right there. I've subjected you to enough tonight."

"And you never speak her name?" she asked.

He shook his head. "Not to anyone. I hope that doesn't bother you. It's the least I can do for her now. Once I say it, I might start forgetting her, forgetting what happened. I don't want to do that."

"Does it ever get better?" she asked.

"It gets dimmer sometimes, not better. This," he said, touching her cheek, "working with you, knowing you. This is the best it's been for me since it happened."

"Good, I'm glad. You're the only person who's been able to help me. When we're together, I feel safe."

"Me, too. You make me feel that way, Gloria."

She wrapped her arms around his neck, used to his harsh kisses now, his need. He lifted her onto his lap, rocking within her until the rhythm quickened into urgency and finally release.

He tasted of her now, of them. There was a them, would always be, regardless of what happened. Within the small room of their joined flesh, she found what she had come seeking.

She stayed longer than she should have, wanting to prolong the moment when she would face Jack and have to acknowledge to herself that she had been unfaithful. Ryder and she didn't have to discuss what the evening meant or the fact that she never intended to repeat it. She knew, and she could tell that he knew, as well. He walked her to the door, pulled her head against his chest.

"I don't know what to say. Just that I'm glad you came over."

"Me, too. I hope it doesn't change anything." She shook her head, laughed. "Who am I trying to kid? It will change everything."

"Yeah, it will, except what we're trying to do."

"No, it won't change that. You're good at what you do, Ryder."

He nodded. "Yes, I am. I just hope I'm good enough to find April."

"Do you think we will?" she asked.

He studied her face with clear eyes that she knew wouldn't allow him to see anything but the truth, regardless of how much both of them might hope.

"I wish I knew," he said.

132 days

The Senator

Eric met with Jerry Mac and the other agricultural leaders four more times in August. They were worried about whether he could carry the party, especially if the governor refused to endorse him. The bitch was holding off on a decision, trying to make him squirm. He knew he could win, with or without her. He knew his constituents, understood them better than they understood themselves. He'd be able to salvage his district the same way he'd salvaged his family.

Sure, Suzanne was still a little chilly, but she'd agreed to come to Sacramento for the weekend, something she would have to do more often now. They'd eat in public places, put up with the craning necks and the cameras. They had to present themselves as a team. Without saying a word to the media, Suzanne had amassed an outpour of tremendous sympathy. Strangers sent her cards, flowers, letters of encouragement.

Instead of hurting them, the rumors about her emotional problems had actually helped their cause. People saw her as loyal and courageous. They knew she'd suffered, and they wanted for her to overcome her demons. Her popularity plus his voting record could win the election for them.

His colleagues treated him with distant congeniality. A few verbalized their support, and several of the Christians said they would pray for him. He treated them all with graciousness, even those who'd been more reserved. They'd change their behavior once he won the election.

Thankfully he had a big war chest. He'd needed it. Melinda had dropped out of school for a semester to run the Pleasant Valley office and keep Suzanne company. He was glad to have her, and she'd learn a hell of a lot more about politics running his office than she would in school.

Cameras followed him up the Capitol steps that morning. Perhaps it was just his imagination, but there didn't seem to be as many of them.

"Senator, any comment?" a reporter shouted.

He mouthed, "Good morning," not bothering to actually say the words. How sick he was of this. It would die down after the election.

Denny waited in his office, talking to the clerks and finishing a doughnut. His gray suit looked new, expensive and anything but subtle. If aftershave were jewelry, whatever he was wearing would be a diamond-studded pinkie ring. "Tried you at home," he said. "Guess you'd already left."

Denny looked at him as if to convey something with his eyes. Eric raised an eyebrow in question. Denny gave a brief nod. This wasn't just a casual visit. Eric invited him in past the clerks, and closed the office door. "What is it?" he asked. "Trouble?"

"Good news, maybe." Denny sank into his favorite leather chair next to a bowl of salted nuts. "Holly Yost just told the world you've had a vasectomy. Said she saw the scars close up."

"That fucking bitch. Why won't she leave me alone?"

"As I said, it could be good news." He leaned forward in his chair, gesturing with his hands as if speaking to someone who didn't fully understand the English language. "Now, why the hell didn't you tell me that, partner? We could have nipped all those pregnancy rumors in the bud. Why didn't you tell me?"

"Because Suzanne doesn't know, that's why."

Denny sank back in the chair. "Wonderful," he said.

He could tell that Suzanne had heard when she arrived. She wouldn't kiss him and barely spoke to either him or Anne Ashley. Anne had scheduled them for photos for his new campaign brochure, candid shots, she'd said, only not candid. Suzanne and he would hold hands, walk through a meadow. He'd shake the hands of eager supporters in an ethnically balanced crowd, stand smiling up at a farmer on a tractor.

Suzanne looked perfect for it. The weight she'd lost had taken off years, and with her hair pulled back, all one noticed were her large, luminous eyes. He wasn't wild about the cream-colored suit. It was a little too professional, too Hilary Clinton, making it look as if she and not he were the one running for office. He'd pictured something sheer, maybe flowered, but he'd leave that up to Anne.

Although slightly overcast, the day was turning out to be another hot one. That was good for the farmers, bad for heart patients, old people and those, like him, who had to spend time outside. He slipped an Etta James CD in the player to smooth out Suzanne's mood. This one was something April had given him, Etta singing Bob Dylan songs.

"I don't want to do this," Suzanne said as they drove the freeway to the photo shoot.

"It's not my favorite thing, either, but we have no choice. It's for the campaign."

"So you really are going to run?"

"Of course. You know that."

"But you haven't officially said so. You're telling everyone you're evaluating the situation."

"That's what I'm telling everyone. No point letting my enemies know any earlier than they have to."

"You don't think what Holly Yost said about you will hurt your chances."

"That woman has said so much about me that I can't believe anyone takes her seriously."

"She says it's because you called her a liar."

"She is a liar. I never had an affair with her." He'd said the words so many times, they came easily now. He hadn't had an affair with her, not really.

"And what about the vasectomy?"

"Suzanne, please."

"It's easy enough to prove. The comedians are going to have a field day with this one. I can hear them now."

He'd already thought about that, and it didn't thrill him, either. "We just have to ignore them the way we have all along."

She leaned across the console, snapped the CD into silence. "There's only one way that woman can know if you have a vasectomy, Eric."

"Not necessarily. Medical people leak information all the time. Look what that shrink did to you."

"Oh, God." She sank back into her seat. "You have one, don't you? You got a vasectomy and didn't even tell me about it."

"It was a long time ago," he said. "We agreed that we didn't want any more children."

She put her hands over her face. "Oh, God," she said again.

"I'm not up for drama and trauma today," he told her as kindly as possible. "These photos are too important."

She sat like that for a mile, at least. He let her stew, turned the CD back on. It was the best thing when she got like this. He couldn't lie about the surgery. As Suzanne had pointed out, it was too easy to prove. After a bit, she calmed down and sat up in the seat, staring straight ahead.

He took the curve off the bridge a little fast. It was a bad habit, one he'd been indulging too frequently. He hit the brakes in time, and they coasted through the curve. Suzanne gasped beside him, slammed an imaginary brake pedal with her foot.

"It's fine," he said.

But it wasn't. She curled up in her seat, fists pressed to her lips, eyes closed, cringing as if she expected someone to strike her any minute.

"Oh shit," he said. Not this again. Not today.

The Girl

The first thing she noticed about Alfonso Trotter was his shaved head. The second was his soft whisper of a voice. He spoke the way some musicians did, kind of like Miles Davis in his last interviews. Before he even sat down, he'd complimented her hair, her outfit and asked Eric how he'd gotten lucky enough to find someone as fine as she was.

The pride on Eric's face made it clear how impressed he was that his friend approved of her. She knew psycho Suzanne wouldn't have gotten this kind of reception. In fact, Eric had said his wife had never even met Alfonso.

"What do you think about this place?" Alfonso asked her.

"I like it—" she glanced up at a bra hanging from the ceiling "—now that I've gotten used to that."

Alfonso looked up at a pair of panties displayed in similar fashion. "And that?"

"Right."

Eric grinned and pulled her close to him. "I told you she's an adventurous girl."

They went to one of the few tables in the place, and Eric returned to the bar to get a round of drinks.

213

"*So you're in love with the man, are you?*" *Alfonso asked with a smile.*

She nodded. "It just happened so suddenly. We couldn't help ourselves."

He grinned and checked her out through thick lashes. "He got himself a pretty one this time."

This time? She didn't want to think about that. "You know a lot about women?" she asked.

"Guess you could say. I got some women working for me right now."

"Doing?"

"Now, you don't expect old Fonso to tell you all his secrets right off the bat, do you?"

Don't judge, she told herself. Don't put him down because of his lifestyle the way Glorious Gloria would. He was Eric's friend, so he wasn't a bad person.

Eric returned with the drinks, and he and Alfonso entertained her with stories of their younger days in places similar to this one. She loved listening to their banter, loved being squashed next to Eric in this wooden booth in this funny little bar. She'd never been in a place with a dirt floor or with women's underwear hanging from the ceiling. She had to admit it gave her a thrill. Adventurous. That's what she was, what he wanted her to be.

She was not one for public display, but with Eric, it was fun. He kissed her with a wet, open mouth, right there in front of everyone. Glorious Gloria always said that after six drinks you were invisible, and that's how she felt. No one could see what was happening in their booth, and if they did, she didn't care, anyway.

The drinks crept up on her. How long had they been here like this? She looked down, realized her skimpy top had slipped down. Her shoulder was naked, exposing part of a breast. She yanked the strap back up. Eric pushed it down again.

"No, honey," she said.

"I like it like that." His eyes were glassy. She'd never seen him with

that much to drink. What had he told her? Everything in moderation, then every now and then go totally crazy.

"This must be one of those times," she said.

"One of what times?"

"That you go totally crazy." She could barely get the words out.

"I'm working on it. What about you?"

"I'm a little drunk," she said. "Maybe we ought to get something to eat pretty soon."

"Think your lady's getting cold feet," Alfonso said from the other side of the table. She looked up, could barely make out his features. He looked blurred and miles away.

"She's not getting cold feet, are you, baby?" Eric squeezed her shoulder hard. "You're my girl, aren't you?"

"Sure, I am." She let him kiss her again, accepted the fresh drink Alfonso delivered. She'd be okay as long as she was with Eric. Still, she'd feel better if someone knew where she was. Maybe she should phone Glorious Gloria again. No, that would just cause more trouble. Glorious would be here in no time, probably calling Eric's wife and everyone else.

"Come on," Eric said, squeezing her arm. "Drink up."

His glass was almost empty, but there was a steadiness to him that made him seem calm and in control. Calm, in control and dead drunk—it was a combination she'd never witnessed before. Maybe she was the problem. Perhaps she was just too drunk herself to evaluate Eric's condition. She'd like to go home, but she'd lose Eric for sure if she tried it. He was right. Just have another drink.

First, though, there was someone she could call, someone who'd keep what she told him to himself.

"Have to go to the ladies' room," she said.

"Rest rooms aren't the best," Eric said. "Go out the back like I did."

Alfonso laughed. "What's wrong with you, man? Ladies can't piss in the back. Someone might get her."

"We could go with her."

"The bathroom's fine," she said. "I'll be right back."

She could barely walk, running into the narrow wooden hall until she finally found the door marked Ladies. It reeked of that deodorizer that smelled like Hawaiian Punch, and for a moment, April feared that she was going to throw up. She'd be fine. She'd pace herself on the drinks, insist on getting something to eat right away.

The cracked mirror on one side of the room made it look as if there were two of her. They both looked pretty good. Except for her eyes, she could have just been stepping out for a night on the town.

On the other wall, someone had scrawled, "I'm sorry," in lipstick.

April locked the door behind her and dialed her cell phone. He answered on the first ring.

"Yeah?"

"Kent?"

"April? Where are you?"

"I think I might be in trouble," she said. "I'm getting a little bit scared."

139 days

The Mother

They met Holly Yost at the Sir Francis Drake. Gloria had been apprehensive about traveling with Ryder to San Francisco, but he insisted that she was essential to his winning Holly's trust. "You'll validate me," he said. "I won't come off as just another nosy reporter."

Gloria wasn't certain if that was the only reason he wanted her with him, but she decided to give Ryder the benefit of the doubt. They had not discussed the night in his apartment, and she did not regret what had happened. Somehow that night Ryder had saved some essential part of her from destruction.

Jack didn't question her when she told him she and Ryder were going to meet Holly.

"Maybe she'll tell you something about April," he said, then looked away as tears filled his eyes. He couldn't speak April's name without tears.

* * *

San Francisco was warm but windy. With a sleeveless top and light sweater her only protection against the weather, Gloria wondered again if she were doing the right thing.

Ryder walked differently from the moment they got off the plane.

"Your feet know this city," she said once they were in the rental car on their way to the Drake.

"They should. I've walked enough of it."

"Do you ever think about coming back here to live?"

"Lately I have." He looked at her. "You'd like it here."

She turned away, toward the window. "I already do like it here," she said.

Holly waited for them in the lobby on one of the Drake's red velvet hassocks. She looked younger than she did on television and more vulnerable. Tall and lean, she wore demure gray slacks and a black pullover. Her hair was short and fluffed across one eyebrow, as if she'd made an attempt to conceal her identity but not her appeal. Once she spotted them across the room, her serious expression broke into a smile.

They introduced themselves, and Holly stood and hugged Gloria. "I feel we know each other," she said in the soft drawl of someone who was born in a slower-paced town. "My heart goes out to you."

"I'm grateful for all you've done," Gloria said. "If it hadn't been for you and Rich, the police would have forgotten this case by now."

They decided to walk outside to reduce the odds of anyone recognizing Holly. With her in the middle, they made their way down crowded Sutter, toward Post Street.

"My lawyer thinks I'm crazy meeting you like this," Holly said. "I want to help you. I know what Eric is like."

"What is he like?" Ryder asked.

"At the best, a liar and a con. At the worst, a sociopath. And before you ask, yes, I was in love with him."

"So was April." Gloria shivered, pulled her sweater closer.

Holly touched her arm. "I wish I'd known about April, wish she'd known about me. He was so adamant that I was the only one. That whole bit with the secret phone number, in case he died when we were together. I felt he trusted me."

"Would you give us the number?" Ryder asked.

She stopped outside a diner decorated to resemble soda fountains of the fifties. "I gave it to the police."

"They won't share their results with me. If I have the number, I'll make it a priority to find out whose it is. I can call a detective friend, have the address in an hour or less."

Holly hesitated.

"Please," Gloria said.

Holly looked at her, and Gloria didn't turn away. Let her see how much it mattered, how much hell she'd been through.

"I don't know what it would hurt," Holly said finally. She reached into her bag, pulled out a yellow piece of paper with a number scribbled on it. Balancing her purse on her knee, she jotted it down on the bottom of the paper, tore it off and handed it to Ryder.

He glanced down at it, then back at her. "Do you know whose number this is?"

Holly's face crumpled, and Gloria wondered what instinct, what talent, showed Ryder exactly where to drill for information.

"I'm not sure," Holly said.

"But you have an idea?"

"I think it might be the person who made the threats."

"A man?"

"Yes."

"Have you met this man?"

Holly turned away from the diner, began walking again, stopped before an art gallery.

"My dad's a minister," she said. "You can imagine what this

has already done to our family. I've got to keep some things quiet. It won't help anyone, anyway."

"You sure about that?"

"Yes," she said, clearly agitated. "Maybe my attorney was right. Maybe the more I give you, the more you'll want."

"That's not true," Ryder said. "I apologize. It's just that you might have the one key to finding April."

"I've got a phone number," Holly said in a crisp voice. "That's the best I can do."

"That's fine," Ryder said. "That's wonderful. Why don't you two wait for me in the gallery there? I need to make a phone call."

He pulled out his cell phone, and they walked inside. The gallery's name was *hang*, lower case, and the work was pretty good, if one were in search of an expressionistic painting and not a missing daughter.

Gloria stood before a sunset-colored painting overlaid on a one-inch plywood frame.

"I'm sorry Ryder was so intense back there," she told Holly. "It's that same intensity that makes him so good at his job."

"Pardon me if I don't value intensity the way I used to. Eric was intense, too."

The sadness in her face aged her before Gloria's eyes. The tiny lines around her lips grew deeper, more defined. She looked ready to burst into tears.

"I'm sorry," Gloria said. "I know you're hurting, too."

"I just want to do the right thing. I want something good to come from this."

"So do I. Come on. Ryder will be just a few minutes more." She pointed at one of the abstracts, reminiscent of the New York school of the sixties. "My husband would love this." She felt it important that she mention Jack to this woman who'd never met him.

"Does he collect?" Holly asked.

"Some. He loves abstracts, the New York school of painters.

At one time, he studied art, but he came from a practical family."

"He's a very successful man," she said. "More so than most painters."

"Success was very important to the Waynes, and he had no idea if his paintings were any good."

"And now he can afford to do whatever he likes," Holly said.

"Yes. Of course, at this point, we don't want to do anything but find our daughter."

"I know. My folks would be the same way."

"There's nothing worse than this, nothing worse than not knowing," Gloria said. "Can you think of anything else that could help us?"

Holly's gaze darted toward the front of the gallery. "Maybe something. I have to be careful, though. My attorney warned me."

Ryder shot through the double doors, a satisfied smile on his face.

"Tell me, please," Gloria said.

"He was very kinky." Holly turned her back as if studying another painting. "Extremely kinky, often to the point of pain. I can't say this publicly. If I'm right, it will come out, anyway."

Gloria thought of April, her baby. "But why?" she whispered. "Why did you do it? Why would anyone?"

Holly looked back at her, over her right shoulder. Her face, fresh and alive when Gloria had first seen her today, was drained of color and emotion. She shook her head as if trying to puzzle out the actions of a much younger and less experienced acquaintance, one for whom she felt a distant affection. "A woman will do a lot of things if she thinks she's in love."

Ryder joined them by a multitextured painting in various shades of purple. "Made the call, got the address," he said, touching Gloria's arm. "What'd I miss?"

"Not much," Holly said, pulling up a splendid smile for

him. "We were just getting acquainted. Gloria was telling me about her husband. He's interested in painting, you know."

It was a proud neighborhood, still managing to keep its head up above the poverty that had set into the area. The fences had all been painted within the past five years. The dogs were chained. Many of the houses had caged front security entrances. This one did.

Ryder parked the rental car across the street, and they both crossed over to Alvina Trotter's house, a small white home set back from a garage in front. Aluminum foil covered the windows on either side of the front door, reflecting the sun. A television show, all boisterous shouting, buzzers and applause, played loudly within.

Ryder pressed the bell. The television noise diminished, and the door cracked open.

"I know you?" a creaky female voice demanded. "Cops already been here."

"We're not cops," Ryder said. "I'm a newspaper reporter. I thought you'd like to tell your side of this."

"Oh, you do, do you?" The door opened, and a large African-American woman stepped outside. She wore a long, yellow T-shirt over a pair of loose-fitting pants, and her feet were bare, the nails painted a deep red.

"And what story do you think I ought to tell, Mr. Newspaper Man?" She looked at Gloria, did a double take. "Oh," she said. "You're that lady."

Gloria met her eyes, one mother looking at another, pleading. "I'm trying to find my daughter."

"I don't know nothing about your daughter, lady." Her expression turned sympathetic, then hardened as she returned her gaze to Ryder. "I had to talk to the cops. I don't have to talk to you."

"I'm just trying to help Mrs. Wayne," he said. "Your phone

number was given to one woman who knew Senator Barry. It's possible he gave it to another one."

She lifted her right hand, shading her eyes against the sun. "Why would some senator be handing out my number? I never even heard of him until that girl disappeared."

"Do you live alone, ma'am?"

"That is none of your business."

"I'm not trying to pry into your personal life."

"Sure you are. I have a man friend stays here sometimes, but he don't know your Senator Barry, either."

"No one else?" Ryder asked. "Please, I'm sure you've already told the police."

"My kids." She squinted at the sun. "My boy was staying here until a few months ago."

"He never mentioned Eric Barry to you?"

"No." She stretched the word out as if to emphasize the ridiculousness of the question. "Fonso don't care about no senators."

"His name's Fonso?"

"Alfonso," she said. "Alfonso Trotter."

"And where is Alfonso living now?"

She smoothed her long shirt with her fingers. "I don't know. He got kicked out of his place here and moved back with me. I helped him get back on his feet, and the first thing he did was run off on me."

"Why would he want to give anyone your number?" Ryder asked.

"'Cause his number changes once a month. I'm the only one knows how to get in touch with him, and now I don't know, either."

"I'd like to talk to him."

"I already told the cops. He just took off."

"I'm not the police. If there's a reason he doesn't want to be found, that's fine. I just want to talk to him."

"So do I," she said. "I told you the truth, though. I ain't seen my son for three months."

"Is it like him to stay out of touch like this?"

"Sometimes," she said. "Usually I'd hear by now. He'd be back, asking for money or a place to stay, at least." She glanced at Gloria again. "I am sorry for what's happening to you. I'm worried about my kid, too." Her lip quivered. She straightened, pulled back her shoulders.

"Did he say where he was going?" Ryder asked.

"Sacramento. Said he had a job there."

"What kind of job?"

"I didn't ask. I don't approve of the life my boy's chosen, so I just don't discuss it with him." She narrowed her eyes at Ryder. "Ain't going to discuss it with you, either."

Ryder gave her a polite smile. "Perhaps another time."

"I've told you all I'm going to," she said. "If you find Fonso, tell him to call me, will you?"

"I'll do that."

She turned to Gloria, and her expression grew solemn. "God bless you then."

"Thank you."

The woman started to say more, but her lip quivered again, and she turned around and went inside, pulling the door shut behind her.

"I believe her," Ryder said, once they were in the car.

"So do I. What do we do next?"

"Try to find Alfonso Trotter."

"You think he knows anything about April?"

"He could. Barry had that phone number for a reason."

She tried to shut out the thoughts of Barry, of April. She had to stop the horrific images that continued to appear in her mind.

"You okay?" Ryder asked.

"Not really. I need to get home."

"We have some time before the plane leaves. Scala, that restaurant inside the Drake, serves deep-fried calamari in a remoulade that tastes right out of New Orleans. Have you ever been to New Orleans?"

"Not for years. Jack and I used to travel a lot when we were younger."

"Do you like calamari?"

"Yes, but I really don't think I could eat anything right now."

He drove in silence for a moment, and she wondered if her comment had hurt his feelings. This tragedy had made her rude, forced her to put her own concerns above anyone else's. He downshifted as he pulled up a steep street.

"Funny, isn't it? We know each other so well, yet I have no idea where you went to school, where you've traveled, nothing outside this situation."

"Dormitory friendship," she said. "It was like that in college. We'd all end up with roommates who were strangers. We bonded instantly, became best friends. It was the way we survived in a strange, frightening environment."

"And after college?"

She shrugged. "Some of the friendships lasted. Most didn't."

"I don't want us to have a dormitory friendship," he said.

"I don't, either."

"I have a confession to make."

"What's that?"

"I invited you to the restaurant because I wanted to get you back to the hotel. I thought maybe I could talk you into spending the night."

He glanced over at her, and she knew he was trying to read her thoughts. But even she wasn't sure how she felt. His words pleased her, yet made her sadder.

"I can't do that, Ryder."

"And I shouldn't ask."

"No, you shouldn't."

"I'll do better in the future."

Although he smiled, she could hear the rejection in his voice.

"You're doing fine," she said.

"I'm trying. I've never been in a situation quite like this."

"Neither have I."

"Sure you don't want to try some of that calamari before we head back?"

He sounded eager, the little kid again, trying to hide his feelings.

"You talked me into it," she said.

146 days

The Wife

He's running for office, and nothing I can do will change his mind. I've spent the weekend at his condo going over strategy with him, Denny and Anne Ashley. By tacit agreement, I've slept in the office room, and he hasn't come near me. He knows I hate being here, knows I'm miserable, and he doesn't care. That's the bottom line, to use Denny's phrase. My husband just doesn't care.

They're gone now, setting up a press conference with Jerry McBride, and I'm supposed to be packing to go home. The police have left the condo a mess, and Eric hasn't taken steps to repair the damage. He speaks of leaving here soon, and I believe that in his mind, he already has.

He still refuses to admit the affair with Holly Yost. He warns me not to push him about his relationship with April, saying that she was an impressionable girl who must have imagined what she'd told her mother. Yet the papers say he admitted the affair to the police.

I have been questioned by two officers two different times. Both were lackluster interviews about my whereabouts the night April disappeared and any knowledge I might have had about my husband's activities. The officers weren't interested in me; I was one more name on a checklist of to-do projects.

While Eric and Denny are gone, I ransack the apartment. I've never been a snoop, never gone through his pockets or his billfold, and he's respected my privacy, as well. This is different. I can live with anything, but I have to know.

I start with the cupboard where I found the pink towel. It is empty. The drain in the sink has been pulled out. I'm sure the police did that. Denny has stated publicly that Eric is not and has never been a suspect in the girl's disappearance, that the police are now trying to locate April's boyfriend. I want to believe that, but the corroded piece of metal lying in the sink makes me doubtful. If he's not a suspect, why are they examining his condo? Why have they talked to me?

Even though the police have been through the entire place, I go over it, looking under the bed, examining the contents of every drawer and closet. There may be something they would overlook that might have meaning for me.

The medicine cabinet in the master bathroom contains only a package of dental floss, a razor, and a tube of toothpaste. The cupboards are crowded with various types of aftershave lotion in phallic-shaped bottles. I've never seen most of these, can't imagine him purchasing them for himself. Many are unopened.

In a velvet box, I find the cuff links Joy gave him last Christmas. I hold it to my chest, remembering last year. We've all been concentrating on the missing girl, the election. What are we going to do about Christmas?

I know I'm being crazy, letting my selfish concerns take precedence over the important ones. But how long can I be fair?

How much longer can I be strong? When can I be a mother, a wife again?

I start to put the cuff links back in the box, then stop, studying the container. A heart is etched on the top of it, pink ribbons flowing from it. April Wayne loves hearts, her mother has told the press. Valentine's Day is her favorite holiday, pink her favorite color. I'm uncomfortable with this intimate knowledge of a girl who may be dead, who did, admit it, probably have sex with my husband.

If this box is hers, why is it in his cupboard? Did she actually keep her toiletries over here, in the master bath?

I know it's hers. I can't help it, don't want to believe it. My hands tremble.

I hear a noise at the front door. They're back. I have to keep this box. I don't know why, only rush through the house to my bag, which hangs over a stool at the bar in the kitchen.

I reach in as he comes through the front door, shove the velvet box deep, beneath my wallet, keys, checkbook. I hear him enter, keep my back turned, trying to compose myself before I turn to face him.

"Where's Denny?" I sound breathless, guilty as hell. He seems to sense it, moving closer across the room.

I shift my weight from one foot to the other and move around to block his view of my handbag hanging from the stool.

"He had to run an errand. What's wrong with you?"

"Just a little nervous."

"You're not going to have a spell again, are you? Denny and Anne are going to be here in an hour."

I put my bag over my shoulder. "I'm going home," I say.

"Are you crazy?" He takes a step toward me, and I back away. "I need you for this meeting."

"I'll stand by you for the election, but I won't stay here another night in the same place where you slept with her."

"I didn't sleep with her." I see the lie in the angry lines of his face. He knows he's lying, doesn't care.

"Tell me the truth, and we'll never discuss it again. I'll support you through the election, and we'll just try to go forward."

"That's shrink talk. Try to go forward but leave me holding the bag in front of Denny and Anne. What am I supposed to tell them?"

"That I had business at home,"

"Suze." He lowers his voice, gives me that earnest look I used to take for love. "Please believe in me. Believe that I'm doing what's best for our family."

"Why won't you tell me?"

"How can I when you don't understand my job," he says. "You never have. It's like the night we saw Mick Jagger in Germany, all those people wanting to touch him. What would you do if you were married to Mick Jagger and someone wrote that kind of trash about him?"

"But I'm not," I say. "I'm married to my college sweetheart, someone I trusted. I wouldn't trust Mick Jagger."

"You know I have pressures an ordinary man doesn't have. A good partner would understand those pressures."

"You're trying to say that I haven't been a good partner to you?"

"I'm beginning to wonder," he says.

I don't know how to respond to that, but I need to get away from this place, and once I do, I'm never coming back.

"You're the one who hasn't been a good partner," I say.

"Suze." He reaches out for me.

I jump back, clutching my bag to my side. "Don't touch me."

I run for the door, hear his voice over my shoulder. "Better call that shrink when you get home. You're really going off the deep end this time."

* * *

The Parlor Game
Barry Says He Won't Drop Out

"I told you," Janie said. "Bet he gets elected, too."

"Absolutely not." Kent shook his head and reached for his beer. "No one would vote for him after what he's done."

"No one knows what he's done, do they, Harold Bear? That's the problem. Looks like you get to keep our bet money when we go back to school. Whitey sure won't be around claiming his."

"He didn't show up at work again, either," Kent said. "He just came by for his paycheck. My dad was pissed."

Janie made a face. "He creeped me out with those weird glasses of his. He's probably miles away from here by now. That means you can keep his share, too, Harold Bear."

"I don't want his money or yours," Harold said. "I'll give it back, and you kids can have a drink before you leave. You heading out the end of the month, darlin'?"

"Yes. I already finished shopping, as much as you can shop in this hick town, that is. My mom and I are going to finish up in the city this weekend."

She was already wearing fall colors and a long duster-type sweater, even though it was still hotter than hell outside.

"Me, too," Heather said. And to Janie, "My clothes have been ready for weeks."

"Mine, too." Kent lifted the sleeve of his T-shirt. "It will be a long trip across town to Shitty College, but I'll still drop by to visit you now and then, Harold."

"I'll visit, too. I'm only at USC." Heather said. "You think they'll ever find out what happened to April?"

"They wouldn't be looking so hard now if her folks weren't loaded," Janie said. "The story will probably die off after the election. I still don't think the wife's telling all she knows. I'd say more, but I don't want to set Kent off again."

She gave him a flirty smile, just asking for it, Harold thought. She couldn't help asking for it. Kent didn't flare up this time, seemed more relaxed, or it might have been the beer.

"She's a nice woman," he said. "It's not fair to say those things about her."

"A nice woman with a cheating husband. That could make anyone pretty irrational."

"How would you know?" Heather asked, and the rest of them laughed.

"I would imagine that's how it would make you. Personally, if any man ever cheated on me, he'd be singing soprano."

She flashed Kent a challenging look, practicing, Harold thought, for when she was back east again with boys who would never see the inside of a city college.

"Janie," Heather said.

"Well, I would. What would you do, Kent, if a woman ever cheated on you?"

He toyed with the lime in his Corona bottle, then looked up to meet her eyes. "I wouldn't do anything at all."

"You wouldn't? Oh, come on."

"I wouldn't," he said. "You can't make someone want you, and you can't stop them from wanting someone else."

Janie gave him a wicked smile over the top of her margarita glass. "Sounds as if you're speaking from experience."

"Maybe I am," he said.

"Tell us more."

"That will be a cold day in hell."

Kent didn't say much else all night, and Harold wondered what could be weighing so heavy on his mind. Probably having the girls go off to college, another year almost shot, and summer on its way out the door. It made him a little sad, too. His little Parlor Game was just about over.

160 days

The Wife

There's no putting this off any longer. If Eric won't meet with the family, I have to. The girls are spending the last two weeks before school at Bass Lake, in the cabin owned by Jill's boyfriend's parents. They've done it for two summers now. This year its appeal is even greater. The media wouldn't dare seek them out there.

When I told them I was coming, Joy offered to drive down and pick me up. Although I've attended parties at Bass Lake, I've never made the drive by myself.

I told her I would be fine on the drive. I have to be. I arrive in the early afternoon, and am not surprised to find a note that they're on the lake. That means I have to walk down there across the wooden pier where the boats are harbored. The sun gleams off the dark water, where I hear young people yelling on skis and in power boats. I never did that, but I'm happy my girls are comfortable in such a setting. When they see me, they come running up the pier. Laguna Beach girls, I think. They could fit in that Southern California city of blond hair, blue eyes and white shorts, everyone in white shorts.

Bass Lake is much less exclusive, a couple of families gather on beach towels with picnic lunches and soft drinks. High school kids in cutoffs are trying to ski barefoot.

My daughters are wet, golden, and when I hug them, I can smell the sun.

"Let's stay down here," Jill says. "Did you bring your suit?"

"I can't stand this heat." I duck a large insect heading straight for me. "What the hell was that?"

"Meat bees," Joy says. "They're all over the place. I had one steal a chunk of salmon right off my plate the other night."

"Where do all these new pests come from? When I was your age, it was June bugs."

"Ick. Remember how they used to buzz on the screen of Grandpa's back door?" Joy puts her arm around me as we walk the shaky decking. "You doing okay?"

"Fine. I want to go back to the cabin, though. I need to talk to you girls."

I relax a bit when we're on solid ground. We walk up a lane to the wood-framed cabin. Joy offers iced tea and artificial sweetener. They're so young, so slim, these daughters of mine, and already they count every calorie. I hope it's because of our culture and not something I did when they were growing up.

We sit at a glass-topped table overlooking the lake.

"We need to have a meeting," I tell them.

"So you said on the phone." Joy holds her glass like a shield.

"It's important. You deserved one sooner. This situation we're in affects you, too."

"We understand, Mom," Jill says. "It's not your fault."

"You might understand, but I sure as hell don't," Joy says. "Our father won't even discuss it with us. He sends you instead."

I gulp my tea, unable to taste it. "He didn't send me, honey. He'd have a fit if he knew I were here, but that's too bad."

"What is it?" Jill says. "You're not going to leave him, are you?"

Joy whirls around to face Jill. "What's the matter? You afraid Gordon Bessey won't propose if your parents are divorced? Why don't you think about Mom? He's publicly humiliating her. You know he slept with April Wayne."

"Leave her alone." Tears well in Jill's eyes. "She doesn't need you to rub her nose in this."

Something in the tone of her voice reminds me of myself. Jill, the pleaser, trying to ignore the problem, hoping it will go away, if everyone will just keep quiet. She's inherited or absorbed my need to please. I hope she never has to deal with the problems that accompany that need.

I take her hand, squeeze it. "Joy's right," I say. "He did just that."

Joy sits straight in her chair. "He admitted it?"

"No, but he did admit that he had a vasectomy years ago, one that I never knew about. Here I was taking birth-control pills, and he had a vasectomy."

"So that Holly woman wasn't lying," Jill said, her expression glum.

"I think she was telling the truth. I have reasons to believe that he was involved with April Wayne, too."

"Oh, Mom," Jill said. "You don't think he did anything to her?"

"Of course not. But he's lied to me and he's lied to the public. He's put his job before anything."

"He always has," Joy said. "Please divorce him. You don't need this."

"Not yet," I said, "maybe not ever. I'm trying to get stronger, but it's hard. I can't remember what happened the night April Wayne disappeared."

Jill gasps. "Mom."

"I didn't do anything to her, of that I'm certain." I don't mention the phone call, that she called me a bitch, and that I exploded with anger. They don't need to hear that right now.

"I'm here for three reasons," I say. "First, because we need this meeting, because you two need answers. Second, because I want you to join me in supporting your father's reelection."

"You've got to be kidding," Joy says. "I hope he loses."

"He hasn't broken the law. He got caught cheating the same way a lot of other politicians have. He's been a wonderful senator and a lousy husband. We need to separate the two."

"Let him get a real job," Joy says. "He's trash just like the rest of his family."

"Don't talk about people who aren't here to defend themselves," I say. "Your grandparents and Aunt Beth were good people, and they loved you." I swallow more tea, amazed to see that my hands are steady. "Your dad and I need to work out our own problems, one way or the other. We can't do that with this election looming over our heads."

Joy leans across the table. "When the election's over, do you think you'll work it out then, or will you just go back to the way it was?"

"I'll never go back." The power in my voice surprises me.

"What's the third reason?" Jill asks.

"I know you've been hurt and humiliated by what's happened. I haven't handled it right, and I don't think your father has, either. I want both of you to get counseling, right away."

They sit silent for a moment. Joy stares down into her iced tea, Jill out the window at the tangle of trees and the lake beyond.

"What if people find out?" she asks in a small voice. "What if they put me on the cover of a tabloid like they did you?"

"There's nothing shameful in seeking help." I see myself in her terrified eyes. "Please don't be afraid."

I'm crying now, unable to stop. What have I done to my

daughter? What can I do, what can I say, to keep her from ending up like me?

"They won't find out." Joy's clear voice stops my tears. "They didn't find out about me."

"You went to counseling?" Jill asks.

"Damn right. I'm still going. I don't know if it's helping, but I'm going to keep doing it until I can figure it out."

Jill looks truly frightened now, alone. "But we tell each other everything."

"I couldn't tell you this," Joy says. "I knew you wouldn't approve."

"I didn't think we needed it. I thought it was just for—" She looks at me, and her eyes fill with tears again. "I didn't think we needed it, Joy."

Joy gets up and hugs her. For how long has she seen the fragility that I've overlooked in her sister?

"I'm proud of you, honey," I say. "It took guts to do that without telling anyone. I want you to go, too, Jill."

The shouts from the lake fill in the empty silence in the room.

Jill looks out at it, then back to Joy, to me. "I don't know. I'll have to think about it."

"Come on," Joy says. "You can go to my shrink. It will be fun."

"Maybe," she says, and I feel that we have made a start. That alone is worth the trip here.

"I'm proud of them," I tell Dr. Kellogg the next day. "I've been so worried that I did something to screw them up, but I think they're going to be okay."

He looks up from his yellow notebook. "Are you going to tell Eric you spoke with them?"

"I don't think so. I don't want him to confront them. After the election, maybe."

"And you're still going to support his reelection?"

"I have to."

"Why?"

"I don't know. Because he's a good senator. Because, for now at least, he's my husband."

"He's done some pretty terrible things to you."

I think of Holly Yost and the vasectomy, of April Wayne's youthful face, of that velvet box with the heart on it. "I know he has."

He leans forward in his chair, the beige cardigan hanging from his bony neck. "Do you really think he'll stop this behavior once he's reelected?"

"He'll have to. What happened to April must have been a wake-up call for him. You don't really think he'd risk that again, do you?"

"It depends," he says.

"On what?"

"On what's behind his actions. In some cases it's impossible to stop the behavior."

I feel myself begin to panic. Eric wouldn't dare do this again. Even if he can't talk about it, he's got to feel awful about what happened. I look into Dr. Kellogg's kind, impassive face and gather the courage to ask my question.

"So," I say. "If there's something really wrong with him, if he's unable to stop the behavior, what happens?"

"It escalates," he says.

162 days

The Mother

Gloria no longer had to wait in the front office when she visited Ryder at the newspaper. The security guard motioned her through the turnstile and clicked the lock even before ringing up Ryder to announce her. She took the elevator to the second floor.

The doors slid open, and there he was, waiting for her. He looked rested, his eyes clear. She wondered what that meant, if it were a sign that he was drinking less, feeling better.

"Sorry I didn't call first," she said.

"You don't have to. Want to go to my desk or talk out here?"

Inside she'd have to sit in Ryder's cubbyhole, pretending to ignore the hive of reporters pretending to ignore her. "Out here's fine." She walked away from the elevator down the hall lined with framed awards. "Jack and I are worried about the election."

He lowered his voice. "So am I. This jerk can't get reelected, but so few people vote in the primaries that it could happen by sheer luck."

"At least those who do vote will be informed voters."

"And farmers."

"We thought of that, too," she said. "What would you say about Jack and I taking out television commercials? We could speak right into the camera, present the facts of what he's done."

He leaned back against the wall. "Something like that could amass even more public empathy for you. It could also backfire. There's a lot of support for Suzanne Barry out there, too. If people feel sorry enough for her, they could vote for her husband out of sympathy."

She took a breath, looked into his eyes. "What if we did something to take away some of that support from Suzanne Barry?"

"Such as?"

"Such as run that story about the housekeeper. Let people know Suzanne doesn't have an alibi for that Friday night."

"I've told the police. They're trying to keep it quiet until they determine how credible the woman is as a witness."

"I don't care, Ryder. I just don't want Barry to be reelected. I don't want him to get away with anything else."

"You think he hurt April?" he said.

"Don't you?"

"I'm not ruling him out."

"Neither am I. There's some reason he's keeping quiet. Once he's back in office, everyone's going to forget this case. Oh, please, there has to be something we can do to stop him."

"I'm not sure," Ryder said. "Let me think about it."

169 days

The Senator

The bitch had finally done it. After all the support Eric had given her, damned near gone on a one-man campaign to get her elected governor, she'd come out with this. And she hadn't even discussed it with Eric first. The statement had been issued a day after Rich Ryder clobbered Suzanne in print. The implication was that Eric's wife, in a jealous rage, had done something to April. The Waynes would love that one.

The cops had been all over him, and he answered as he always had. He and Suzanne had spent that Friday together. The housekeeper must have been mistaken, or perhaps someone had convinced her to lie.

Eric crumpled the newspaper, threw it at the fireplace in Denny's office. It was a marble fireplace that burned a fake fire every day of the year, "for ambiance," Denny said.

Denny pulled a chair up to the conference table. Beside them, a year-round garden bloomed in a glassed-in atrium. The antiques were real, the marble-topped, inlaid tables Denny had picked out in Greece. Above his desk, sunlight streamed in through hand-etched glass. Denny liked to brag that he'd started in a basement office where he never saw the sun. This was the only place he didn't allow food.

"Fucking women," Eric said.

"Take it easy, partner. It's not the end of the world."

"My political career is my world."

"There are other worlds out there. You just need to look around." He waved an expansive hand toward the atrium and the traffic beyond. "The governor stuck it to you. What do you expect?"

"A little loyalty, perhaps?"

"What's she supposed to do? Rich Ryder's a bulldog. He's not going to let this story die. What he wrote about Suzanne—"

"A cheap shot," Eric said. "She was with me that night. An open suitcase and a few broken plates don't prove a thing."

"He crucified her in print. And as for you, that vasectomy story painted you as a adulterer."

"So we have my wife painted as a suspect, for what? Murder? And me painted as an adulterer." Eric picked up a silver letter opener, touched its cool surface. "Other than use this on my wrists, what would you do?"

"Before I answer that, I have more bad news," Denny said. "Anne Ashley quit."

"That bitch." Eric tossed the letter opener back on the table. "She couldn't come to me? She had to tell you?"

"She said you never followed her advice, partner. Said she's tired of hearing what lousy PR people you have."

"Her advice sucked. Good riddance. We don't need her for this election."

"That's what we need to discuss." Denny grew solemn, his

undertaker face, Eric called it. "I think we need to explore other avenues."

"Other avenues? Other than politics?"

"For now."

"And what am I supposed to do in the meantime?"

Denny's grave expression melted into a smile. "Guess who I've been meeting with? Junior LaRue's agent. He wants to arrange something with you and Junior."

Eric couldn't follow Denny's logic. He searched his eyes, trying to determine if this were his idea of a joke. But he saw only excitement.

"Junior LaRue killed his wife in cold blood, and he wants to arrange something with me?" Eric said. "You can't be serious. Where would you hold this media side show? Springer?"

"Of course not," Denny said. "You think I'd put you on with a bunch of people who'd sell their grandmothers for a trip to Disneyland? I'm on retainer for a major entertainment company that has several shows in production. The independent networks are looking for something controversial to grab the spotlight. You and Junior could be co-hosts like Robert Stack on *Unsolved Mysteries*."

"And you'd be another Merv Griffin, syndicating the packages for big bucks."

"Big bucks for both of us, partner. Buy you some time."

"Money isn't my goal." He looked with disgust at Denny's permanently tanned face, a new addition since his appearances on the talk shows. "And hosting my own TV show isn't my goal, either, difficult as that may be for you to understand."

"No, your goal is power." Denny made it sound like a disease.

Eric got up from the table. It couldn't be this bad, couldn't have come to this. "Your little taste of fame is rotting your brain," he said. "What you're suggesting is political suicide."

Denny jumped to his feet as well, his pudgy face florid. "You've already committed political suicide," he said. "You

243

did that when you got involved with April Wayne. They're calling you Senator Sleazy now. The lamest opposition can defeat you."

"Stop judging me," he said. "If that girl had thrown herself at you, you'd have been all over her like one of your ten-dollar pizzas."

Denny leaned across the table, supporting himself on his knuckles. "I don't like that kind of talk."

"And I don't like that kind of fair-weather loyalty, counselor."

Denny heaved a sigh, tried for his usual grin but couldn't quite pull it off. "I'm trying to help you. You're my friend. I don't want to see you fuck up anymore."

Where did this parasite get off calling him a fuck-up? Eric bit back a rush of angry words, calmly gave him his best senator's face. No point in getting mad. It wouldn't solve anything.

"Listen carefully," he said. "I'm staying in the race regardless of what you or anyone else thinks. I'm going to run, and I'm going to win this son of a bitch. If you don't like it, find yourself another client."

With that, he picked up his briefcase, walked to the door and left.

170 days

The Wife

I smelled fall in the air for the first time today. It's really coming, and this election is going to happen, with or without me. Labor Day is behind us now, and the campaign is on in earnest. Melinda brought me a list of fund-raisers. I told her I'd attend only the ones that were most crucial, and only briefly.

I've opened the sliding glass doors to the patio so that I can smell the cooling air and watch the setting sun from my kitchen. My appetite has returned with the change of weather. I heat a pasta pot of water on the stove, and kick off my shoes as I busy myself in the kitchen.

I put on the Eva Cassidy CD with "Let the Good Times Roll" and "Gee Baby, Ain't I Good to You" on it. My intent is to lose myself in Eva's amazing voice. Instead the music reminds me that she was another young woman of tragedy, dead of cancer in 1996, at the age of thirty-three, before she knew how close she was to stardom. Don't start that, I chide myself. Just listen.

The table is a mess with college brochures Berta dropped by and this velvet box I took from Eric's condo. I pick it up, touch the pink ribbons that stream from it. It's mine, in my care. And that's why I took it, I realize, because if I didn't, he would have surely destroyed it. What do I do with it now?

I've taken to hiding out again. Rich Ryder's article all but accused me of murdering April Wayne. No one knows for sure that she's dead, and he has found me guilty of her murder. Would I have killed her, I wonder, that night when she called me a bitch? If she had been here and I'd had a weapon in my hand instead of a china plate, would I have used it?

The white heat of that moment returns to me. I can hear her youthful voice, petulant and sure. Yes, like one of my daughters.

I'd been packing on and off all day. Remembering that the Sacramento refrigerator was always bare, I decided to prepare a snack before I left. Turnoffs in strange places could sometimes set off anxiety attacks.

First, I'd call to let Eric know I was ready to leave. I remember it now, word for word, thought for thought.

"Is Eric there?"

Startled to hear a woman's voice, I assured myself she had to be one of his aides.

"Who?"

She sounded strange, confused. I grew impatient. It was my condo, too. She had no right to screen my phone call.

"Eric Barry. Who is this?"

Then the sharp intake of breath, the words I'll never forget.

"Who the hell do you think it is, you crazy bitch."

I sink down into the kitchen chair, put my head into my hands, urge the memories forward. I'd gone into a fury, shouting in the emptiness of the house, wailing, a woman in pain. What next? I see pills, a handful of them. I had not been trying to kill myself, I know. Suicide is murder. I wouldn't do that. But what had I done? I picked up the phone again, shouted into the answering machine that I was going over there. And I did go there, didn't I? Yes, I drove to Sacramento that night. Or I started to. I woke up in the garage, slumped in the front seat, car door open. I stumbled inside, grabbed one of my bags, left in a panic. Was that when Rachel, the housekeeper, saw me?

I hear a noise behind me, see that it's just the boy with the groceries, standing in the open doorway.

"You gave me a start," I say. "Could you put the bag on the drain board? The table's a mess."

He crosses the room, stops in front of the table, staring at the box. Something in his face gives me a chill. Recognition. He knows this velvet container, knows its owner.

As he sets the bag on the counter, I chatter about the store, ask how his father is. I've never really looked at him before. He's tall and muscular with blond hair, a face that girls probably find handsome. What's wrong with his eyes? Why is he staring? I try to recall his name. Kenny, like his dad? No, shorter than that. Now I remember.

"Guess you're back in school now, Kent," I say. "Still at City College?"

He nods, touches the box.

"Where'd you get this?"

"I don't know."

"Don't lie." He steps forward, snatches it from the table, clutching it to his chest. "It's hers. You know it is." The smell of alcohol is strong on his breath.

I glance out the back door. It's growing dark. I could scream, but I don't know if anyone would hear me over the music. Besides, a scream might set him off.

"Calm down," I say in a firm voice, as if he's one of my children. "I found it in Sacramento. I think it belongs to one of my husband's aides."

"It belongs to April," he says. "April Wayne. I know because

247

I gave it to her." He looks slowly from it to me. "Did you take it from her?"

"No," I say. "She must have left it in Sacramento. The aides used my husband's condo as a second office."

"I know what goes on there. And I know who does the using." He places the box on the table. "You were going to get rid of it, weren't you?"

"No." I back up against the drain board. If I can keep him preoccupied, I just might be able to make it to the door, into the backyard, the gate to our neighbors' patio. "If I wanted to get rid of it, I wouldn't have brought it home with me, would I?" My logic disarms him momentarily. As I inch along the drain board, unrelated facts fall into place. "Are you the young man the papers wrote about? The one she was seeing?"

"I'm not supposed to say. She made me promise."

"But it's okay now. She won't mind. You might know something that can help them find her."

"I don't know where she is. She was supposed to be back before school started."

"When did you talk to her, Kent?"

He jerks to attention. "Didn't say I talked to her. You're trying to put words in my mouth. I thought you were a nice lady. I stick up for you all the time in the bar, even stood up to Janie Stuart. She thinks you hurt April."

"I didn't," I say. "I don't know what happened to her, either."

He turns his back on the table, watching me intently, moving closer. "I'm the only one she trusts. She told me about your husband. She didn't tell him about me, even though our thing was all over in high school."

"Kent," I say. "We need to call someone. You have to tell your story."

"I'm the only one who can keep a secret. That's what April says. What did you do to her?"

"I didn't do anything. Please believe me. I want to help. Why do you think I brought that box of hers back here?"

I point at the table. He does what I hoped he would, slowly turning to look at it.

I run for the door, scream, "Help." I'm almost there, my legs churning, carrying me toward the patio. "Help me, please."

His strong fingers grip my arm, drag me back inside. I continue to scream for help as he jerks me across my kitchen floor, flopping me like a doll as he shoves me against the counter.

"Was Janie right? Did you do something to hurt April?" He lowers his face to mine, his expression fierce.

"No, damn it. Who's Janie? Let me go."

I will fight, even if he kills me. In my mind, I see Kellogg's watery eyes, hear his words about my dream of driving over a cliff.

"It doesn't matter if you crashed," he tells me. *"All that matters is how you handled it. Did you fight for control, or did you throw up your hands and scream all the way down?"*

I'm not about to throw up my hands and cave in for this little punk. I lift my foot, kick like hell at his balls, hit his shin instead. He yelps. Good. Very good.

He drops for a moment, then stands upright, his face like that of an animal that doesn't understand the consequences of its actions. He seems fueled by something primal, something completely irrational. He begins to sob.

"April said she talked to you on the phone before she went to that bar. She was afraid. She said that, too. Why did you scare her? What did you do to her?"

He grabs me by both arms, yanking me to his chest.

"How many times do you have to hear it? I didn't come near April that night. I've never met April."

"You're lying. Someone hurt her, or she'd be home by now."

He slams me against the sink. I catch my breath, I look him in the eyes, realize he is beyond reason. I've got to get away, or he will kill me. His rage is building, coming back to him in a wave as he reaches to grip me again.

The pot of pasta water bubbles just to my right. With all of the strength I can muster, I whirl around, grab it and throw it at his face.

His high-pitched shriek is worse than anything from my most terrifying nightmares. I freeze for a moment, gaping at his scalded flesh. Then, I scream, too, drop the pot to the floor and run barefoot into the night.

The Girl

"*Listen,*" she told Kent. "*You've got to keep this to yourself, okay?*"

"*You know I will, April.*"

"*I'm going to be back to see you before school starts. Don't say anything to anyone until we talk, no matter what.*"

"*You know you can trust me.*" He paused. "*What's all that noise? Where are you calling from?*"

She looked around at the dismal room, the gray stone walls, the lipstick scrawl apologizing to the world. "*A stupid pisser in the middle of the boondocks. You wouldn't believe it. I'll tell you all about it when I'm home.*"

"*Are you sure you're okay?*"

Hearing his voice made her feel better now. The horrible room deodorizer had cleared her sinuses, and she could breathe again. She just needed food, and Eric would see to that.

"*I got to feeling lonely, is all,*" she said. Here she was, an intern in the Capitol, most likely to succeed. What was she doing calling her high school boyfriend from a bar like this?

"You said you were scared."

"That's just because of what you-know-who's wife said. I'm not scared now. I feel pretty good, actually, ready to party all night. Too bad you're not here. I'd buy you a Corona. Next time you're in Sacramento, let's get drunk on chocolate martinis."

"You're not with that guy, are you, April?"

"No, of course not, and remember, you're not supposed to know anything about him. Don't ever say a word to anybody. Promise."

"I won't."

Listening to his sweet little-kid voice made her want to cry. She probably should tell him more, explain what was going on, but he was too simple and way too loyal. He'd be calling the paramedics before Eric could order the next round.

"You always manage to calm me down," she said. "Thank you."

She could picture his face, the wide eyes, the earnest smile. She'd loved him back once, when they'd been younger, but she didn't want to end up with a grocery store clerk, even if his dad did own the store. She wanted just what she had—Senator Eric Barry.

"I love you more than all those high-class guys," he said. "You know that, don't you?"

"Sure, honey. You prove it all the time. You're like a brother to me, and that's better than some guy. You and I are forever, Kent. I need to get going now."

"Talk to me longer, April. You sound funny."

"Maybe I'll call you back later. I've got to piss right now."

She could always make him laugh when she used crude talk, and this was no exception. Crude talk. If he only knew.

"If you need anything, you can call anytime, day or night."

"I might take you up on it," she said. "We'll talk soon."

"And you'll get down here before I go back to school?"

"Promise. Hey, I really do have to pee. Catch you later, honey. Bye."

She snapped off the phone before he could reply. Damn, that was a stupid thing to do. What had gotten into her, anyway? She was getting to be a real wuss with booze. She hoped she hadn't come off like a creep in front of Eric and his friend.

She lifted her skirt and stood over the toilet. No way was her ass coming close to that nasty-looking seat. Eric would laugh when she told him about it later. Just one of the many advantages of going without panties, she'd tell him.

She'd been holding it too long. She released a stream into the toilet feeling the painful pressure leave her bladder.

She heard a click from the other side of the door. The knob turned. Someone was trying to get in.

"I'll be out in a minute," she called, stepping away from the bowl.

The knob twisted again harder. Something hit the door. Stupid drunks.

"I said, I'll be right out." She raised her voice, trying to be heard over the racket.

The door shuddered with the weight of impact, and fell away from its hinges. April backed against the sink. Alfonso stood facing her.

"What are you doing?" she demanded.

"We got worried about you, little girl," Alfonso said in his rasping voice. "Your men don't like it when you leave them alone too long."

173 days

The Mother

The story broke that morning. Kent Dishman, April's high school boyfriend, had attacked Suzanne Barry at her home.

Kent, an air-conditioning and refrigeration major at Pleasant View Community College, refused to make any comment, but a photo of Kent's father, his face broken with shock, accompanied the story.

"Kent's a good boy," Ryder had reported him as saying. "He never even mentioned that he knew April Wayne."

Gloria tried to work that morning and couldn't. They had a big order for a private school, and she wanted Karen to have her support, at least physically. Their business had almost tripled, and the thought that her increased visibility was part of the reason sickened her. Still, she couldn't let Karen take it all on herself.

She could at least unpack the shipment of Thanksgiving decorations that had come in. The Orange Season, she called it, not her favorite, but it came every year, like it or not, before summer had even burned itself out. She would unpack some of the less fragile items, but first she needed to hire Karen some help. That was her first job of the day, draft a classified ad in the *Valley Voice*.

Gloria steadied the ladder and looked up to where Karen was unfastening two shell-shaped sconces from the wall. "Did April ever mention Kent Dishman to you?"

"I've been trying to remember since you called, and I don't think so." Karen handed one down to her, and Gloria balanced the ladder with her knee. "He might have been at some of the swim parties, though. April invited a cast of thousands to those things."

Gloria remembered the constant swarm coming in and out of the house. April had always been surrounded by kids.

"We were around for all of those parties," she said. "How could she be so secretive?"

"Some girls are just that way. It's no reflection on the parents. Hey, would you hold it steady, please."

Gloria concentrated until Karen was back on the floor beside her. "That box?" she said. "The velvet one? It's hers. I've seen it in her room as far back as I can remember."

"That boy must have given it to her then."

"And Suzanne Barry admitted taking it from Eric's condominium. That proves April was telling me the truth that night."

Karen ran a hand through her dark hair. "I never doubted it."

"If she could tell me that, why couldn't she tell me about the Dishman boy?"

"Stop blaming yourself. April didn't tell you about Kent because she didn't want to. It's as simple as that. Maybe the relationship just wasn't important enough to her."

"Or maybe she thought I'd judge her for being with a grocery store clerk. Maybe that's why she went after someone more important."

Karen put her arm around her. "Gloria, you're the least judgmental person I know. There's no way you'd care what kind of boy April dated, not as long as he was a nice person."

"You're right," she said. "I wouldn't care."

"Now, Jack might be a different story."

"I don't think so."

No, she thought, it was true. April adored her dad. She used him as a standard against which she measured everyone else, even Gloria. Jack would never say anything against anyone. The most he'd venture about a potential boyfriend was, "What's his dad do?" Maybe that was enough.

"What's the matter?" Karen asked. "Did I say something to make it worse?"

"No."

Gloria went to the stock table and began unpacking gourds and wicker cornucopia. She was too frantic to understand the importance of Kent Dishman, too eager to place blame anywhere but with herself. None of this would help her find her daughter. She had to think, try to imagine what April would have done after they'd argued on the phone that night. According to Suzanne Wayne, Kent suggested that April had called him from a bar. The police knew that. She'd been seen at a bar that Friday with Eric Wayne. But what bar? Maybe something had happened there.

She phoned Ryder at work and got a recording saying he was out of the office. His voice on the machine sounded as if he were trying to sleep off a rough night.

When he opened the door of his apartment, she knew she'd been right. Van Morrison blasted from the stereo, "Back on Top Again." Ryder looked anything but.

"Come on in," he said. "Just let me warn you, I'm not in the best mood."

"So I see." She sat on the leather couch, remembering the

night of lovemaking as she touched its soft surface. "You feel pretty bad?"

"Like shit. You realize that story of mine was probably the reason that kid went to the Waynes' house. I shouldn't have run it."

"Don't beat yourself up."

"I did it against my better judgment, Gloria."

"I know why," she said. "I shouldn't have asked you."

"I talked myself into thinking that the public had a right to know. It was horse shit. That kid could have killed Suzanne Barry."

"Ryder—" she got up from the sofa and put her arms around him "—I didn't try to use what happened between us as a way to get you to run that story."

He squeezed her bare arm, ran his stubbled skin against it. "I'm not trying to blame you. I'm a grown-up."

Gloria looked down at his bloodshot eyes. It would be easy to lean a little closer and let it happen all over again. She straightened up, returned to the safety of the sofa. "I came here because I had an idea," she said. "Remember when April first disappeared? There was a report that she'd been seen at a local bar that night with Eric Barry."

"Right."

"Do you have the name of that bar?"

"Sure, in my notes somewhere. It's a man's name, Rick's Place, Joe's Place, something like that."

"Did you ever go there?"

He started to look interested. "No. The cops probably did, though. In fact I think I saw a report somewhere."

"I've decided to. Today."

"That's not a good idea. You don't want to put yourself through it."

"I don't have any choice," she said. "I'm going crazy sitting at home, trying to help Karen at the showroom. It will make me feel that I'm helping."

257

He nodded, rubbing his grizzled chin. "Then I'm going with you."

"I hoped you'd say that." She looked at her watch. "It isn't even ten o'clock. If we hurry, we can be there by one."

The Senator

This was insane. Suzanne had called in the middle of the night, hysterical, claiming she'd been attacked by April's old boyfriend. April didn't even have an old boyfriend, not that he knew of. Still he needed to get down there right away.

He had a meeting that morning but promised to be home as soon as he could. He picked up a paper on the way. He'd have a wait before the meeting, and could fill in the details while he drank his coffee. As he sat in the coffee shop, he went over the story. Damn crazy. Suzanne shouldn't leave the back door open when she was by herself like that.

She claimed the Dishman boy said April had called him from the bar. He said he had given April a box, which Suzanne Barry had taken from her husband's Sacramento condominium that served as a second office for his staff.

Eric sat motionless, unable to lift his coffee cup. Suzanne had betrayed him. She'd taken something of April's from his condo. When had she done it? Why? What had she planned on doing with it? She'd acted strangely the last time she'd been there, insisted on hurrying home, even though he'd wanted her involved in the strategy meetings with Anne Ashley and Denny.

He'd been afraid that she was going into one of her spells. Maybe this was part of the spells, some kind of advanced paranoia. Eric looked down at his hands, watched them flex, then clinch into fists. Whatever it was, she was not going to get away with it.

173 days

The Mother

Ryder and Gloria drove into Sacramento with Van Morrison blaring on the CD player. They'd stopped off Highway 99 for coffee, and Ryder seemed more alert. From the stereo, Morrison launched into a rhythmic, ambiguous refrain.

"'Rough God Riding,'" Gloria said. "That's your song. You're the rough god."

Ryder lifted the cup of coffee to his lips, took a swallow and put it back in the holder. "Thanks, I think. I feel rough today."

"It becomes you. Makes you look like the long-suffering reporter."

He glanced across at her. "Just for the record, I've about had it with suffering."

He sounded as if he meant it. "Good for you," she said.

She thought of herself, couldn't imagine arriving at a place where she could let go of her suffering. She would be in pain for the rest of her life unless she could find April.

She played navigator, reading Ryder instructions she'd written down when she called Nick's. The street was one of those with numerous dead ends that picked up again several blocks later. They ended up at road's end beneath an underpass.

"Warehouse district," Ryder said.

She looked down the street, saw a storefront with a crudely lettered sign on the door. "Nick's."

Several motorcycles were parked side by side in a parking lot adjacent to the building.

"Damn," Ryder said. "It's not what I expected."

Gloria's mouth went dry. She didn't want to think of April in a place like this. "It looks pretty seedy," she said.

"You'd better wait in the car."

"No, I have to go in there, no matter what."

He started to say more, then looked at her, his pale eyes washed of color by the sunlight. "Come on."

He knew she wouldn't listen to logic, that she hadn't traveled this far to sit in the car. And, she marveled, he knew all of this without having to invest an entire conversation on the subject. He understood her.

She'd been in a few dives in her day. This one struck her differently. It was the last place anyone had seen her daughter.

Although the sun shone outside, the windowless hole was as dark as midnight. There was no time here. No clock, no windows, only the one wooden door through which they stepped into the darkness.

Ryder took her arm, glanced over at a couple of empty tables. "I think we better sit at the bar."

"That's fine."

A kitchen chair was suspended from the ceiling mobile style, and from it, a woman's bra and panties.

"Some decor," she said under her breath.

"I wouldn't be offering any advice along those lines if I were you."

Daytime drinkers downing red beers and boilermakers glanced up when they sat down, then went back to their conversations, gesturing with beer bottles, swallowing shots of liquor. A huge man in leather chaps fed coins to the jukebox. A Johnny Cash song cut through the stale air.

The bartender hummed along with it as he made his way behind the bar. He'd tucked his lanky brown hair behind his ears, and he looked too young for the roll around his middle. The way he walked made Gloria think of the men who operated the rides at carnivals.

Ryder ordered their beers. The man slapped down two bottles before them, hers on a napkin. Gloria looked down, hoping he wouldn't recognize her, but he was too full of whatever he was serving to pay much attention.

"Are you Nick?" Ryder asked.

"Ain't no Nick," the man said. "I been running it two years. Name's Morgan."

"First or last?"

"Just Morgan."

"Okay, Morgan. This is Gloria. I'm Ryder. I'm with the *Valley Voice* in Pleasant View."

"I could've guessed that." He scratched his head. "You don't look like no narc to me."

"Thanks."

"Didn't mean it as a compliment," he said. "Just meant you don't look like one. I can tell a cop a mile away."

"You must have had some practice."

"Some. They haven't been around lately, though." He knocked three times on the bar. "You're here about the girl, aren't you?"

"I was hoping to talk to someone who'd seen her that night."

"You're talking to him."

Gloria's stomach lurched. She reached for the sweaty bottle, tried to look preoccupied. Ryder squeezed her arm.

"Buy you a beer, Morgan?"

"A shot of Crown Royal wouldn't kill me."

Ryder put the money on the bar, and Morgan filled his shot glass. "All I care about's keeping this place out of the papers," he said. "It gets a little rowdy at times, but we do our best to settle our differences ourselves, if you know what I mean."

"I'm not trying to cause trouble for you," Ryder told him. "I just want to know about April Wayne."

"Like I told the cops, I saw the girl here that Friday. Don't ask me how I recognized the guy. I've never voted in my life."

He spun out the story with the skill of someone who'd had a few rehearsals. Gloria guessed this wasn't the first time someone had bought him a drink to hear him tell it.

"Did he give you his name?"

"No, but I did hear her call him Eric, and it just clicked. I'd seen him on the news when they were making that big fuss about whether or not gays could get married, and I remembered him."

"And the girl?"

"Good-looking." He tilted his hand from side to side. "A little tipsy. They were right over there."

He pointed behind her, and Gloria turned, staring at the table and its empty booth.

"Where?" she asked. "Where exactly did she sit?"

"Right there, next to the wall. The senator guy sat next to her, and the other guy across from her there."

Ryder took a drink of his beer, and she sensed he was slowing down the conversation, making the bartender comfortable again. "What other guy?" he asked.

"Black guy. I told the cops about him."

"Can you describe him?"

"Tall, shaved head, white T-shirt, jeans. Very clean-cut."

"Had she been in here before?" Gloria asked. They'd agreed

that Ryder would handle the questions, but she couldn't stop herself.

"No, ma'am. I would have remembered her."

"Oh." This was more difficult than she'd imagined. She swallowed some bitter beer, trying to compose herself.

"What about the men?" Ryder said.

"Not the senator, but the black dude, he might have been."

"What makes you say that?"

"The way he talked. I thought I'd heard him in here before. Course it could have been someone else with a voice like his."

Ryder leaned over the bar. Gloria felt his even breathing, tried to match hers with it, to calm down and just let the man tell his story at his own pace.

"He had one of them raspy voices, you know, like he'd smoked his share of weed."

Gloria sat impatiently while Ryder bought the man two more Crown Royals and asked the same questions a number of different ways.

"You helped us a lot, Morgan," he finally said.

The bartender grinned. "Just remember what I told you. We don't need any trouble around here."

"Understood." Ryder rose, put some bills on the bar. "Do you remember what time they left?"

The bartender scratched his head, frowning. "Sorry. I was half shit-faced myself that night. She left before they did, I think."

Ryder stopped. "You sure?"

"I remember seeing the two guys at the table by themselves. I think she went out the back."

"Mind showing it to us?"

"Sure. Not much to see."

He led them down a narrow hall that smelled of cigarette smoke, stale beer and urine. A screen door with a latch lay straight ahead. Before that, to the left, was a door marked, Keep Out. To the right, matching doors announced Gents and Ladies.

Gloria moved closer to the ladies' room. Its door hung ajar from a broken hinge, the wood around it shattered.

"Was there a fight in here?" Ryder asked.

"Not that I know of." Morgan crossed his arms. "Like I said, we settle our own differences."

Gloria stepped into the room. Graffiti littered the walls. A broken mirror hung on one wall. Such a narrow, cramped room. The smell of the deodorizer had to be as bad as whatever it was trying to cover. For a moment, she felt she was going to be sick, and she didn't want to go in.

"Come on," Ryder said from the doorway. "We need to get going."

Morgan unlocked a screen door at the end of the hall. They both thanked him, and they stepped outside. Finally Gloria could breathe. She felt her head begin to clear.

"I can't tell you how I feel right now," she said.

"I can only imagine." He put his arm around her as they crossed the parking lot to the car. "You did great. I know it wasn't easy."

"It was terrible, maybe one of the worst times for me, visualizing her in that place with him."

"Before we do anything else," Ryder said, "we need to make a phone call."

"To Oakland?" she asked.

They sat in the car, and Ryder took out his phone and notebook. After a moment, he gave Gloria a thumbs-up.

"Mrs. Trotter?" he asked. "It's Rich Ryder with the *Valley Voice* in Pleasant View. When we spoke the other day, you said to ask your son Alfonso to get in touch with you if I saw him. No, I didn't see him myself, but a friend of mine thinks he did. The description is similar, but I'm wondering—does Alfonso have an unusual voice?" He scribbled on his notebook, then looked up at Gloria with a grin. "He does? Stuck with a pencil as a child? Sounds as if he might be the person my friend saw. I'll be in touch. Goodbye."

"It's Trotter, isn't it?" she said.

"Sure sounds like it."

And he was with April the night before she disappeared. "What do we do now, Ryder?"

"Go to the police," he said. "I want to be sure they know everything we do, and I want to make it known that I'll kick their asses in print if they even try to drag their feet on this. Alfonso Trotter's the link to Barry. They've got to find him."

The Parlor Game
April's Former Boyfriend Has Alibi For Night Of Disappearance

At least he could do that for the kid, Harold thought, folding the newspaper. As he'd told the cops, Kent Dishman had been sitting right here at this bar the Friday night April Wayne disappeared. Of that, he was sure.

None of the regulars were around tonight. Sometimes it was like that, a bar full of strange faces that never again returned. Other nights it was as familiar as a living room.

"Hey, Harold."

He heard the voice before he realized someone had come in.

Whitey stood inside the open door. Didn't he know he'd been eighty-sixed?

"It was our group's fault what Kent Dishman tried to do to the Barry woman," he said. "The kid just blew."

Harold turned slowly to face him. "Thought you'd left town."

"Just got back." He started toward his usual stool.

"Whitey, look." Harold moved closer to the bar, speaking in a quiet voice. "I told you the last time you were here we couldn't have any more trouble."

"That wasn't my fault what happened that night. It was Kent. You can see that now. Look what he tried to do to Suzanne Barry. Not that it's all his fault. That's how two-faced this fucked-up state is."

"Whitey, listen." His voice stopped the barrage of words. At least Whitey was sober. Harold had handled worse in his day. "That's better," he said.

"What I'm saying is true." His eyes looked narrow through the thick gray glasses. "Anyone's ever made a mistake has to register as a sex offender to live here. Mothers won't let their kids even walk by your house, you know that? But a swinging dick like Senator Barry can go anywhere he wants, screw anybody's daughter. He's the real sex offender. Women aren't safe with him on the street."

"Keep your voice down," Harold said. "I'm not going to serve you anymore, Whitey. I'm sorry. You're a good guy, but I just don't need the hassle."

"You fucking coward." Whitey started to come around the bar.

"Don't try it," Harold shouted. "I'll call the cops, and I've got a gun right here."

"Stick your gun and the cops, too, Harold Bear. You suck just like the rest of this town. You wouldn't survive anywhere but California with a bunch of weirdoes just like you."

"Get out." Harold reached for the phone.

"Nobody kicks me out," Whitey said. "Nobody treats me like dirt. I'll be seeing you again, old man. Just wait."

Harold sagged against the bar and watched him head for the street. California sure didn't have a corner on weirdoes, not anymore. Something in the tone of Whitey's threat sounded just nutty enough to be real. That's why Harold kept a gun, for guys like this. Damn, maybe he was getting too old for this business.

176 days

The Senator

Eric was flying in his car, breaking into the curves hard, barely slowing for them, bending in the wind. They had tried to take his life from him, the Waynes, that bastard Ryder. He'd been a good senator. He'd earned the office, and without it, he'd be nothing, not a fucking thing.

The road narrowed as he neared the Delta, and he bumped over it. Better cut the antics or he'd be wearing his Jag, and that would make too many people happy.

He parked next to Fonso's car on the road and walked up to the dock. Although he wasn't one for boating, he liked the Delta. "Mystery and history," Fonso had said, "heavy on the mystery."

Anyone could get lost here and did, some permanently. Since the Gold Rush of the mid-1800s, the waterways between San

Francisco and Sacramento had laid open many legends and hidden even more secrets.

A party was going on several boats down, but the majority of them sat dark. Mostly just RVs out here this time of year on the other end of the campgrounds. It was a perfect place to get lost, and Alfonso wasn't the first to use it. Some people made their livings hiding people out here.

Eric climbed on board, then shouted, "You in there?"

"Well, ain't it about time?" Fonso stood in the entrance in a circle of light from the lantern.

Eric nearly twisted his ankle as he scrambled inside. "Damn boat. Shut the door, would you? We don't need to be issuing any open invitations tonight."

Fonso chuckled and stretched out on the short sofa bed. "No parties for the senator? There's gin in the galley in case you change your mind. Your favorite kind, man."

He'd helped himself to some of it, Eric could tell. The glassy cast to his eyes wasn't all due to the lamplight. He wore navy sweats, the top unzipped, that clung to his sinewy body. His subtle scent filled the tiny area, like the aroma of a candle. Eric shucked off his jacket and went to the galley. Get rid of the tension, he thought. Whatever it takes, just get rid of the tension. He lifted a glass from the netting and filled it with ice and Bombay. The boat's rhythmic rocking combined with the gin would settle him down in a hurry.

"Thanks for remembering my brand. It was thoughtful of you."

"Brought it from my apartment. We still had some left from the last time. If you hadn't gotten here pretty soon, I would have had to drink it all alone."

"I tried. I had to make sure no one saw me."

He sat across on a similar sofa, a nubby brown fabric that blended with the wood of the boat. "Who owns this, anyway?"

Fonso stretched out his long legs and leaned against the back of the sofa. "Friend of mine, name of Ivory."

"You didn't tell him about me?"

"Do I look like a fool to you? I told him I didn't want to be seen for a spell."

"He must know why."

"He knows, but I told him I had bigger troubles than some pussy-crazy senator. He said he understood. Last guy who stayed here was that frogman who hit hotels up in the city then swam across the bay. I'm small-time to Ivory."

"Can you trust him?"

"We both can. But it's going to cost you."

"I brought cash."

"Praise the Lord. I was starting to get worried."

"You knew you could count on me."

"I was hoping." His gaze swept over Eric. "You two need to get together, you know what I mean. Ivory can give out what you like."

"I like it all."

"Don't bullshit your brother. You like it rough."

His voice grated out the word so that Eric could feel it reverberate in his groin. "Sometimes," he said, trying to hide his smile.

"You like it rough, and Ivory gives it rough."

"As rough as you?"

Fonso sipped his drink and nodded toward Eric with a sleepy-eyed smile. "Rougher. He'll make you weep, my man."

"Did he make you weep?"

"I'm not into that weeping shit, as you know."

"That's not what I'm asking."

"I know what you're asking."

"So answer me."

Fonso got up, strutted to the galley for a refill. On the way back to the sofa, he stopped, tousled Eric's hair with his fingers.

"The answer," he said, in his taunting whisper. "You're better."

The gin had melted away some of the tightness in Eric's

shoulders. He considered joining Fonso on the sofa. One more time. Who the hell would ever find out? No. That kind of logic was what had gotten him in trouble. He had to think about his job, about where he'd be without it. And his family. Hell, what would happen to them?

"I'm worried," he said.

Fonso threw up his hands. "Hey, man, if anyone should be worried it's Alfonso Trotter here. I'm the one they're looking for."

"Only because they want to get to me."

"Don't worry," he said. "I took care of everything. They'll never find her. By now, there's a house built over where she's buried. Watched them lay the concrete myself."

"That's not what I'm worried about."

"Okay, Eric, tell Papa. What the fuck you worried about? That chicken-shit election? I don't think you got a fool's chance, anyway."

"You're not exactly a political analyst."

"Don't have too many of them on your side, either, right now." He stretched out again and yawned, not bothering to cover his mouth. "Give it a few years, why don't you? Come back when it's forgot and they're crucifying someone else."

Eric rose from the sofa and drained his glass. "There's more at stake than the election, Fonso."

"No shit."

He glanced down at his hands, his perfectly shaped fingers tapering into blunt nails. Perhaps it was just the trick of lamp-light, the swaying boat, but they seemed detached from him, as if they had an existence independent from his.

"What are you thinking?" Fonso asked. "You got a funny look."

"You think you can tell the shape of someone's dick by the shape of his fingers?"

The rasp was Fonso's way of laughing. "Man, you can come up with some crazy shit sometimes."

"As I said, there's a lot at stake."

Eric had the gun out before Fonso could respond, firing it into his face. It was the only way for sure, to blast his beautiful face, the evil brain it hid.

Fonso's expression went from astonishment to a frozen stare. Eric couldn't stop watching his face, the awful black hole above his eyes, the whispered message of death from his lips. Blood and tissue dripped off the wall behind the sofa. Eric had to get away.

He walked up the stairs, careful not to twist an ankle. When he slammed the door and started the car, he was surprised how strong his legs felt.

Farther up the Delta, he'd toss the gun Fonso had given him, and the last link would be broken. He looked at his hands, reflected in the dim light. They'd acted almost without any instruction from him. How could they have done this?

There was no choice, that's how. That scum in the boat would have ruined him. Sooner or later, he would have gotten caught and told all he knew. He might have turned to blackmail. It would have ruined Eric's family. A man had a right to protect his family.

It was the right thing, the only thing, yet tears burned his eyes and ran down his face as he drove. He'd never been able to cry anywhere but in his car, not even since all this shit started happening around him. He cried now, though, sobbing out his anguish to a God that never seemed to be there when he was needed.

Eric glanced down at his hands again then looked up into the darkness, the black wind that blew his tears back into his face. He missed Fonso already, mourned him as he would a brother.

178 days

The Mother

"Guess you know you killed my boy."

Alvina Trotter sat across the desk from Ryder, her face set in grief. She'd phoned that morning, demanding to talk to him and Gloria.

One look at Ryder, and Gloria knew he hadn't slept. Except for a thirty-minute or so stretch between five-thirty and six, she hadn't, either. She sat next to Alvina, across from Ryder in the newsroom, crossing her legs within her long skirt. She'd retreated back into the batik dress in which she'd lived in June and July, trying to hide, she supposed. There was nowhere to hide anymore. Alfonso Trotter had been blasted to death while staying on the houseboat of a friend. No one, not even Ryder, could link him to Eric Barry now.

"Could I get you some coffee?" Ryder asked the woman.

"You can get me my son back. Why don't you do that, Mr. Newspaper Man?"

Ryder rested his jaw in his hand. "I had no idea he was in danger, ma'am, believe me."

She pulled her heavy body out of her chair. "They said it was a drug deal. My son had his problems, but he never dealt drugs."

"I believe you."

Ryder's voice was raw. Gloria wanted to reach out for him, but she wanted to reach out for this woman more. Before she could, Alvina turned to face Ryder, hands on her hips, face alive with pain.

"Who cares what you believe? You just wanted to lay something on that senator. You didn't give one damn about my boy. You know what his body looked like when I had to identify it?"

Gloria gasped. She wasn't sure she could stay in this office. The woman's grief hurt too much.

"You, lady." The woman turned on her now. "You know how it feels, don't you?"

Gloria nodded. "Yes, I do. I'm so sorry."

"Then why'd you let him do this to me?"

"We were trying to find my daughter. Trying to find out what happened to her."

"Oh, Lord." The woman nodded and moaned, appealing to a power that seemed to have forsaken her. "It didn't do no good. My son's gone, your daughter." She motioned to Ryder. "And he just sits here and keeps on writing his stories."

Ryder rose now, his jaw tight. "Don't you care who murdered your son, Mrs. Trotter? Don't you want to know?"

"I already do know."

Tears blurred her eyes. She let them run down her shiny cheeks.

Gloria knew the sensation. That's how it felt. Force the world to feel your rage, witness your pain. It wouldn't help this woman any more than it had helped her. Nothing did. Not pain, not anger, not even love.

Alvina spoke the last words in a whisper. "You killed my son, Mr. Ryder. You just live with that, because I'm going to have to."

"Mrs. Trotter."

Before he could stop her, she was running down the hall, her shoulders shaking, bent forward, like someone carrying too heavy a weight.

Gloria watched her go, her shoulders stooped under the long, dark jacket.

She looked to Ryder, feeling his helplessness before she saw it in his face.

"Ryder," she said. "What have we done?"

He reached out for her. She pulled away, unable to say another word. She walked down the hall, then ran. The elevator was all the way to the end, around the corner. Alvina was just stepping on as Gloria reached it.

"Wait," she shouted. "Don't go."

Alvina stood there, glaring at her with flat dead eyes. Gloria knew the eyes. The doors started to close, but before they clamped together, a hand reached out. Fingers pried them apart. Thank God. Slowly the doors opened, and Alvina stepped out.

"I ran all the way," Gloria said. "I was afraid you'd left."

Alvina's face shown with tears. "You got something to say to me?"

Gloria nodded and put out her arms. "Oh, God," she said. "Yes."

182 days

The Wife

This town is flypaper. It catches people from all over. Although the favorite topic of those who live here is where they'd like to move, Valley lethargy soon sets in, talk replaces action, and no one ever goes anywhere.

Our downtown, which in the sixties served as a model for malls all over the country, sits like an abandoned movie set populated by hookers, druggies and those either too old or too poor to get out.

Among this squalor and hopelessness are brick and stone city offices that would be considered historical in a city that values its past. Our new city hall is located here, an imposing glass structure that rises within a maze of one-way streets.

So is our police department. A forlorn building grim as the adjoining jail, it's an accumulation of federal gray chairs and tables and cheap indoor-outdoor carpeting.

I've purposely worn low shoes to help prevent the sudden dizziness that comes when I have to walk on shiny surfaces. For years I wore nothing but heels, because Eric said they made my legs look better. I had no idea the difference a pair of shoes could make, how much easier it is to walk closer to the ground.

I sit in the same room I did the last time, questioned by the same two officers. One, his name is Larimore, has well-tended gray curls and a body that looks as if it's never missed a work-out. Coleman, his partner, is a large black man with thin, bronze-rimmed glasses and an accent that sounds East Coast.

I sit across from them at a gray metal table that looks like a World War II relic. A history of names, numbers and cryptic witticisms have been carved into its imitation wood surface. I've dressed for the occasion in a crepe suit of seafoam-green. I don't want to look like a murderer, and I know that's why I'm here again. They think I might have killed April Wayne.

Coleman is in charge. He makes a general statement about additional information and how they hope I can be of assistance. They ask for help. That's how they do it, pretending I'm a resource and not a suspect.

Kent Dishman is the subject today. They express their concern about what happened in my kitchen the night I threw the scalding water in his face. I'd run to the neighbors, and by the time the police arrived, Kent was still in my house, in a fury of pain and grief. He has cooperated totally, they say. He withheld information only out of loyalty to April and because, until she didn't return by the date she'd promised, he believed she was in hiding.

After being treated at the hospital for his burns, Kent told the police what he told me, that April said she had spoken to me on the phone that Friday and was afraid of me.

"She didn't sound afraid," I say.

"So you did talk to her?" Coleman asks.

"I was trying to reach my husband. He wasn't there, and the

second or third time I called back, a young woman answered the phone."

Coleman leans across the table so that he can get a better look at my face, my eyes. "And what did you do when you heard this young lady's voice?"

"I assumed it was one of his aides working late." I feel my voice begin to shake. I can't get enough oxygen. "I asked who she was, and she became upset. Her exact words were, 'Who the hell do you think it is, you crazy bitch.'"

"And that's when you got angry?" Larimore asks.

"Yes, I got angry. A woman in my husband's condominium—our condominium—had just called me a crazy bitch. I was furious."

More than furious, I think, staring down at this marred table-top. "I knew that night on the phone that my husband had been cheating on me all along, that my marriage was a joke."

"What did you do then?" Coleman's evaluating gaze makes me blink. I try not to, certain he must read it as a sign of guilt.

"I took some tranquilizers."

"Prescription drugs?"

"Yes. We discussed that before, the last time I was here. My thought was to drive to Sacramento and confront them both."

"And that's what you said you'd do. We have the answering machine tape, ma'am."

"I was hysterical." I feel the trembling start again and hang on to the edge of the table. Just pretend I'm talking to Kellogg. Pretend I'm in a safe place. "I must have blacked out in the car. I woke up there the next morning, early."

"And then you drove to Sacramento?" Coleman asks.

"Yes."

"And you and your husband decided to lie about when you arrived?"

"The media pressure was unbearable. We didn't know what else to do."

"So then." Coleman reviews his notes and looks back at me

as if he is trying to understand my statement, but he's clearly looking for a reaction. This must be his contribution to the team. Larimore is the soft-spoken one, Coleman the human lie detector. "You couldn't remember what happened that night, but now you can."

"That's right."

"What caused you to have this sudden return of memory?"

"It started coming back that night with Kent Dishman," I say. "I was terrified, trying to tell him the truth, and it just began coming back."

"So you're convinced you didn't spend that Friday night at the Sacramento condominium with your husband?" Larimore asks.

"I know I didn't. I was home."

"Can anyone verify that, ma'am?"

I see where the question is leading, but I have no answer for it. "Not that I know of," I say.

Coleman adjusts his glasses, cocks his large head as he watches me. "So, at this time, there's no one who can corroborate your statement regarding your whereabouts that night?"

"That's what I just told you."

"Nor where your husband was?"

The question hangs in the air, and I look into Coleman's eyes, unable to answer.

I nearly stumble down the steps when I leave, although I grip the rail with sweat-slick fingers. It's all coming down around me, my lies, my life, all coming down.

I make it to my car and collapse inside, my heart beating so rapidly that my burning chest constricts. "Please," I beg God, the universe, any power that will listen. Not even the Xanax answers, but I know it is there, waiting in the safe darkness of my purse. My fingers go to the vial, and I swallow a pill without water. I've become adept at that.

I'll have to wait to start the car. That's all right. I'll sit here and watch the people walking in and out of Courthouse Park. These individuals are the public, the individuals of our community who elect my husband, those who vote, at any rate. Right now they're just people on their way to traffic court, on their way to jury duty, on their way to file for a marriage license or a divorce. Oh, God, it's happening again.

I close my eyes, unable to watch them, and what I see is worse, the movie I can't turn off now that it's started, the one that only Dr. Kellogg knows about.

July, the sweetest month for a twelve-year-old girl. The tamarack trees on our ranch almost met in the middle of the road as I walked through them. The air was ripe with the smell of peaches, melons. Best of all, the house was mine. My parents wouldn't be back until next week. Daddy was flying in first for some meetings. Mama would follow a few days later.

I was supposed to be in San José visiting my cousin Lisa, but her dad had to come to the Valley for a meeting, and he dropped me off at our neighbors' house. I had no intention of staying there. Daddy would be back at anytime, I explained to Ginny McBride, our neighbor, and my folks' good friend.

I was twelve, and I wasn't afraid of anything.

I ignored the buzzing June bugs on the screen, let myself in the front door and started toward the back of the house. Good that I'd come home early. I remember thinking that as I smelled the locked-up mustiness and felt wise about my early return. I'd clean, I thought, make it nice for Daddy. Maybe I'd fix a tuna casserole and some cupcakes. He loved my chocolate-chip cupcakes.

The noise stopped me, something I'd never heard before, yet at the same time, familiar. A pain noise, only worse, echoed from upstairs. I knew before I took one step up that I shouldn't. It was the feeling, the knowing, that comes right before you cut your finger with a knife. Yet in spite of the knowledge, it's already too late to stop the movement your body has put in motion.

They didn't see me at first, their bodies tangled, their voices rising in the hot room. Mama and Daddy's bed, I thought. They were doing this on Mama and Daddy's bed, the white chenille spread kicked off onto the floor, a partially full bottle of whiskey on the doily on Mama's nightstand.

I had seen the woman at church. Elisha, I forced myself to remember. Her name was Elisha. She was married to Daddy's banker. She used eyeliner, and she smoked and drank in public. That was all I knew. I never even thought she was pretty.

What they were doing plays before my eyes right now as if they were both here in front of me. Her naked legs around him, his thrusting, muscular buttocks, her scarlet nails raking his hairy back. All of this I saw in that split second.

A noise escaped me, a kind of gasp, and they stopped, motionless, as if I'd fired a gun.

I turned, ran, hearing him bellow behind me. "Suzanne."

I ran for my life, ran down the stairs, through the front door out through the canopy of the tamaracks.

"What's wrong, honey?" Ginny, our neighbor, asked, as I dashed into her house, sobbing and out of breath. "Whatever happened to you?"

I had to calm down, had to get myself back in control. If not, I'd ruin my life. I'd destroy our family forever. "I got scared," I said through heavy breaths.

"What scared you?" Ginny frowned with concern.

"The house," I said. "I'm afraid to stay by myself alone."

"But I thought—" She looked at me, at my trembling body and nodded. "That's okay. You just stay here 'til your daddy gets home. It will be all right."

I did as she said, and the next day, my father came over and picked me up. I heard his voice sing out on the porch when Ginny opened the door.

"Is my girl here?"

"She's here."

I walked into the living room, and he scooped me into a hug

before I could squeak out a greeting. His features were the same: his eyes, his bushy, sun-bleached eyebrows, his ruddy face, his ready smile. He looked no different than before.

"Let's go home," he said, putting his arm around me.

And we did. And we never spoke of it. And I began having dizzy spells every time I climbed the stairs.

And for many years, I convinced myself I had imagined what I had seen that day.

All that talking to Dr. Kellogg, and I just now understand that it was no accident that I never saw what was happening in my own marriage, either, never allowed myself to admit that I was married to a stranger.

I wipe the tears from my cheeks. I think I can drive away from this place now, and I'm not even sure I need the Xanax to do it.

The Girl

They walked up the steps, the three of them, their arms around each other. How had they gotten out of that bar? It didn't matter. They were here now, at Alfonso's new apartment, her arm tucked around Eric.

"I need some food," she said.

"I'll get us a pizza." Alfonso's voice sounded as if it must hurt him to speak. She wondered if he were born that way.

Once inside, he poured drinks for them. The apartment was small but tidy, as if no one lived here. A zebra-print pillow the size of a mattress covered the floor. There was no sofa, only one chair, and a small kitchen in the back of the room. It smelled as if someone had been smoking cigarettes.

Alfonso took out a book of matches and lit a candle.

Eric couldn't keep his hands off her. They settled into the zebra-print cushion, while Alfonso put on some music. The cushion felt soft against her legs. Eric pulled her to him with one arm, sliding his hand up her skirt.

"He's watching," she whispered. From the corner of her eye, she could see Alfonso walking around the room, lighting more candles.

"Does that turn you on?"

"If it turns you on, it turns me on."

"He digs you. You know it's making him horny as hell to see me touching you like this."

Alfonso glanced over, winked at her, then leaned down to the stereo and turned the music up.

The room smelled of fragrant candles, melting wax. April lost herself in Eric's kiss, sliding under him, letting him slip her skirt up along her leg. Beside them, Alfonso slowly began unzipping his pants.

She pressed her lips to Eric's ear. "Do you see what he's doing?"

"Does it bother you?"

Although she'd never done anything this kinky, she had known that she might sooner or later for him. It was the one way she could make Eric her man for good.

"I'll do anything you want," she said, "as wild as you want it, any way you want it."

"That's my baby." He gathered her bare buttocks in both hands and began nibbling on her flesh through her sheer blouse.

"How about some oil?" Alfonso's whispery voice sounded sexy and sensual now. "This stuff heats up when you blow on it. On you it will smoke." He stood above her, totally naked, his body gleaming in the candlelight.

She extended her bare arm to him.

"Let's try it."

183 days

The Mother

"What happened to you the other day?"

Ryder caught up with Karen and Gloria in the parking lot of the gym.

"I've been trying to call you," he said, "went by your business. I just got this."

He held up the flier she'd faxed to him at the paper.

"Karen designed it. Looks great, doesn't it?"

"When did this all happen?"

"Last minute," she said. "I know you're not sure it will work, but it's our last hope. We'll appreciate whatever you can do."

Ryder shook the flier in the still air. "*Down With Eric Barry.* That's the whole campaign?"

"That's right."

"That should please his opponent Jenine Durison."

"She may be a little light on experience, but at least she's honest," Gloria said, "And God knows Eric Barry shouldn't ever again hold a public office."

Ryder's face turned an angry red. "Why haven't you returned my phone calls? Why do I get this off the fax like the rest of the media?"

"Hey." Karen touched her arm, slung her gym bag over her shoulder. "Mind if I wait in the car?"

"I can give her a lift back," Ryder said.

Gloria looked into Karen's eyes. "Wait for me, okay?"

"Sure thing. See you, Rich." Karen nodded and strode in the direction of the car.

Ryder turned her around to face him. "It's about Alvina Trotter, isn't it? You blame me for what happened to her son."

His pale eyes defied her to deny it.

"I just hurt for her, that's all. I hurt."

"Trotter was seen with your daughter and Barry. Now, he's dead. Doesn't that tell you he was probably connected to her disappearance? Barry may have even killed him or had him killed."

"I know that, and I understand why you ran the story. But it's just a job to you. You can't begin to know how that woman feels."

"I don't pretend to. You knew I was going to run that story. Hell, you talked me into running that piece about Suzanne Barry. If Kent Dishman had been more than a misguided kid, she could have been hurt."

"I know," she said. "I hate it. I hate it in me, and I hate it in you."

Ryder let go of her shoulders and dropped his hands to his sides. "It's what's kept your daughter's case in front of the public."

"I'm grateful for that. Working with you made me think I was taking positive steps to make something happen. I wasn't being a victim."

"And now? Are you going to tell me it was a dormitory

friendship, after all, something to get you from Point A to Point B?"

"That's ridiculous." She walked away from him in the direction of her car. He followed.

"I care about you, Gloria."

"I care about you, too." She stopped, turned back to him. "Working with you has kept me from going crazy," she said. "You saved me, but it's put me into some kind of attack mode that I can't turn off. It's not helping me heal."

He gave her the rueful smile she remembered from the first day she'd seen him. "In this world, attack mode's not all that bad."

"It works for you. I don't think it's going to work for me in the long run. This campaign is my last attempt to stop Eric Barry. Once the election's over, I'm going to put my energy in a new direction."

She turned quickly before he could see her tears and walked into the afternoon, its air already scented with fall. It smelled like hope, like promise, for everyone but her.

There were others like her who had to live through every season with no closure, with a hole in their lives where love had been. Ryder had tried to tell her once, but it had been too soon. Now she was starting to understand, and she had an idea what to do next. But first, she had to keep Eric Barry from being re-elected.

The Girl

Ruby-red. The strawberry-scented oil in the glass bottle glowed in the light. April closed her eyes. Her flesh felt warm and buttery where Alfonso stroked it into her legs and her shoulders where Eric kneaded.

Ruby-red. Eric was naked now, too, and erect. Knowing that watching her was driving him into a frenzy aroused her even more. She moaned louder, feeling his fingers dig deeper into her flesh. Now she knew why Alfonso had turned up the stereo.

Her first threesome, and she was actually enjoying it. People had been doing this for years. Her parents had probably done it in the sixties. Eric wanted it; he wanted her. She could do this for him. She'd never let him get bored the way Suzanne had.

They spread her out on her back. Eric leaned over her shoulders kissing her from above.

"You like this?"

"I love it."

From below, Alfonso chuckled. "Pretty little heart you got here."
He slid his fingers into her. His hot breath felt as if it had ignited her
skin where the oil had left its heat.

"I'm on fire," she said. "Ruby-red."

"We're all going to be on fire," Alfonso said.

She was full, full of man. Alfonso's tongue between her legs cir-
cled her in heat. Eric in her mouth, gasped with a passion she'd never
witnessed in him. She'd never been able to make it this good for him.
But now she could.

Alfonso moved away from her, stood and picked up a candle.

"Yes," Eric said. He lifted his arms up into the air, as if he were
praying.

April watched as Alfonso dripped hot candle wax onto Eric's nip-
ples.

"No," she said, pulling away from him.

"It's all right." Eric grabbed her wrist tightly. This was part of it
then. It hurt him, but he liked it.

"Pull the wax off, baby," Alfonso said.

She slid her fingernail under a piece of wax. Eric moaned with such
passion that she thought he would shoot right then. All he said was,
"More."

Eric lifted an arm to Alfonso. She watched in horror as he lowered
the candle to his armpit. The hair burst into a dancing fire. April
screamed.

"Don't stop." Eric's eyes had rolled back. His mouth was twisted
with grim pleasure. The smell choked her. Eric liked this. He needed
it.

The fire ended as instantly as it had started. April tried to get used
to the smell, tried not to let it gag her.

"Now you," he said, his voice as harsh as Alfonso's. She took the
candle, held it to the pale hair under his other arm. The flame again,
the smell. Aroused to frenzy now, Eric grabbed her, poured the burn-
ing wax to her breast.

She screamed and struggled to get away from him.

"Cool it." Alfonso's voice boomed out of nowhere. He got to his feet, took the matches out of Eric's hand. "She don't dig it."

"You like it, don't you, baby?"

She fought tears as she pulled the searing wax from her breast. "I'm not used to it. I can't."

"That's okay," Alfonso said. "We got lots left to do. You like my oil, don't you?"

"Oh, yes." No more wax, she thought. She could do anything but more wax.

Alfonso began rubbing the oil into Eric's buttocks.

Eric took her in his arms.

"Didn't mean to hurt you."

"It's okay."

"I thought you liked it a little rough."

"I do, honey." She leaned over, bit his neck hard.

He shoved her against the pillow and entered her. Alfonso moved behind him, and she knew what was happening, didn't care.

She let Eric press her legs against his shoulders. This part she could handle. The fire was too frightening.

It reminded her of something. The first time they were together, lying in his bed like this. She had looked at his naked body that night and wondered why he had no hair under his arm.

"Oh baby." Eric cried out, his voice, high and shrill. He wrapped his fingers around her throat, pounding into her. She reached up to pull his hands away, but he threw her back against the mattress. "Struggle," he said.

"Oh, yes. I'll fight." This was what they'd started earlier. Scratch, scream, fight. Tie her up and strangle her until one moment before she passed out. It was the sure way to get him off every time. Now they had Alfonso. That would just make it better for him. "I'm struggling," she said. "I'm going to get away."

"You can't. I've got you." He grabbed her throat again driving into her, rising above her to dig his fingers in. He was just about there. She began to pass out, saw the jagged lights behind her eyes.

He groaned. His fingers wrenched the air from her.

No.

You're going too far.

I can't breathe.

Her lips stretched around the words, but no sound came. The lights splintered and ignited, burning her eyes, her eardrums, her scalding throat, and she exploded into an ocean of fire.

194 days

The Wife

Eric's committee holds the election party in a downtown restaurant, the old Pleasant View icehouse, near the Santa Fe Railroad tracks. The selection underscores his longtime support to revitalize the area, and should at least be worth a few local votes.

Joy and Jill have refused to come home for the election. Eric is furious, certain a malevolent force is scheming to turn them against him. I assure him that they love him, but that they're adults now.

I'm glad they're making their own decisions and doing what's right for them instead of trying to please us. The Waynes have launched a vicious campaign against Eric, and I am relieved the girls won't be here to see it escalate.

I worked with the caterer all day, checking appetizers, increasing orders for everything. Jerry McBride and his West

Side farmers picked up the tab for a tri-tip barbecue in back of election headquarters.

Win or lose, the so-called victory party will be packed tonight. The entire country will be viewing the results of this election.

The national media have already hit town in an explosion of cameras, phone calls, even knocks on my front door. Oh, please don't let that start again.

I watched Rich Ryder being interviewed last night on a segment of a talk show.

"The true question in this election," he said, "is do the voters care about a politician's—in this case Eric Barry's—personal life, as long as he's serving the needs of his constituents? That's the issue they're really voting on tomorrow."

When questioned, Ryder admitted that he believes Jenine Durison is the better choice for senator. She doesn't have Eric's experience, he said, but she does have moral integrity.

I turned off the television after that. I didn't want to think about moral integrity and this embittered reporter's—or anyone's—interpretation of it.

Denny Petroni has been all over the news, too, predicting what he calls, "a landslide loss" for Eric. I'm not sure what went wrong with them, and Eric can't really explain it, other than to say Denny has "gone Hollywood" on him, and that he had to fire him. He has another attorney now, much more serious and low profile.

Denny also managed to mention that he's landed a six-figure book contract to write about Eric's personal and political downfall, "a tragedy worthy of Lear or Hamlet," he said, his face aglow with self-love.

I know Eric trusted him, and feel sorry. I don't know what else I feel. I need to get through tonight.

As a blatant attempt to endear Eric to voters, the Pleasant View staff rented an abandoned bank building for election headquarters. I arrive early, but the cameras have beaten me there. The weather is freezing, too cold for the rain that was promised last week, and the leaden sky looks stubbornly set in place.

I've dressed carefully. As long as I'm Eric's wife, it's my job to make him look good. My wool dress and matching duster of winter white aren't as flattering now as they were in the lights of the store where I bought them. I'm paler than I realized. I hope I've been able to conceal the fact with makeup.

Berta did my hair this morning, insisting that she come tonight to support me. I didn't ask if she would vote for Eric. I know the answer.

"He's in the back," Melinda tells me, waiting until everyone arrives.

He doesn't want to be cornered by the cameras. That makes sense. But without him, they sweep the room, and find only me.

"No interviews until after the election," Melinda explains in a sharp, clear voice. She's grown up over the summer and fall. Tonight in her long black skirt and top, her strawberry-blond hair knotted at the back of her neck, she looks like a woman.

She takes me in the back, where Jerry and Ginny McBride stand with their plastic glasses of bourbon, surrounded by a contingent of farmers. They cheer as I arrive, and I feel myself blush.

Ginny's wearing a long skirt and embroidered red, white and blue sweater adorned with glitter. Jerry Mac has shoved his rangy body into a suit. He moves from one foot to the other, as if he's attending a wedding and still looking for the bride and groom. Once he spots me, his face gets parental, protective.

"Come here, beautiful," he says, and hugs me so tightly that I'm afraid he'll pop a button off his suit. "This is our night, kiddo."

"Your night, kiddo," I say, as if my late father has just turned on a tape recorder. "A victory for agriculture."

"Barry's our man." Jerry Mac slings an arm around Ginny. "He's our man, right, honey?"

"Sure thing." She bobs her head like a sparkling, slightly off-center doll, then, with a smile, removes his hand. "Those protesters were already out back when we got here, Jer. I'd better go check again."

"They'll be pissing in the wind tonight," Jerry Mac says. "We're going to kick us some butt."

I try not to think about what we're discussing. At first, I thought only Gloria Wayne and Rich Ryder would protest this election. Now, I realize that a crowd has turned out; it's going to be a football game of us versus them. I look through one of the upstairs windows, see the signs below me.

One looms through the outside light into my face. *Bury Barry.*

"This isn't going to be an easy one," I say.

"I agree." Jerry Mac pats my shoulder in his paternal way. "By the way, where the hell is Eric?"

"He'll be here," I say.

That's all I know.

Jerry points proudly around the room. "See how many of our people came out tonight?" he asks. "We support the people who support us, and unlike those lazy Mexicans, we're legal. We can vote."

I've heard this kind of talk for years, and I don't want to hear it tonight. "Jerry," I say. "Mexican isn't a dirty word."

"Not unless you're a farmer, and you have to deal with their jacked-up union."

I know little about unions but a bit about history. "Chavez started the United Farm Workers for some pretty basic reasons," I say. "Fresh drinking water, toilet facilities, the banishment of the short-handled hoe."

His face sags with disbelief. "You know what that kind of talk would do to your dad?"

"I never talked that way in front of him," I say. "I knew he wouldn't understand. I thought you might."

He frowns agreement, stares down in his bourbon. "Different times back then," he says. "A lot of smart people did some stupid things."

I see the hurt and confusion in his face and realize that I have spoken out of turn to someone who considers me family, something I never did with my father. I don't need to say more. I've made my point.

Eric arrives in a flurry of lights and cameras. I'm reminded of what he said to me that other time when I found out about his vasectomy. "Like being married to Mick Jagger," he'd told me. What would I do if I were married to Mick Jagger and someone wrote a story like that about him?

Funny that I can remember Eric's questions, and I've forgotten my answers. Maybe I didn't have any.

I do know this. I've never seen my husband look better, not at any age. His eyes burn from within. His skin glows.

Election results filter in slowly. In the first precincts, Eric's losing. The female opponent with little experience has trounced him all the way. Eric's committee members remind us of Clinton and Gore in Florida. They talk about human and technical frailty. I'm not surprised when he takes the lead again, and I share more hugs with Jerry and Ginny McBride.

Victory is momentary. He's down again. The television sets on the far wall are already spelling out doom. One flashes an interview with Holly Yost. She's talking about the telephone threats she received months ago, says they have stopped. Melinda quickly changes the station.

"Don't pay any attention to the early predictions," she tells me. "They're wrong as often as they're right. Eric has a good chance."

Do I want my husband to win?

I suppose I do. He is a good politician. Perhaps after the scare he had, he'll be an even better one.

But do I want my husband to win? Does adrenaline pump

through me each time new returns come in? Do I feel justice will be served if he is elected?

No.

He moves through the crowd as if he owns it, and he does. He's a star in this arena and knows it, but in many ways, he's been a star all of his life. Nights like this—the tension, the doubts, the promise of victory—this is how he comes alive. Throw an election, and Eric Barry will show up.

He gives me a quick kiss. "We'll win this," he says, then moves back into the throng of supporters, shining like silver.

I need fresh air, step out in the back, carrying a glass of Merlot from the university's enology department. Jerry Mac follows. From the other side of the building, we hear chants, "Bury Barry, Bury Barry." The air smells of seared meat.

"We'll stick with Eric, no matter what," Jerry says. "There will be other elections if this one goes bad."

I know he means it. His loyalty is as strong as the earth. Farming is his life, his history, as it was to my dad, and Eric has always been a part of that.

"He appreciates you," I say. "We both do."

He clears his throat, walks out closer to where volunteers are barbecuing the meat.

"Forgiveness is a beautiful thing, Suze."

I move my head in the direction of the chanting. "You talking to them or me?"

"You, beautiful. I'm talking about forgiveness."

"What are you trying to say?"

"That Eric's a fine politician. That he loves you and the kids."

I cross my arms across my chest. "Will you tell me the truth about something?" I ask. "I need to know."

Jerry Mac raises his whiskey glass. "On your dad's life."

"Have you ever cheated on Ginny?"

"Hell, no." A blush covers his face. He shakes his head as if to rid himself of it. "Not on your life."

"And Eric?"

"Honey." The word and the way he says it is an accusation. "I don't keep track of a man's personal business."

"Not as long as he votes ag."

"Don't make it sound like that." He loosens his jacket, stares into the night. He'll never admit it. He doesn't care what my father did. He doesn't care what Eric did. They've already negotiated it between themselves, where it will stay.

I turn my back on Jerry, take a sip of the wine.

Suddenly, from behind us, I hear an excited screech. It's Ginny McBride, rushing, sparkling shirt and all, to join us out here.

My heart quickens in spite of myself.

"Get in here," she says, grabbing Jerry's arm. "It's turned around all of a sudden. It looks like Eric's going to take it, after all." She throws her arms around my neck. "He's winning, honey. It's a miracle, isn't it? A miracle."

204 days

The Wife

I need to get away.

The media attention after the election hasn't lessened at all. They're hungrier than ever for Eric now, but he no longer seems to mind. The victory has made him belligerent. He issues officious statements like, "The people have spoken," and "It was God's will."

He's still angry at our daughters. "I did it without anyone," he said to me after he won, the fire of victory in his eyes. "I put this together alone, and I won the son of a bitch, just the way I said I would."

Melinda has decided to return home for the holidays until she goes back to college in the spring. She must be sick of the press, the election and probably her boss.

I'm spending the week in Noyo Harbor with nothing but the

bark of the seals for company. Perhaps I'll be able to make some decisions.

But the news follows me. Today I saw on the television that Gloria and Jack Wayne have launched a major foundation to assist the police in cases such as theirs. The director, a gay man who lost a partner to AIDS, calls Gloria "an angel and an inspiration."

I can't imagine the living torment her life must be. She's hurt my family, hurt me, but she's not the stereotypical wealthy woman I always thought she was. Her daughter's disappearance has shown the kind of person she is, and I envy her toughness.

Melinda and I have dinner at Noyo Harbor the night we arrive, the same restaurant where Eric and I ate that terrible first night after I learned about April. We sit on the heated patio with our wine, watching the lumberjack types drinking their Red Dog Ale and eating their fish and chips.

"This is still my favorite place on earth," I say. "The corruption hasn't touched it yet."

"You should move here," she says, then puts her hand over her mouth.

"You think I should leave him?"

She pulls her sweater around her and looks down into her wine. "I didn't know if you'd made a decision. You've been through so much."

"Maybe it will get better."

She tries to smile, but says nothing. She knows something. I sense it. She's seen something at the office.

"I know now that regardless of what he maintains that he did have an affair with April Wayne," I say. "That's tough to take."

She nods. "I know it must be."

I think of how it felt to hear April Wayne's voice that night, to want to kill her, actually want to kill her.

"Holly Yost made it worse. I don't believe she's lying, do you?"

Melinda shakes her head, her expression so sad it breaks my heart. She's lost faith in him, too, he, who was once her hero. I drink my wine, look out over the indigo water as if the answers drifted out there, waiting.

"I was the only brunette he ever dated," I say. "He always went for the redheads. April's hair is that coppery-red. Holly Yost's is a light red."

"He wants to dominate them."

Her voice is so thin I can barely hear it over the roar of the ocean. I look across at her, the narrow face, intense eyes, and the frizzy curls pinned to the top of her head. Where the sun hits it, the red highlights glint like coins.

I begin to tremble but I can't let her see it. I have to be strong. "He does?" I ask. "Tell me."

"They have to be redheads." She pulls her sweater close, hugging herself. Tears fill her eyes. "He hurts them, too, Suzanne. He does things to them. Makes them afraid to talk."

I feel the breath leave me, and with it the last bit of hope. We sit there for a moment as I try to control the rapid beating of my heart.

"How long ago?" I ask. "When did he do it to you?"

"Since I was sixteen." Tears trail down her face. She wipes at them with the backs of her hands. "Oh, Suze, I'm so sorry. I tried to make it up to you a hundred times."

I'm too numb to know what I'm doing, but my body does. Somehow I'm crouched beside her chair, rocking her in my arms like a child. I couldn't save the other girl, but I will save this one.

"It will be all right, honey." I say. "It will, I promise you."

The Girl

I sing. My music travels with me, even here in this vortex. You can't get away from me, although you want to. You will hear me singing in your sleep.

Others will say they have seen me, standing at a bridge, appearing in the travelogue of a dream. But you will hear me. You have no choice, nor do I. I must sing until you notice and until you tell those who must be told.

You will speak to those who think of me and see the equivalent of tulle. They see the fingernails, nipple pink, looking as if I have just taken them out of my mouth. They see the breasts begging for attention and more ass than I'd like to show, but no one ever complained, not until him. They will never hear me, but you will.

You must listen to the fingers of love strangling my last plea into silence. You must listen to the slap of solid wood above me. There are messages to carry back, and you know what they are. I am not the messenger. You are.

I sing, not for remorse, nor for revenge. I sing betrayal. It is the only song I know.

The Mother

Gloria always closed the door to her home office when she worked, and Jack always knocked. Today he didn't.

"There's someone for you at the door." His voice strained to finish. "That psychic."

Gloria shoved aside the press release she was editing. "What did she say?"

"Just that she wants to see you. I invited her in, but she refused. She was pretty definite about it."

When Gloria reached the entry, she found Berta leaning against the door in a tweed jacket the color of her hair. She wore no makeup, and her skin was sallow.

"It's cold out there," Gloria said. "Please come in."

"I can't do that. I came here because I had to."

"You said you wouldn't work with me."

"I didn't want to. I never wanted anything to do with your sorrow, but she won't leave me alone."

"April?"

"Just listen. Here's what I know. A dream almost strangled me to death last night. I'm just going to tell you about it, and then I'm going home."

Gloria grew cold with fear, motioned Berta in, closed the door to the severe weather.

"Under wood," Berta said, shuffling into the room.

Gloria touched the rough fabric of her coat. "What?"

"I'm telling you what I heard. Under wood, she said. He did it, the one she loved, and now she's under wood. She wants you to know that. There, I've told you. Now, I'm going to leave."

Gloria stood with her hands reaching out, watching her open the door, slowly retrace her footsteps down the driveway back to her car. The door felt so heavy she could hardly push it closed. When she turned around, she realized Jack had been standing behind her.

He held out his arms, and she went to them, hanging on for dear life.

205 days

The Parlor Game

Janie Stuart arrived late that night, after the magpies had tottered out. Harold was both surprised to see her and not surprised. That was what this business did to you.

A gray hat the same color as her long coat hiding her hair, her lips a stripe of red, she strolled up to the bar just as she had all summer. He'd been playing John Prine on his stereo, the TV off, everyone, even the servers gone home.

"What a sight for sore eyes you are," Harold said. "One margarita in the blender?"

"On the rocks." She slid onto her usual stool.

"You changed your drinking habits."

"I like variety." She didn't look as if she liked much right then.

"Your first one's on the house," he said.

That made her smile. "And if it's my only one?"

"Still on the house. When'd you get in?"

"Late last night. What did you think about that screwed-up election? I can't believe that monster actually got reelected."

"Living in the Valley all these years, I can believe anything. They elected him. Now they can live with him."

Her perfume was too strong for someone so blond and fair. Harold served her drink and poured a quick one for himself. "What are you doing in town?" he asked. "Thanksgiving break come this early back there?"

She slipped the gray coat off her shoulders, let it settle around her like a blanket. "I'm taking the next semester off, looking into some other opportunities. School just isn't doing it for me right now. How've you been?"

His drink tasted flat. He could see only her face. "Same-o, same-o. It was a nothing night."

Her sweater was black with a silver zipper to the chin. She stretched and unzipped it a couple of inches. "It's kind of warm in here, isn't it? You know, all of the nights I've been coming in here, and I don't know diddly about you. Like are you married? Do you have any kids?"

"Not married anymore," he said. "Kids are grown."

"Grandkids?"

The question made him uncomfortable. "A couple."

"That's nice." She took the straw out of her drink, sipped from the glass, chewing on the ice. "I read about Kent."

"A shame," he said. "His folks are standing by him."

"Who would have believed April would be with a dolt like him?"

"I thought you liked him," Harold said.

She laughed and stretched again, catlike. Somehow her zipper had slipped farther down, exposing the curves of her breasts. "You don't really think I'd go out with him, do you?"

"I didn't know what you were thinking."

"Just trying to get through the summer. You know how that

goes." She glanced at her watch. "Which reminds me, I've got to hit the road."

Little tease. As if he cared. He'd seen her type come and go as long as he could remember. He'd like to tell her that nothing that happened in this bar could shock him. Instead he said, "Something wrong with the drink?"

"No." She slipped off the stool, as if her coming or going could make a difference in his or anyone's life. "Take care, Harold Bear."

He watched her go, knowing long after he'd forgotten her name, he'd remember her face as part of the summer of the missing girl—the period of time when the only topic of conversation was April Wayne.

He turned up John Prine, blasted the mother. Then he sat down on the customer side of the bar, the bottle of tequila beside his glass. Minutes passed. He drank alone, listening to Prine. Then behind him, he heard a whoosh, felt a cold breeze. He started to turn, but someone grabbed his head, forced it back. He felt something cold and sharp at his throat.

"Open your fucking cash register."

The mumble sounded familiar. Before he could identify it, Harold was pulled off the chair, shoved across the room to the register.

He'd always planned what he'd say in a situation such as this, but the plans were far removed from the reality. He tried to move his lips, to tell the intruder that he could have it all, every bit of it.

He hit the cash register hard.

"Open it, now." The knife rode close to his throat. Harold turned, got a glimpse of his assailant—his smoky glasses, his Beach Boys T-shirt.

"Whitey," he said.

"Shut up, old man. Just give it all to me, the money, the gun."

He held out a fabric bag, like the kind Harold used to transport cash to the bank. "Put it in here." He tried to take his time.

Once Whitey had what he wanted, he would no longer need Harold. "Hurry up, damn it."

He did as he was told, trying to remember how to pray. "That's all of it. Here's my gun."

Whitey snatched it out of his hands. "Turn and face the mirror."

"Please."

"Face it, right now. Count to one hundred, and don't do anything until then. If you do, you're dead."

Harold stared into the mirror, no longer able to see anything but glass.

"One, two, three, four..."

206 days

The Senator

"You can't be serious." Eric carried the phone into the kitchen, the only room he hadn't packed in his rush to vacate the condominium. Moving day tomorrow, and now this. One more hysterical woman to placate. Would it never end? "You can't do this, Suze," he said, "not after everything we've been through together."

"Most of what we've been through is your fault," she said in a calm voice. "I know what happened with Melinda. I'm divorcing you."

He perched on a bar stool gripping the phone. "If you're trying to destroy my career, you're a little late."

"I'm not trying to do anything to you. I'm trying to save myself."

She was as bad as Denny and just as ungrateful. "You'll be

back," he said. "You're just upset. I'll be moved tomorrow. Why not come for the weekend? We'll work it out."

"I'm filing for divorce, Eric. Don't be surprised when you're served with papers."

"We need to talk," he said. "Don't do anything while you're angry."

The line clicked, went dead. She'd hung up on him.

Eric stared at the phone. Suzanne couldn't pull this off. She wouldn't dare. Even if she did, he could just point to her medical record, show how crazy she was. He got up and fixed himself a drink. If she really left, it wouldn't be the worst thing that had ever happened to him. The rules of politics had changed. Having his wife walk out after what he'd been through might actually swing the sympathy his direction for once. Now, that would be a welcome change. Lord knows, he had it coming.

He made himself another drink while he waited for the guy who was coming to look at the condo. He resented having to act like a damned rental agent, but the property management company had set it up, and he'd do anything to get out of his lease as soon as possible. He was glad now that he didn't purchase the condo when he had the chance. It was tainted. He needed a fresh start.

He wouldn't have agreed to show it while he was still packing, but the property manager had talked him into it. She was a cute little redhead who seemed genuinely sympathetic when he said he had personal reasons for wanting to move as soon as he could. Once he got settled, maybe he'd give her a call.

The doorbell rang.

"Pardon the boxes," he said as he let the guy in. Then he took a closer look. Something was wrong. He'd seen him somewhere before, in a crowd, watching him. There was no mistaking the weird glasses and T-shirt.

The man slammed the door behind him, then shoved Eric against it. Before he could react, a powerful fist drove into his stomach. Eric crumbled to the floor. He grabbed his stomach trying to hold in the hurt, to keep his pain from spilling all over the room.

"You've got the wrong person."

"I got a killer."

"A killer? No. Never even been a suspect."

"Liar." He kicked him again. Pain bled through him as the heavy boot crushed his jaw. When he looked up, the man was pointing a gun at him. "You killed April Wayne. Everybody knows it, and they elected you, anyway. Me, I get caught feeling up a girl back home, and her mother makes sure I'm put away. What about you? Who's going to protect the women from guys like you?"

Eric tried to explain, but blood gurgled out of his mouth. He pushed himself onto his knees. If he could just make it to the phone on the bar, he'd be all right. He grabbed the stool, tried to pull himself up. The man watched. He might be able to make it, after all, if he could just keep from screaming out.

"Apologize to her parents," the man demanded.

Eric couldn't fight him anymore. He'd do whatever he had to do to save himself.

"I apologize," he said, spitting blood.

"No, not like that. Say, Mr. and Mrs. Wayne, I'm sorry that I killed April."

"I'm sorry," he said.

"Mr. and Mrs. Wayne."

"Mr. and Mrs. Wayne, I'm sorry."

"Say the rest."

"Sorry that I killed April."

"That's what I wanted to hear you say."

The man lowered the gun. Thank God. He would be all right. It all would be all right. Eric would let him get away. He wouldn't even report this.

The man put out his hand. "I'd like to introduce myself, Senator. I'm Warren White. They call me Whitey." A blast sounded from close outside the window. Eric jumped, then relaxed.

Probably the construction job across the street. Nothing to fear now.

"Nice to meet you. Thank you, thank you so much."

He reached up to shake his hand, but he couldn't make his arm move. What happened to his hands, his beautiful hands? There had to be a mistake. This couldn't be happening to him. He was a senator. Senator Eric Barry.

His bowels twisted. A red spray covered his stomach. Odd, so red and yet so cold.

Whitey's face danced above him, the dark object in his hand moving down. This was the time to run. No forgiveness. No remorse. *Oh, God, Daddy, no, please no.*

"Let me go," he begged. *"I'll never do it again. I'll be a good man, a good husband."*

The words sounded funny. Had he spoken them at all? He must have because Whitey crouched down, moved closer to him, as if ready to whisper something very important.

He lifted his lips, but only the cold metal met them.

"Can you hear me, Barry? Can you hear what I'm saying?"

Through the blood in his eyes, he tried to make out the face. *"Yes, sweetheart."*

"I'm going to kill you, Barry, do you know that? I'm going to kill you for what you did to those women."

"No, please."

The cold lips moved to his temples. Eric tried to scream, to beg for mercy, to call for Suzanne, for Fonso. He choked on his pleas, gagging blood, until the excruciating blast rained red through his bursting body.

240 days

The Mother

Gloria had said to her husband, to Karen, to Ryder that she wanted to kill Eric Barry. Yet his murder gave her no satisfaction. The tabloids at first claimed that she and Jack had hired his killer, but soon even they dropped that and began publishing stories of Warren White's troubled past.

April Avenged read one headline. Parents Say Justice Is Done. April was not avenged, and justice was a concept Gloria could no longer hope to define, let alone discuss.

Denny Petroni's book, *Tragic Hero: The Eric Barry Story*, was sold for a television movie. A literary agent had already approached Jack and her for rights to their story.

"I think we ought to do it," she said.

They had spent New Year's in Santa Barbara, trying to escape the sounds and sights of celebration. The following day they walked out on the pier, along the rows of boats.

Jack had aged in the past few months. His face was drawn, the lines around his mouth deeper. His hair blew wild in the wind. He stopped and leaned against the pier, looking at her with doubt.

"A book would bring it all back, sweetheart."

"It's not going away, anyway. We need to tell our side. The truth."

"We don't need the money," he said.

"I already thought about that. We can donate it to the victims' fund."

His eyes filled with pain. She knew he was thinking about April. He stared out at the boats, then back at her.

"That's a good idea," he said. "We could go bigger with the project, national. Hire staff, get the word out."

"It will take everything we have," she said, "and I don't mean money."

"I know." He took her hand. "But it could offer people like us some hope."

The water glistened before them in the sunlight. Gloria choked back tears. "Jack," she said.

"What, sweetheart?"

"I love you."

She and Ryder met in the newspaper cafeteria the following week. It was the first time since their confrontation after Alfonso Trotter's murder. Ryder wore the same purple shirt he had on the first time she'd seen him. His pale eyes were clear, curious.

The rain had finally come, washing clean the leaden skies. They sat inside watching it stream down on the patio, and Gloria told Ryder their plans about the book.

"And we want you to write it," she said.

He couldn't conceal the smile that melted his serious expression. "It would be an honor. I wouldn't do it without your permission."

"I know that. You're the only person who could tell the story the way it should be told."

"Not the only person." He leaned across the table so close that she could smell his clean, soapy scent. "Write it with me, Gloria."

"I can't."

"I could help you. I understand how you think, how you feel."

"I can't get involved in another emotional project with you."

He raised an eyebrow. "Dormitory friendship?"

"If it were that, I wouldn't have a problem working closely with you."

"We'll still have to see each other, talk."

"I want you in my life, Ryder. And my husband and I trust you to write this story that means so much to us."

He nodded understanding. She could always count on his knowing exactly what she meant without her having to say it.

"I've been thinking about trying to get a job in San Francisco," he said.

"That's what you should do. You're a wonderful reporter. You're ready to go back."

"I don't need to be here to write the book."

"Of course not," she said. "I've made Karen a partner in the business. I can give the project all the time it requires. You could make it good, Ryder, something we could all be proud of."

"Spoken like a true Crusader Rabbit," he said.

He walked her to her car, and as always, she fell into rhythm with his steps.

"I have something to say to you," he said.

"What's that?"

"Diana." His eyes changed when he said it, lightening somehow. Gloria felt a chill.

"What exactly are you trying to tell me?" she asked, but she felt the answer before he spoke.

"I told you once I'd never speak her name to anyone, and I never have."

"That's a good first step." She could barely get the words out. "I'm glad you chose me to tell."

"And I'm glad you chose me. For everything."

She wanted to say something, to explain why she had chosen him, and why she couldn't anymore, but she didn't know how, and he probably understood, anyway.

"When I met you, I was in shock," she said. "I had nowhere to go."

He put up a hand. "From now on, let's talk about the book. I promise you I'll give it everything I have."

"Thank you. I know you will."

He hugged her then, quickly, and turned back toward his office, too quickly, before she was ready to let him go. But it was time. It was past time.

Gloria watched him walk inside, then drove through the rain, home to her husband.

387 days

Suzanne

The college here is the size of the elementary schools in Pleasant View, only in Pleasant View it would be caged in chain-link fences, not open and free at the top of a hill like this. I often eat lunch on the patio with the other instructors, looking out into the sea. *The other instructors.* I still find it hard to say, even to myself.

Concrete steps cut into the side of the hill take me up over water and lawn overlooking the walkway that leads to the entrance of the college. I've slung the book bag over my shoulder and am wearing soft, rubber-soled shoes that make a sucking noise on the ground as I walk. I threw out my high heels when I moved.

September in Mendocino smells of beginnings. We have a small staff, and our classes are crowded. I don't mind. Just one week into the semester, and I already know the names of most of my students. I can tell by the way they look at me that some know my story, but most either don't know or don't care. Like my daughters, they are fascinated by their own young lives. I am, too. I am excited by those who know just what they want, and I relate to those who are lost.

Yesterday in a California history class, we talked about the Grape Strike of 1965. Except for a bearded man with a ponytail and a woman enrolled in the senior-citizen degree program, my students found it amazing that I had been alive when the strike took place.

"I didn't participate in it," I said. "My father was a farmer, and farmers considered it a threat. But Cesar Chavez told his people, *'Si, se puede.'* Can anyone tell me what that means?"

A blond girl in the front row raised her hand. "*'Yes, it's possible.' 'Yes, it can be done.'* Isn't that right?"

"Yes," I said. "Yes."

I have a house now, a job, students, a tree-lined walk to work every day. Carefully making my way up the hill, I breathe in the autumn air of anticipation. Perhaps one day there will be room for more in my life, but for now, it's this dazzling expanse of ocean stretching out before me, this concrete step ahead of me. And the next.